THE RED HOUSE

ON ISLA VISTA

M. Eli Milakovich

Metropolitan Executive Management Publishers

Printed in the United States of America

ISBN-13: 978-1542872959

ISBN-10: 1542872952

DISCLAIMER: This is a work of historical fiction based on events allegedly taking place at or near locations pictured above. The fictional stories (which may or may not have occurred) loosely based on the misadventures of a group of romantic paternalists who lived, learned, and loved in the neighborhoods adjacent to this campus during the tortured decade of the 1960s. All composite characters are fictional and any similarity with the names of those, living or dead, or the situations described, is purely co-incidental.

DEDICATION: "To my Mother who made up great stories and my Father who patiently listened to them; and to all of those who think they survived the Sixties, but can't remember."

ACKNOWLEDGMENTS: To Mike, Ron, Marsh, Phil, Dave, Jim, Greg, Tom, Tog, Jud, Jeff, Bill, Dennis, Bob, Brian, Tyler, Norm, Ross, "Willie," Leo, Steve, Jack, and Beto, all those who participated in the Red Barn Tales projects, and helped keep Isla Vista legends alive.

Table of Contents

FORWARD

The decade that began so brilliantly for so many young Americans ended in a drug-induced inner-space nightmare on the streets of America and in the rice paddies of Southeast Asia. Militant anticommunist politicians took full advantage of this generation's inherited patriotism with few moral boundaries or even fewer consistent values.

The Sixties produced the best music and the worst politicians ever. Nobel Laureate Bob Dylan, The Beatles, Country Joe McDonald and the Fish, Jefferson Airplane, Jim Morrison and the Doors, Joan Baez, and the Rolling Stones would have never achieved fame during the ensemble brassiness of the Big Band Era or within the confines of the syncopated rhythms of the Fifties. Rock musicians offered the truth, but politicians deceived in the cruelest way—using the draft as a stick and patriotism as a carrot—to engage in bloody crusades against imaginary threats to capitalism, democracy, and freedom which blew in from Southeast Asian windmills.

During this twisted decade, American society was fundamentally and irreparably shattered by three prominent occupants of the White House: John F. Kennedy, the visionary scion too rich and too bold for his own survival; Lyndon "how many kids have you killed today" Johnson, the Texas cornpone fascist with a guilt-ridden conscience; and Richard Milhous Nixon, the Shakespearian self-destructive over-achiever consumed by alcohol and ambition. These three political leaders set the stage for today's divisive, dysfunctional and identity-driven deep pocket plutocracy. Sadly, JFK's New Frontier, LBJ'S Great Society, and 'Nixonland' were populist fairy tales foisted on a paranoid society hungry for security from Russian satellites beeping overhead and Cuban communists poised to invade just 90 miles from Key West. God help us if those Commies ever launched those nukes and land on our shores!

DUCK AND COVER!

Three naïve post-adolescents imagine "Isla Vista" as a seductive playground, an undiscovered paradise where they can consume alcohol underage, receive tuition-free quality higher education, and experience erotic sexual freedom. Instead, their futures purloined by events beyond their control: among them, civil rights struggles, drugs, political assassinations, threat of nuclear war, and fighting for a cause in Vietnam that few understood.

As they and their friends nervously reflect upon their pasts at a reunion, their lives mirror the trials and triumphs of an entire generation. They remember how war, psychotropic drugs, and struggles for equal rights and social justice affected entire families. They recall how some listened more intently, became political activists and marched against discrimination, militarism, and segregation. Many silently confess that they were troubled by violence triggered by war, inequality and racism, but instead sought economic security and joined the academic, business and legal establishments. Meanwhile, the agenda for change initiated in the Sixties remains incomplete.

The Sixties shattered attitudes about civil rights, drugs, gender roles, race, sex, sexism, war, and paternalistic authority—causing deep rifts in families, politics and morality and doubts about the American Dream.

From a pristine and unspoiled environment known as "Isla Vista," three naïve post-adolescents cope with uncertain futures. Personal choices play out against a larger world stage filled with multiple obstacles and intense struggles. Like many others, futures compromised by the constant drumbeat of nuclear Cold War and by "fake news" offered by political leaders. Unbeknownst to them at the time, their lives would be guided by the actions of corrupt politicians who sacrificed open democracy and willing workers for a closed system of money-driven deep pocket economic plutocracy. The fragile fault lines of American identity politics began to crack in Sixties, deepened in the ensuing decades, and eventually fractured with the anti-establishment electoral tsunami and the ensuing seismic transition of power in 2016.

Our leaders failed us and American politics still suffers from the social malaise that began in this jumbled decade—the music is still the greatest!

Chapter 1: Legends, Myths and Half-Truths about Isla Vista

On cold winter mornings, a gentle grey mist settles over the narrow coastal promontory jutting out into the Pacific Ocean. Ships bells and deep-throated horns heard in the distant fog-shrouded waters. Old-growth eucalyptus trees whisper softly in the cool late afternoon breezes. On warm afternoons, testosterone-filled guys and eager young girls dressed in Halloween costumes roll around Deveraux sand dunes, grabbing ass, swilling beer and thinking only of sexual satisfaction. Large white storks nest on saltwater marshes surrounding a sheltered movie-set lagoon. It was all so perfect…too perfect.

During certain seasons, cool mountain breezes drift down the canyons of the San Ynez Mountains and the sweet smells of lemon and orange blossoms waft through the night air. Herds of cattle and goats graze in open fields and packs of wild dogs roam the barren plateau at night. Residents still tell mythical stories about drunken cheerleaders, goat parties, kidnappings, taitfrenchers, and harrowing trips to Mexico. Others harbor lurid accounts of anarchist cults, jointrolling contests, police repression, Viking parties, and voluptuous young girls roaming the streets alone and sexually frustrated. Most of these legends are "kind of" true…if perhaps somewhat exaggerated with time.

The hippie movement was rumored to have begun here when groups of young 'free-lovers' camped out in tents along the ice plant covered cliffs above College Beach. The movement first became popular in the Sixties, but declined rapidly the 1970's due to violent demonstrations, police repression, mass murders, drugs, and the end of the Vietnam War.

Comely young girls with bleach-blond hair wander the streets with their dogs, but without their boyfriends. Thousands of luscious young men and women cloistered in an isolated one-mile square known as Isla Vista: trouble was inevitable then and still is today.

In less than a decade, this affluent and formerly hidden 'student ghetto' would degenerate from an upper-middle class playground for oversexed teenagers to a violent revolutionary battlefield. This upheaval did not happen overnight or without contributory negligence. This compact square mile of protected geography would mutate from an adolescent's erotic dreamland into a dangerous compound for addicts, cults, murderers, revolutionaries, surfers, terrorists and rioters. History offers some clues, but few definitive answers why this regression-in-paradise occurred.

Among the obvious explanations: a volatile combination of drugs, police brutality, sexual freedom, and lack of adult supervision exploded into a full-blown violent rebellion. Buildings burned in protest, riot police and National Guard troops besieged protesting students, and university staff members and students were bludgeoned and killed. Simultaneously, millions of confused and emotionally scarred baby boomers (underline denotes glossary term), the dutiful children of the Greatest Generation who instinctively supported U.S. involvement in the Vietnam War, began to question the rationale for war. In time, many would find the moral fortitude to question the motives of politicians, university officials and civil authorities—protesting escalation of the war by the Nixon administration.

Complicit university administrators, corrupt local officials, and greedy landowners kept Isla Vista ghettoized and separated from its more stable surrounding communities. Meanwhile, projected student enrollments at the newly funded campus of the University of California at Santa Barbara (UCSB) created a building boom and an absentee property owner's goldmine. Students were (and still are) victimized by both overpriced rental apartments and under-patrolled streets: grass-roots efforts to incorporate for self-governance repeatedly thwarted by landowners reaping huge profits from overpriced and under-maintained rental apartments. Student safety issues routinely swept under the rug by administrators who opined that student apartments on IV were "privately owned" and therefore not under university supervision. Everyone in authority turned a blind eye to the inevitability of violent mass behavior, emphasizing only the curb appeal of the campus-by-the-sea. According to full-color real estate websites, IV is a "sun-drenched cluster of beachside apartments, fraternity houses, and pricy student accommodations" just west of the University of California at Santa Barbara campus-by-the-sea (cover): Isla Vista is also a neighborhood that has experienced unspeakable violence.

IV burst into national prominence in February 1970 when a Bank of America branch burned down following months of student anti-war demonstrations. Residents rebelled after witnessing Santa Barbara County Sheriff's deputies brutally beat a student suspected of carrying a Molotov cocktail. It was a bottle of wine, hardly a dangerous weapon. More protests and overly aggressive police behavior interrupted classes for over a year. At one demonstration, a student was shot and killed. The police blamed his death on a sniper among demonstrators, but an autopsy later revealed that police killed him. Politicians railed against the protesters and blamed the mayhem on "outside agitators." Local authorities investigated the killing and ruled it an "accident." Does this cover up sound familiar?

Governor Ronald Reagan blamed "communist-inspired left-wing hippie radicals" and declared a State of Emergency, as if he were rehearing for his big show a decade later. Hundreds of students arrested and detained, thousands more abused and harassed—individual attitudes about authority and politics permanently altered.

By the end of the decade, Isla Vista would replace Berkeley and Columbia as the epicenter of student protests. The anti-war movement would expand, escalate and disrupt learning at college and university campuses worldwide. There were an estimated 175 bombings on U.S. colleges by the late-1960s. Many campuses resembled occupied war zones, not unlike the troubling images recently broadcast from the streets of American cities (Charleston, Charlotte, Chicago, Baltimore, Dallas, Ferguson, Milwaukee, and Orlando among them) after killings by domestic terrorists or police. Impressionable young minds would be hardened by similar images of street riots, forced conscription for a cause that many doubted, and by the influx of mind-altering substances. National leaders escalated protests by forcing young men to fight an unwinnable war while simultaneously undermining their futures by making side deals with foreign opportunists.

Politics of the twisted era would reflect the continuing decline of youthful idealism accompanied by political battles for America's heart and soul. Frustrated by the apparent failure of politicians to maintain 'law and order' at home, voters would entrust their country's future to an ambitious fully certified ego-driven Master of Deceit.

Nothing symbolized the rise of reactionary politics more than the career of one obsessively driven politician—Richard Milhous Nixon. Just eight years after he had failed in his *mano-a-mano* media driven contest against the suave and polished John F. Kennedy, a "new" Nixon emerged in 1968 and succeeded in his quest to become president. How could Nixon's blind ambition and misplaced passion lead to tragic consequences in such an idyllic place? Why did this political catastrophe happen to a free and open country? Could such a breach of public trust have happened again?

In myriad ways, Isla Vista was an insular refuge for frisky young boomers seeking to avoid the grim realities occurring in what most thought to be "other" places. Young residents of Isla Vista sought shelter from an uncertain world, especially after the bubble-shattering assassination of President Kennedy in November 1963. Nixon, Reagan and their political allies seized the opportunity to crackdown on civil rights leaders and hippie anti-war protesters while selling-out willing U.S. workers to foreign interests. Repressive police tactics forever hardened attitudes towards "big government," politicians, representative political institutions and democratic traditions, setting the stage for selfish economic interests to reassert power.

Pessimism about the complex relationship between access to information, political democratization, and economic growth has infected Western democratic societies since this volatile decade. Boomers' descendants, <u>millennials</u> born from the 1980s to the 2000s, now outnumber their elderly ancestors (born from the mid-1940s to the mid-1960s) and are a potent economic, political, and social force. Ironically, they suffer from some of the same generation skipping negative stereotypes as their boomer grandparents. Like their elders, many have become so dejected that they eschew even the most basic civil obligations such as voting.

Despite lower voting turnouts than earlier generations, millennials are smart, wired and deeply committed to supporting others via personal networks. Renewed interest in politics among younger left-leaning voters did increase turnouts slightly in recent presidential elections, but participation plummeted in 2016.[1] Without defined interests and confidence in their ability to influence "the system," electoral participation is unsustainable. Making it easier to register online, easing residency restrictions on voting, encouraging the use of early voting and mail ballots could contribute to increased voter turnout. As witnessed by the 2016 Presidential Election, voting alone will not draw younger citizens into democratic processes.[2]

In retrospect, past events and individual experiences on Isla Vista "in the Sixties" seem almost quaint when compared to the horrific realities facing today's campus-by-sea and many other institutions: panty raids, <u>gotcha parties</u>, <u>goat parties</u> and street demonstrations were replaced by the violent acts of drug dealers, police crack-downs, mass murderers and self-indulgent student social rejects. External threats once faced by boomers hiding in enclaves like Isla Vista pale in comparison to internal threats against their millennial offspring by disaffected youth who turn violently against their own culture. Lone wolf killers have infested numerous communities once considered safe havens for learning. Internal terrorism and increasing instances of school violence have further driven families to protect their children at all costs.

Compounding these tragedies, the United States abandoned one of its founding principles and the cornerstone of its 240-year tradition of open participatory democracy: an educated population. Thomas Jefferson and other architects of our Democratic Republic believed strongly that education provided the training for democracy. Writing in 1776, Jefferson asserted that: *"no one more sincerely wishes the spread of information among mankind than I do, and none has greater confidence in its effect toward supporting free and good government."*

This transformation represents far more than just a failure of our democratic institutions. The bi-polarization of representative government no longer provides fair and equitable mechanisms for Americans to pursue a better life. The hollow shell of merit-based higher education that once worked so well to mitigate the effects of poverty and income inequality still exists, but many institutions have deteriorated to a point that they no longer function as vehicles for either economic or social mobility. We are squandering one of our finest accomplishments and historic legacies: a system of education long characterized by excellence, equality and wide accessibility. The country sacrificed its own willing workers for a closed system of money-driven deep pocket democracy and unrepresentative economic plutocracy.

Events during the late-1960s fundamentally altered the relationship between citizen and state, changing America's collective consciousness forever. Contemporary relations between government and the not-as-greats (now disparaged senior citizens) are far worse now than they were two generations ago. Deep down, most boomers know the establishment fooled them: predictably, younger generations X, Y, and Z inherited a deep sense of suspicion about government.

This is the story of how and why that happened, as told by those who participated either by choice or by chance.

CHAPTER 2: The IV Reunion Blues

I can't give you the grip 'because I've got arthritis,
I've also got jaundice, gout and phlebitis;
Now that I'm here at this lavish reunion
I seem to be suffering from mental confusion.

I have no recollection of half of the brothers,
And those I remember I confuse with some others.
When I asked about Joe there were several long pauses:
He was carried away by natural causes.

Some of the time you're a little pretentious,
You react to my story like I might be infectious.
You've slowly revealed you've been pretty successful;
Trying to frame a rejoinder was a bit too stressful.

It was in the mid-Sixties before I dropped out of school,
I never worried, I was playing it cool.
It was during that time that I joined the fraternity;
My only anxiety was avoiding paternity

We'd go down to the beach and pick up some chicks
Build us a fire and throw on some sticks,
Down a few beers and wrap us in blankets,
Watch the sun rise and head back to campus

You were one of those who were into achievement;
I feared overworking would lead to bereavement;
I always intended to get my degree
But somehow or other I just hung out in IV.

Over the years you've grown sentimental
While my worry is that I'm going mental.
You tell me IV seems a place of effusion,
But to me an IV means I need a transfusion

But I'll be back on my feet in a few more semesters,
Then I'll get that degree that the Dean has sequestered.
At our next reunion I'll be feeling so wealthy
Somehow being with you has made me feel healthy.

P.T. Jameson

For those fortunate enough to attend UCSB during its formative years, the campus was a pristine and undiscovered Southern California gem located just west of the ultra-affluent and conservative Old Spanish City of Santa Barbara. The newest campus joined the UC system in the late 1950s as part of the University of California Master Plan for expansion of statewide higher education. Known as the Campus-by-the-Sea, it sits on a headland overlooking the Pacific Ocean on all three sides. From the air, it looks more like a swanky resort than an academic institution (below). Just below the dormitories, the campus surrounded by sandy beaches dotted with eucalyptus and palm trees swaying in the breeze. Surfboard racks provided for the 'gremmies' who favored the curl off College Beach just below dormitory row. What is there not to like?

"If there's a more beautiful campus than this one at the edge of the Pacific, we haven't seen it," said Newsweek.

Despite the external comforts, internal conflicts plagued many of school age who listened to pleas for social justice and fair treatment for all Americans. As their futures began to fragment, some went underground to avoid the inevitability of the draft and others found new and sometimes high-risk pathways to prosperity. Most silently coped with fears of violent domestic civic disorder triggered by poverty and racial hatred. The vast majority followed their parent's footsteps and joined the academic, business, education, legal, or medical professions.

These characters and their stories offer an inside look at how boomers responded to expectations of their parents (aka the "Greatest Generation") and coped with the realities of political changes and campus life: sex, sexism, racism, relationships, Vietnam, segregation, and the universal desire to avoid inescapable maturity (and paternity). Personalities molded by external behavioral choices, enlistments in the military, marriage, silent protests, and exotic new forms of escape: internal rebellion accelerated by alcohol, drugs and other delusional and self-destructive escapes. Life choices channeled by anti-communism, drugs, racism and changing gender relationships. For most, these years would form and mold adult personalities and sustain lifetime friendships. Who knew?

✶ ✶

Strange thoughts race through your mind when you are about to reconnect with friends, some of whom you have not seen for nearly a half-century. Although you try to lose weight for the occasion, you still wonder if others are thinner, have more hair, or look younger than you. Obviously, everyone is older. Which ones have aged the most?

Upon entering the event venue, the overly cheerful host, Ross Rosenbloom, said, "I remember you; you used to be Mark McGinnis."

Misplaced humor at best.

"Good to see you, man, it's been a few years."

"Yeah, just a few. I was surprised that so many of us lived long enough to have a reunion," morbidly joked Rosenbloom.

An understatement at best, thought McGinnis.

That was just the opening gambit for a long night of cynicism, pimping, sarcasm and nostalgic reflection.

After a few awkward introductions and drinks, you melt in with the group and, as each new/old face arrives, you oddly begin to feel the same sense of camaraderie from decades ago. Wives, guests, girlfriends and significant others, who have never met any of the others before, stunned by the transformation that takes place almost immediately. Between the casual banter, serious talk of tours of duty in Vietnam, campus demonstrations, children's achievements, ex-girlfriends, marriages new and old, harrowing trips to Mexico, and post-UCSB careers. Surprisingly, most of free-thinking mid-Sixties legends survived the draft, free love, Nixon and the war, and coped in various and creative ways with their futures after leaving Isla Vista. For aging war baby boomers like Mark McGinnis and his friends David Eggert and Richard Morgan, cynicism about the direction of the country began for different reasons at various times during their lives.

For McGinnis, that revelation came sometime between the grinding schedule of studying for doctoral exams in graduate school and Air Force flight training missions over the Pacific Ocean off the coast of Santa Barbara. While viewing his lost paradise from 10,000 feet, he wondered whatever happened to our isolated square mile of seclusion. Why are we now so vulnerable? When and why did our country relinquish our national sovereignty to multi-national corporations and foreign powers? Why so hateful of one another because of race, gender or ethnicity? Questions unanswerable then and even more difficult to comprehend now.

For David Eggert, pessimism began at a much earlier age when his father died. He was 14 years old and felt the profound loss of security for the rest of his life. Eggert was a serious but disobedient ex-Catholic, confounded by internal conflicts as one of two surviving sons whose father died in military service. While in graduate school, he immersed himself in the civil rights and anti-war movements. After a stint in the Peace Corps interrupted his flirtation with radical leftwing politics, he settled down as a professor in a small liberal arts college in the Midwest.

Richard Pierpont Morgan was an affluent Northern Californian rejected for admission to prestigious Cal-Berkeley and Stanford who had to settle instead for the lowly upstart UC-Santa Barbara. Most of his family members were conservative and conceited Berkeley or Stanford graduates who looked down their noses at any college south of San Francisco Bay especially "Sun Tan U" as UCSB was known as because of its reputation as a party school. Rick was an obedient Catholic scholar-athlete from an affluent two-parent family who raised with strict traditional values, none of which prevented him from partying with the lowly Southern Californians. His father had been a gunnery officer on a Navy destroyer in South Pacific who settled in San Francisco after the war. As the first-born son, his younger brother and sister worshipped him and would later follow his lead in selecting UCSB—a decision which would lead to tragic consequences for his family. His personal values and loyalty to friends would distinguish his later life and service to country.

Dennis "Jailbait" O'Malley was one of the many who avoided military service, but in an unusual way. He joined a Hindu cult in Nepal, where he mediated and chanted in search of personal self-awareness. In desperation, he went to an ashram (meditation center) near Kathmandu in the Himalayas. He realized that his desires were creating negative experiences and he could not change: he neither ate, nor preyed, nor loved. Just sat around depressed. After returning, he moved from Santa Monica to Oakland in 1978 to be near the cult's mediation center—he has yet to discover the meaning of life.

John Lambright never thought too much or too deeply about the meaning of life, but was grateful to have lived in the animal house wing of the old Red House in the last year before it was bulldozed into oblivion.

Few habitable structures existed on the barren property in the 1960s, some weathered beach houses, a few apartments and a barn-like Red House hastily abandoned some years earlier. Its occupants experienced a rich and varied social life from the late 1940s until the late-1960s, when it was demolished to make way for a newer and far less friendly dormitory-style building.

Nostalgically John recalls: "What a contrast when we moved into the new red brick building with the snazzy red door. I missed the old house and the sand and seaweed spread over the chapter room floor for parties, the goat, and Sully's dogs. The parties were great."

"Does anyone remember whose date it was who actually passed out in a bathtub full of wine?" asked Lambright.

"That would be me," chimed Eggert.

"The funny part about it was that none of the brothers helped her, all they wanted to do was to dip their cups in the tub for more wine."

"Who was the girl in the tub?" asked a curious Lambright.

"To be honest, I can't remember," said Eggert with a huge shit-eating grin on his face.

Another adventurous member, John Holger, claimed to have run into Sir Edmund Hillary near the Tibetan Plateau (around 10,000 feet) in 1978. He bragged that he had "walked in valleys of undulating wheat fields surrounded by 25,000 foot peaks and visited Esalen many times. Sat in baths. Got massaged. Meditated. It didn't work. Took EST and LSD, but not at the same time."

Holger concluded with one of his famous non-sequiturs: "It was all a waste of time—that Snowden fucker defected to Russia."

Vietnam vet and helicopter pilot Sam Cormack interjected: "Can you believe we now actively trade with those communist bastards in countries like Vietnam? What bullshit is that after we risked our lives to save that jungle rot gook-infested place from the commies"

"Yeah, it's worse than that, our government employs the same damn authoritarian tactics we swore to fight and die for," commented Eggert.

"Bullshit, man, you should see how some of those countries are run. One bad comment about their leaders and 'off with your head,'" Cormack shot back.

17

Not only Vietnam, but also the Cold War and the Cuban Missile Crisis disaffected many of us, but some more directly than others. Dennis Finch was a Marine Reservist and remembers the call to active duty in the fall of 1962.

"They told us to prepare for a D-Day style amphibious invasion of Cuba, if high-level negotiations with the Russians failed. Can you believe that they were actually considering a 'preemptive tactical nuclear strike' against Cuba? The Russians would have retaliated with bigger nukes against Miami, New York or Washington. World War III. The land invasion, even though it would have probably killed us, was considered a *moderately risky* choice. That is so scary to think about now."

Fortunately, Kennedy's advisors chose a naval blockade of Russian ships carrying missiles to Cuba instead. This was still a risky option because it cut off Russian transport ships from entering Havana harbor. Any contact between U.S. and Russian vessels, accidental or incidental, would have been a hostile act of war and prompted retaliation. The rest of the story is bitter Cold War history. Robert F. Kennedy, who was in war rooms as the drama unfolded, estimated a 50:50 chance of nuclear war with the Russians. Cooler heads prevailed, Dennis stayed in California and nuclear war averted.

"Obviously, Iraq and Afghanistan are this generation's Vietnam, huge payoffs to Bush and Cheney's allies in the military industrial complex. The only result was greater losses of American lives and less respect from our allies," injected Norm Cedrick.

"No one was surprised that so much Defense Department money found its way back to the pockets of Republican candidates as campaign contributions," complained Cedrick, another Army Vet who served with the 101st Airborne Division.

Norm chuckles as he remembers how all the "peace nicks," who were about to be drafted, joined the Army and volunteered for Special Forces. They wanted to be medics and knew the Army required two and a half years of training before they would be deployed. They figured the war would be over by then. Some made it ok and some didn't.

After getting married to avoid the draft, Bill Richardson started a wheatgrass juice business. Juiced wheatgrass daily, 6 days a week and delivered it to health food stores in Oakland and Berkeley. He lamented, "I never had a solid shit for 5 years and still feel unhealthy. I should have sold weed and made some decent money instead."

Because pot was illegal, the reefer (hopefully without the madness) had to be tried in safer surroundings: where else but Mexico, where it was both an appetizer and after-dinner aperitif. Conservative attorney Bob Roth interrupted, "Hey, do you remember that bar fight we had Tijuana? They really fucked us up."

"Yes," said McGinnis, "how could I forget, but it wasn't much of a fight. We were sipping beers minding our own business when the next thing I remember, a large wooden chair splintered over Freddie Navarone's head. All hell broke loose in the Long Bar and chairs and tables flew across the beer-soaked floor, blood gushed from an open wound in Freddie's head, the music died and the lights went black. We all hit the deck (customary in bar fights) as bodies, chairs and people flew in all directions. Large glass beer mugs whizzed past our heads, exploding on the glass mirrors and sending shards of glass flying everywhere."

"How did we get out of Tijuana alive?" Roth asked.

McGinnis recalled, "Some of us tried to fight back, but a wave of gang members descended upon us, and we mostly huddled in fear under the table on the beer and blood soaked floor. We pulled Freddie unconscious from under the table and crawled across the floor, trying unsuccessfully to avoid being cut, kicked and stomped. We reached the exit and escaped without paying for the beers."

Nervous laughter followed the story as others remembered similar 'close calls' on road trips to Mexico.

"By the way, what ever happened to Oxnard Freddie? Why doesn't he come to these events?"

"Maybe he never recovered from that bar fight in TJ?" said McGinnis jokingly but half seriously.

"Do you remember Bill Wierman, 'Weirdman' as we used to call him, the guy who dropped out of USC Dental School after one quarter when he had to give another student Novocain shots and dissect a cadaver? He apparently never recovered either." "Hell yes, I sure remember him," said Morgan.

"He attended UCLA Film School for one quarter when it was still possible to get into UCLA with a B- average. The last we heard he became a hippie living in a commune in Malibu Canyon."

"Yeah, I remember seeing him once while in law school. He was in a long flowing robe and long hair. Looked like Jesus and stoned to the max," said McGinnis.

"What ever happened to him?"

"Do you think he would show up at one of these things?"

Morgan laughed again and said, "I doubt it. He probably forgot everything at the rate he was smoking weed."

"Speaking of forgetting, remember when I was kidnapped, tied up and put on an airplane to Chicago?" Morgan said, almost enthusiastically.

"Oh my God, that was so illegal, probably now a federal anti-terrorism crime if they didn't shoot you in the airport first," said Eggert.

"Yeah, it's funny to think about now, how good-natured the Captain was about the whole thing. Especially after they wheeled me through the airport gagged and tied up and one of the pledges, I think Adam Ross, carefully explained to security personnel that 'my medical condition required treatment in the Midwest and that I was bound and gagged' for the safety of other passengers!"

Morgan bragged that, "The pilot would have let me off the plane, but I was determined to get back on my own just to show them up."

At one point around 1986, Steven Taylor became disillusioned with teaching, wanted to earn more money and became a "book buyer" at San Jose State College. During a book fair, he ran into Scott Peters.

"Peters told me that he was living off the profits from the 100 pounds of heroin he had smuggled out of Vietnam in 2 porcelain monkeys. I felt envious," said Taylor.

"Yes, Peters never quite learned his lesson, did he? Rather than just peddle the stuff and get filthy rich, he started using too much of it himself, just like Al Pacino in my favorite film, *Scarface*. Similar outcome, too, unfortunately for him," said Taylor.

"How did he die?" asked McGinnis.

"No one I talked to was quite sure, but I heard he made 7 "hash runs" to Afghanistan before he overdosed in Mexico. Supposedly, he bought a VW camper in Wolfsburg, drove to Afghanistan to pick up hashish. Stuffed VW side panels with 100 kilos of hash, enough to kill an elephant then shipped the car thru Marseilles to Mexico. Apparently, he exchanged hash for cash to supply San Francisco Fillmore Auditorium entrepreneurs to entertain rock n' rollers. On last trip he was busted in Mexico," explained Taylor.

"I'm not sure who turned him in, but the rest of the story is even harder to believe," said Holger, "believe it or not, he got sympathetic lawyer to recommend him as part of rehab program. Can you believe that?"

"Sounds like bullshit to me, since when do lawyers became mentors?" said a skeptical Bill Roth.

"I don't know, he said he got 50 letters of recommendation from Senators and Congressmen when applying for graduate school. He said he kept in touch with sponsors until he died (Catch me if you can, reward me if you do). The weird part is that he told me that he gave business to Larry Woodson and Mike Shelby (an SAE) who got busted in Bulgaria, and sent to prison in Greece,"

Taylor explained skeptically "Yeah, I heard Woodson tried to smuggle coke out of Columbia, but got caught, jailed and escaped from cops in Colombian jungle.

How strange is that?" said Eggert.

"Even weirder, since he got away, Larry lives most of the year in Cuba away from the U.S. narcs. We keep in touch. It is a crazy story. He pays the Cuban government to have sex with a bunch of women. He thought he had fathered 10 children hoping for U.S. citizenship when diplomatic relations were re-established. Every time he tested one of the new kids, it was not his DNA! How weird is that."

As laughter erupted, some were obviously nervous about their own lapses of judgement and lack of birth control.

After Obama's diplomatic *rapprochement* between Cuba and the United States, we might even see the advent of affirmative action programs for Cuban youth fathered by ex-pats Americans who might be eligible for citizenship. It is even weirder to think of Cuban "*hermanitos*" receiving special treatment seeking asylum in the U.S. while children of Americans continue to be excluded from the American Dream.

"Does anyone remember super straight Mark Foote, another ROTY guy?" He actually said to me once, "if I knew any of them were smoking pot, I would turn them in. What a prick," said Pete Fowler.

During a bus trip to a job as a desktop publisher for IBM in Palo Alto around 1991, Fowler read that Josh Bentley had become CFO of a big Silicon Valley hardware company.

"I felt so jealous. Tried to forget by backpacking in the Sierra, snowboarded many times before it attracted riff-raff. Climbed 14,000 feet to top of Mt. Shasta 3 times, failed on another attempt due to rain. Still pisses me off."

Joe Leishman volunteered at local elementary school in Berkeley for the 8 years where he coached sports teams, taught a science class, videotaped classes, taught computer classes, and coached flag football on the playground. He made over 30 videos of the school activities and personalities. These 15-minute videos each took over 20 hours to make and were shown once a month at the all-school meetings.

"I felt used and quit."

"Isla Vista has really changed, hasn't it? Streets jammed with chicks in bikinis and I bet most of the stuff we had to go to Mexico for is available here," observed Jim McNabe.

"Yeah, except all the UCSB kids are freaked-out about those social reject mass murderers. They were 'under privileged' Hollywood brats, don't you know?"

"That reminds me of the stories about the girls having sex with donkeys in TJ?" said Tog Roberts.

"That was bullshit, man, just a rumor," answered a skeptical Sam Cormack.

"It is not a myth. I personally witnessed it at least three times. The most famous of the donkey girls could take about three quarters of that critter's considerable dong. Amazing, and at the same time disgusting."

"Speaking of dongs, do you remember Alan Harrison's "flaming dick" trick?" which was painful to watch and even more difficult to describe. Al poured lighter fluid on his penis and carefully lit it with a cigarette lighter. The trick was not to over dip or under dip the organ in lighter fluid as this could cause severe burns and a lifetime of celibacy," said McNabe.

McGinnis interjected, "Do you remember the time we took Jaime Sherman to TJ? I think he was a virgin because he totally freaked out when the dancer came up to him on the rail at the Blue Fox."

Jamie was a somewhat naïve lad whom we had regaled with stories about the forbidden fruit available a few hours away just south of the border. For some of the more naïve (i.e.

Catholic) brothers, the first trip to TJ also constituted their first taste of beer and pussy. After several bottles of Tecate, we beckoned a "dancer" over and paid her to give Jamie a private lap dance. What happened next shocked even the most battle-hardened veterans of the Tijuana Bar Scene.

After stripping right in front of Jamie's eyes, she not only performed a lap dance, rubbing him on the front and back, but removed his glasses and slowly inserted them in her well-lubricated pussy. As we cheered her on to do more, she removed them slowly and returned his glasses. Flustered by all the unanticipated attention, he put the gooey glasses back on! Disgusting to watch and, at the same time, unforgettable. Not surprisingly, after that private tease, Jamie lost whatever inhibitions were left and preceded to the rail, whereupon another *senorita* provided him the house special—a "hot box lunch." After that, she escorted him upstairs to the second floor for dessert.

"That is really gross, but I think the initiation rituals we used to perform on the pledges were even worse. I wonder if they still do that shit today?" ask a curious George "Crowbar" Jenkins.

Part of the ritual was lighting a cross on the guy's chest, something about our Southern KKK heritage. We thought this part of the ceremony was funny because of the rank smell created when those with hairy chests were set on fire. A brother stood by with a bucket of water just in case the initiate panicked or his robe caught on fire. In another instance, the fire burned too long on a pledge with a sunken chest and we had to be dosed him with water.

Jason Alexander became a computer network administrator for a big real estate development corporation in San Francisco in 1998. He didn't need the money because he became trust-fund-baby when father died in 1996.

"Supposedly, it is impossible for him to get married or have a girlfriend for any length of time. One astrologer said that, with his chart, she didn't even see how he could have a one-night stand. I know you don't believe in astrology but that is not doing me any good! At least he had a couple of ex-girlfriends to get him over the rough spots," added Norm Cedrick.

"Many of the guys were so hard up for dates that they became hashers in sorority houses and ended up married to one of the sisters."

"I remember when Dave Newman got caught in bed with a DG and was summarily dismissed by the House Mother. Can you imagine how those raging house mothers would treat guys these days?"

Dick Gozinya, an original member of the infamous Red House Dining Club, never married but remained close to his two godchildren.

"I bicycled around England and Ireland with a stricter vegan than I am, who graduated high school valedictorian, is a cross country runner and going for a triple major at Cal with Japanese, Chinese and math. We get together regularly and still bicycle. Even though I have more money, jealous that kids smarter today and I feel still feel inferior.

On December 15, 2007, Tim Neckragel collected his first social security check.

"At first, it didn't seem like much for all those years of forced savings," he remarked, "but now it looks pretty good. Definitely a Baby Boomer. Feel old now."

Dave Johnson boosts that he likes to trade options and collect iron condors (his high school mascot).

"You mean those ugly South American vultures?" said McGinnis.

"They are graceful birds, maybe a little gangly, but in the air, magnificent."

"They love to feed on dead animal carcasses, right?"

Speaking of animals, Ross Rosenbloom recalls how cleaver we were about hiding new pledges who were not quite the right ethnicity, race or religion.

"We outfoxed the national rep or, as we called him, the Travelling Fuck (TF), who would visit and overnight at the House. We had to provide dinner and chit-chat about the great work of our national leaders who were looking for any non-Christians who would be purged from the pledge class," said Ross boastfully.

The TF's pathetic job was to visit the local chapters, inspect the membership rolls, protect their racial purity and ensure that the locals measured up to the lofty segregationist standards of the National Headquarters. Lots of creative thought went into creating what turned out to be a win win solution: all the non-Christians got money to dine out when the TF was in town. Risky move for the segregated Sixties.

"That reminds me of the time we tried to sail a homemade raft from College Beach to the Channel Islands and almost drowned? If the Coast Guard hadn't rescued us, we would have gone down for sure," said Rick Morgan.

"Yeah, speaking of drowning, have you seen how the Deltopia thing has grown and exported to places like Miami Beach?' I heard there were 20,000 people on the beach and they made a huge mess."

"Bitchin,' man, at least IV is known for something more than casual sex, keg parties, and mass murders," said Eggert.

YOLO. Be here now and go Heat.

As we broke up into smaller groups to reminisce about our being seduced by Isla Vista, we tried to convince ourselves that nothing much has changed, that we were all equal in achievement, hairline, fame, income, mental state, prison records, physique, procreation, health or personal stability—but that was a fantasy. Despite obvious differences, the bond of friendship formed in the Red House on Isla Vista a half a century ago exceeded any status inconsistency or career regrets we might have about our present world. We loved it, and respect all of those who practiced determined individuality, the Red House ethos that guided and enriched our lives. In our minds, we imagined ourselves as young men in Isla Vista, living holographs, hungover and staggering toward College Beach to play volleyball. Life was good.

For Eggert, McGuinness and Morgan and the millions of other Sixties survivors, reflecting on the seductive events a half-century ago brings up bittersweet memories of new experiences, lost opportunities, past loves, reckless adventures, and grand—but now distant— delusions.

CHAPTER 3: Generations X-Y-Z

Generalizing about entire generations is politically *in*correct, but who doesn't do it? Baby boomers are too old, too rich, and too spoiled. Millennials are selfish and narcissistic. Generation X, born from the mid-1960s to early 1980s are money-driven and socially unconscious. Nonetheless, those who came of age during the Sixties share much in common with today's millennials. Both generations are highly educated, experienced revolutionary and reactionary politics, and witnessed sharp economic decline, political paranoia and social upheaval. Both have seen continuous global warfare, horrific acts of terrorism, militant anti-communism (then) and anti-terrorism (today). Clashing countercultures, shifting political values, overt gay bashing, sexism and racism—all affected war baby boomers and millennials in similar ways. Many boomers have not saved enough for retirement and most millennials have "failed to launch" their careers because of higher unemployment, lower incomes, less accumulated wealth, and greater debt.

Even the term "millennial" carries with it an assortment of pejorative connotations: selfish, self-indulging, self-serving, self-absorbed and other less flattering "self-gratifying" adjectives. Their love affair with all forms of technology has even spurred a ubiquitous worldwide narcissistic phenomenon—the "selfie." Predictably, millennials (ages 18-35) have become prime targets for intergenerational political warfare: right-wing conservatives have initiated campaigns to seize the hearts and minds of the younger left-leaning idealistic voters.

Eager politicians, the mysterious Koch brothers, and presidential wannabes stir intergenerational conflict by proposing to gut age-based and social programs, meager subsidies benefitting boomers, the poor, minorities, and women. Their "solutions" for other social problems such as women's freedom of choice, marriage equality, and unwed pregnancies even more draconian: repeal *Roe vs. Wade,* shutdown women's health clinics, and overturn recent Supreme Court decisions applying First and Fourteenth Amendment freedoms to gay couples seeking the legal protection of marriage.

For the first time in American history, those under 35 expect a lower standard of living than that of their elders; confidence in the American Dream reached the lowest point ever recorded.[1] Both generations have seen job prospects, savings, and retirement accounts dissipate rapidly—

economic insecurity now binds them together. What used to the American Dream of upward economic and social mobility has darkened into an expanding shadow of politically induced class warfare. Two-thirds of American GenXers believe that their children will have fewer opportunities to succeed than they did.[2] The most disaffected groups formed the heart of what was once called the Obama Coalition, dubbed the rising American electorate in 2008 and cast aside by Donald Trump's election victory in 2016. Even before this radical realignment election, Americans believed that millennials faced greater challenges than older generations in their efforts to reach the middle class.[3]

More than one-third of millennials still live with their parents after college, delay marriage, family rearing, and home purchases—all traditional socialization rituals that could stimulate an otherwise moribund economy. Not all, but most, seem to get along fine with their parents, even sharing the same tastes in music: The *Beatles* and the *Eagles* among the favorite bands of both generations and extended home stays have strengthened generational bonds. Millennials reluctantly help their clueless non-techie elders with Internet glitches in exchange for room and board. As a result, both share a passion for anything technological, from home theatre systems to Buzz Feed, to Google, to *Facebook*, Kendall Readers and I-pads.

Unlike today's "techno-hippie" generation, most boomers coped with rapid social change in traditional ways by getting married, buying houses, starting businesses, having children, going into law, medicine or the military—while secretly harboring deep reservations about career and cause. Many learned too late in life that a passive existence is a wasted one, and that activism in the name of individual rights and political freedom is legitimate: unless constitutional rights are tested by conflict, they will not protect you when needed.

Since the founding of our Constitutional Republic, absolute freedom from the power of the state has been a clarion call for a balance in favor of individual rights over government power. Such liberties are difficult to enforce and subject to abuse. Among the "rights" considered off-limits for government in some regions include freedom of choice for local elites to decide who should vote, religious traditions such as burning Qur'ans, segregated private schools, and any form of gun registration. The balance of power to enforce such freedoms has clearly shifted from protecting individuals to defending the collective rights of society.

All generations share a mistrust of government. Skepticism has a long history in the United States, even though widespread grassroots distrust has less to do with the relative size of government *per se* than with deep political divisions concerning those areas considered off-limits for the state to invest financial, technological, or human resources.

Prior to November 8, 2016, we depended on government to solve society's complex, overwhelming problems such as debt, deficits, domestic terrorism, education, gun safety, access to healthcare, homeland security, immigration, pollution control, unemployment, and energy conservation, to name just a few. Republican-dominated Congressional deficit hawks have tried for decades to divest this dependency and dismantle vital governmental and human assets, insisting on cuts in public revenue and spending while shifting public responsibilities to the private sector. This happened during a recessionary period when infrastructure was crumbling, security threatened and Americans of all generations had difficulty meeting basic needs.

Among the other differences between generations is the avalanche of Internet communication technologies and their impact on individual behavior, career choices, education, sex, and politics. Obtaining information via the Internet in real time may make one's voice heard through social media, but also spreads anger, dissatisfaction, frustration, gridlock, hate, and misinformation in countries where modern democracy evolved—particularity in the United States and Europe. For millennials, invasive technologies have replaced nearly all forms of interpersonal relationships, political activism, and created a generation of 'armchair hacktivists' who possess the knowledge and moral conviction to act, but are reticent to engage in real civic participation, protests or political change. Thanks mainly to their high-quality low-cost higher education, boomers benefitted from higher rates of college graduation than previous generations. For millennials, that advantage no longer exists.

Eleven other nations—in not only Western Europe but also Poland and South Korea—have leapfrogged the United States in the percentage of their college-age citizens obtaining four-year degrees. When boomers graduated, only 5% of the population had college degrees and nearly all college graduates employed—a stark contrast to the frustrations plaguing millions of recent graduates in overcrowded job searches. War baby boomers did not worry about the effects of globalization, BREXIT, the EU, 401Ks, Trump, or finding a decent paying job as do millennials in the current post-recessionary economy.

Boomers were more willing to demonstrate on campus and in the streets because they gained confidence from high quality public education and the government subsidies their fathers received under the GI bill. Women who utilized student loans and federal Pell Grants gained more-advanced education and subsequently took part in politics at higher rates, helping to close the gender gap in commerce and political involvement. Families of male WWII veterans who used government resources experienced leaps in occupational status: a dockworker's son became a lawyer, a coal miner's daughter became an accountant, and an electrician's son became an engineer.

Boomers never thought about the availability of health insurance or retirement funds. Fringe benefits accompanied jobs and employment opportunities were plentiful. Collective anger was still outer-directed towards Russians, Chinese, North Koreans and other Evil Communists bent on conquering us. We were not worried about home invasions, murders in classrooms or walking in our own neighborhoods. We felt safe to demonstrate peacefully, protest and work inside or outside the system to achieve our idealistic social goals.

Today, overpriced and undervalued college degrees are viewed as investments, much like home mortgages, that yield benefits only to individual owners. This is significant change from the promises of the mid-20th century college and housing construction booms, when public officials promoted state-supported higher education as a vehicle for community economic development and social change. Based on the idea of a liberal education as the foundation for higher learning (since the founding of Harvard College in 1636), encouraging and subsidizing access would foster knowledge, creativity, dynamism, leadership, and other skills necessary to spur economic growth, technological innovation, and social advances. Other institutions assumed the responsibility of providing workers for the industrial age.

All that began to change on February 28, 1967 when California Governor Ronald Reagan declared that higher education as an *"intellectual luxury that perhaps we could do without."* Reagan was plainly staking out a competing vision for higher education and pandering to those who resented paying the bill for an educated workforce. Reagan changed the relationship between state government and higher education and crystalized what has since become Republican Party "conventional wisdom" about college education.

In the early 1970s, nearly three-quarters of college freshmen still said it was essential for them to "develop a meaningful philosophy of life." About one-third felt the same way about being "well off" financially. Those percentages have now completely reversed. Today, only one-third of college students believe in exploring guiding life principles while two-thirds seek financial security. This reversal began with the neo-conservative movement in the late-sixties and has accelerated in recent decades with the prolonged economic recession. The intellectual developmental purpose of higher education has all but disappeared due to government budget cuts and the rise of expensive private "for-profit" colleges. Advanced education, in turn, no longer emphasizes liberal arts or guarantees upward social mobility.

On the contrary, liberal education has become a joke with too many recent graduates co-opted by corporate interests, giving up on social causes, and willing to tolerate regressive social policies so long as government actions do not affect them personally. Many colleges and universities cooperate by eliminating so-called "low-enrollment" courses in the arts, classics, history, humanities, philosophy, and social sciences. Rather than envisioning idealistic goals for themselves and society, too many millennials concentrate instead and by necessity on mere survival, a good paying job and minimal recognition for organizational loyalty.

We continue to pay a high price for economic inequality and concentrations of wealth in the hands of the top 1% already uber-wealthy elites. Despite Bernie Saunders brief success in framing the issue of economic inequality as the 99% versus the 1%, many still blame government interventions for causing deep rifts in society. The Occupy Wall Street movement was the closest surrogate for generation-comparable political activism. The movement focused attention on society's still unmet challenges, but emerged and dissipated quickly. Millennial anger and idealism popped up briefly over shootings of Blacks by police, but many saw how quickly peaceful demonstration can turn violent and hesitated to participate. Subtle fear of surveillance that someone…somewhere…is watching, combined with cynicism and distrust of authority in general, inhibits activism on college campuses and in electoral processes. Anger rekindled after Trump's Electoral College win and Clinton's 2.8 million-vote victory in the popular vote. If this has happened in 40% of our recent presidential elections (2 out of 5), why even bother to vote?

****

Boomers were not always as comfortable or so paranoid about their futures. Despite the relative ease of their early years, many grew up with affluent inferiority complexes, always comparing themselves with the exploits of their parents' generation, aka "the greatest." Their formative years did not remotely resemble the life-and-death struggles faced by their parents, stalwart men and women who came of age during the Great Depression of the 1930s.

The now-mythical "Greatest Generation" (GG) experienced personal hardships and achieved heroic conquests during World War II. They accepted challenges from their political leaders willingly and endured the lean years with courage, dignity and grace. Many of them believed wrongly that their sacrifices would be rewarded later in life with the admiration and respect of their offspring, the anxiety-ridden and "not-as-great" boomers.

On the surface, boomers seemed to have it all: good neighborhood public schools, robust economic growth, prosperity, and peace from the end of the Second World War until the grim reality that U.S. armed forces were caught in the bloody quagmire of Vietnam. Between the wars, they and their parents enjoyed unprecedented economic growth and relative domestic tranquility. They were brainwashed into believing that the declared war in Southeast Asia and covert wars elsewhere were "just" and their leaders were trustworthy. However, these leaders and conflicts were different.

Vietnam was a protracted 20-year nightmare that produced no definitive outcomes and few victories. Unlike previous conflicts between equally matched combatants fought to liberate other countries from fascist dictators (and protect capitalism, democracy, and freedom), this conflict was a bloody prelude to the continuous state of terror-induced warfare that has existed for the past three decades. Except for the personal bravery displayed on the battlefield by those caught in the jaws of war, excuses for militarism in Southeast Asia were false in nearly every respect. This ideological conflict drained resources, demoralized the entire nation, and began the steady decline of America's post-World War II Golden Era.

Among the benefits of obliterating Germany and Japan—along with much of Asia and Europe—American economic prosperity and political dominance flourished during the post-war years. Our manufacturing prowess and military strength annihilated all global competitors and our economy prospered because our heavy energy-dependent industries were still intact after the war. Panic replaced complacency in early-1970s when the Organization of Petroleum Exporting Countries (OPEC) Middle East oil cartel hit us where it hurts—in the pocketbook.

Despite their soft Dr. Spock up bringing (the pediatrician, not the Star Trek robot), boomers were nonetheless imbued with their parents' fierce sense of loyalty, patriotism and gut-level opposition to all foreign "isms." They hated fascism, nihilism, imperialism, nudism, socialism, and especially communism—all viewed with distain as enemies of capitalism, democracy, freedom, truth, justice and the American Way.[4]

Thousands of books, documentaries, feature films, newsreels, and television series depict the GGs as stalwarts bravely defending democracy against foreign aggressors and preserving capitalism and economic freedom for future generations. They did just that with stoic resolve and at great personal cost: no one doubted their courage, fortitude or heroism. Boomers and their families were the primary beneficiaries of a robust post-war economic recovery, but their parents were not without their faults.

They degraded women, punished their children, segregated blacks, and despised Asians, Jews, Hispanics and other ethnic and racial minorities. They perpetuated income inequalities and persecuted gays. Invincible male veterans of the GG dressed in grey suits, drank whiskey, smoked cigarettes and, despite the occasional office romance, got married, and stayed married. They also maintained white male-superiority, occasionally "spanked" their daughters and frequently used "the buckle end of the belt" to punish their sons. When asked about their war records, many claimed they were with the Marines in the South Pacific or part of the first wave assaulting the Normandy beaches on D-Day. Some were genuine heroes, but many others lied about their service to the country.

The GG's emotionally (and physically) bruised sons and daughters grew up fat, happy and depressed—wrapped in the pseudo-security blanket of the American Dream and slumbering in the shadows of their victorious parents. Boomers were the first generation to witness shocking images of modern war machines devouring Freedom-Fighting Americans and Godless Vietnamese Communists. They tried, but somehow never quite measured up to their parents' accomplishments. Cowed by constant reminders of past, most of the not-as-greats acknowledged inequities caused by laissez-faire capitalism, gay bashing, poverty, segregation and racism. Many of them supported idealistic liberal political, social and religious causes, which sought to remedy these societal ills—others were conflicted by the threat of the draft, empathy for the civil rights movement, and fearful of the bloody battles televised nightly from the streets of America and the jungles of South Vietnam.

Opposition to the Vietnam War and support for civil rights was at first viewed as unpatriotic. By the late 1960s, resistance to the War merged with much broader social movement, reflecting a wider recognition that everyone deserves an equal opportunity regardless of age, gender, race or religion, as well as questioning conspicuous consumption, the role of banks and corporate interests supplying machines and materials for the War. The hardcore left re-emerged again during the spring of 2016 with candidate Sanders railing against the excesses of Wall Street and big banks. Too little, far too late.

Boomers were perhaps the last generation to grow up in an era of economic expansion with public resources (tax money) available to invest in domestic infrastructure and higher education. As they matured, many isolated themselves from the external chaos by hiding behind pretentious societal divisions: education level, income, gender, race, collage ranking, and religious stratification all played major roles in maintaining a rigidly segregated universe. Throughout this volatile decade, public schools and state universities were adequately funded and almost everyone (except ultra-conservatives) believed in the value of publically supported higher education. Public colleges opened to qualified candidates seeking personal and social betterment: many still trusted governments to provide support based on qualifications. In a bold departure from the past, public education promised equality of opportunity, economic benefits and upward social mobility never before accessible to America's lower and middle classes.

We were the "Great Society," Lyndon Baines Johnson's egalitarian social vision and linear descendent of Roosevelt's New Deal. Access to higher education supported economic elitism. Children from wealthy families could always pay steep prep school and college tuitions, attend graduate school, or take paid internships to beef up their résumés–without accumulating enormous debt. Not so for those in the middle or bottom rungs of society systemically excluded from college until the creation of the Scholastic Aptitude Test (SAT) in the mid-1960s.

Nothing manifested the aspirations of boomers more than the 4-tiered California higher education system. Only the best and brightest high school students admitted to the University of California, regardless of race, social class, or family income; if high school grades were slightly less than the top 12% in rigorous academic subjects, state colleges were next; community colleges third in the pecking order; and absolutely last were trade or vocational schools...dead last. In theory, those with exceptional abilities could "upgrade" from one level to the next, but the vast majority remained in the same institution for economic and family support reasons.

Public education served multiple purposes, but would never be isolated from the long knives of budget-conscious tax-cutting state politicians. Politicians heard the not-so-subtle message from taxpayers rejected from the top-tier and responded: Why should "we" pay for "them" to move up the economic and social status ladder? Right-wing politicians were quick to react. To paraphrase then Governor Ronald Reagan's belligerent attitude towards the University of California in 1967: *"Learning for learning's sake might be nice, but the rest of us shouldn't have to pay for it...higher education should prepare students for jobs."*

Resentment from the UC rejects built, simmered over, and helped to accelerate aggressive actions to reverse most progressive policy achieved during the expansionist eras of the 1930s and 1960s.

Little has changed since. Political invective against the "tax-consuming class," together with so-called "supply-side" tax cuts to prime the economy (and benefit billionaires), always the mantra of Republicans. Wisconsin's right-wing governor, Scott Walker, a Reagan-clone and brief GOP presidential aspirant, proposed rewriting the mission statement of his state's public-university system from one that emphasizes the public good to one that puts meeting "the state's workforce needs" front and center. How original. The self-serving and subtle message was that "government is to blame" for just about anything and everything wrong with our economy and society. This kill-the-beast rhetoric resonates with disaffected voters, many of whom themselves benefited from generous state-supported higher education subsidies in the past. Today, all but the brightest low-income scholarship-eligible are denied the promise of social mobility through higher education...sowing the seeds of an even less equal and more violent society in the future. Most boomers believed that higher education would improve income and social status but, as they grew older, they became more reluctant to pay the taxes necessary to achieve these and other goals. Darker and more tempting forces altered lifestyles: forced military conscription (the draft); glimpses of total sexual freedom (before the AIDs scare); idealism and fear of political violence (personified by the anti-war movement); segregation and racism; and the infusion of first soft, then hard, drugs into society. Many survived and prospered, but others did not.

Aging boomers who hid under their school desks fearing nuclear holocaust in 1950s can now afford to ignore the fetid reality outside and "enjoy the view" from their idyllic beach houses, mountain top retreats, Upper East Side co-ops, or gated suburban Mc-mansions. They cannot,

34

escape past memories, nor can they or their descendants avoid the ominous warning signs of present realities.

Plainly, some of the stories presented here happened in the past: others are blunt warnings about our present polarized political climate and its negative impact on future generations.

CHAPTER 4: America's Last Open Political Convention

Mark James McGinnis was a wisecracking 15-year-old suburban Southern California (SoCal) high school kid who was only vaguely aware that an election was underway during that hot LA summer of 1960. The issues, candidates, and parties competing for the presidential nominations escaped him and most of his compatriots almost entirely. He remembers his parents' friends and high school teachers mumbling something about Eisenhower, Kennedy, Nixon, Stevenson and the Republican Party, but his definition of a 'party' differed considerably from its political meaning. He and his friends were not oblivious; they just weren't interested in politics or politicians. (In this regard, as well as others, nothing has changed during the past half century.) Fifteen-year old SoCal males had far more important things on their minds than politics and political conventions: girls, drive-ins, football, surfing, wheels and…just maybe… college.

His parents were transplanted Midwestern suburban "I like Ike" Republicans who were content with the post-war status quo. They had endured bitterly cold upper Midwest winters during their early years. Depression-era hunger, military service and wartime rationing were still fresh in their memories. Like millions of others, they had moved to California after the war for warmer weather, steady work, decent neighborhoods and safe schools for their children. They were college graduates and constantly preached the value of higher education and civic responsibility as the only sure vehicles for upward economic and social mobility.

McGinnis was blessed with a middle-class upbringing in suburban SoCal during the go-go Fifties, but saw the world differently than his parents did. His best memory of high school was discovering Holden Caulfield in an English class.[1] Rather than studying after football practice, he preferred cruising Bob's Big Boy on Whittier Boulevard in his lowered '57 Chevy Bel Air. (Like Richard Dreyfuss in *American Graffiti.*) Nevertheless, there was a price to pay for such a leisurely and pointless adolescence.

"Stop fooling with that greasy car and go to your room and study," repeated his mother almost daily. She was right, but who listens to their mother's nagging at that age?

The political talk around the dinner table usually ended abruptly with the damning Franklin Roosevelt and all Democrats, extoling hometown hero Vice-President Richard M. Nixon, and paying homage to Ike and Mammie Eisenhower, the perfect Republican couple.

"Why can't you be more like Ike?" his father would say.

"Try harder, join the Army and make something of yourself."

Military service was a tempting prospect for patriotic young able-bodied red-blooded White American males, who tried to live up to their fathers' expectations, hardline attitudes, and alleged war records. Victories in Europe and in the Pacific were still celebrated and veterans of these conflicts revered by a grateful population. Before the passage of Civil Rights laws and enforcement of Title IX equal opportunity regulations, young white men of the male-dominated American culture of the 1950s and 60s were eager to become war heroes, G-men, or Rocket boys.

Heroic images were emblazoned into their adolescent imaginations after listening to their father's war stories and seeing endless media images of war heroes in public office, John Wayne movies, WWII propaganda films, and television series like "Victory at Sea" and the "Big Picture," all reinforced aggressive neuron receptors in their young brains. The emerging power of the mass media made it nearly impossible for young white males not to consider careers in military service: they were a willing cadre of Boy Scouts eager to arm themselves with heavy weapons.

For no apparent reason and with nothing else to do on a hot July day, Mark, his brother, and a childhood friend decided to attend the Democratic National Convention held at the Biltmore Hotel at 5th and Grand Avenue in downtown Los Angeles. Why they decided to make this epic 30-mile sojourn remains as much of a mystery as how they were able to find the convention hotel, enter without credentials, pass for delegates, and roam freely amidst the crowds of delegates, journalists and politicians. They were anything but strong partisans, had no press passes, and barely knew where the Biltmore Hotel was located.

None of the boys knew who would be speaking just a few days later at the Los Angeles Coliseum or how the challenges presented by an energetic young presidential candidate and authentic war hero would affect their futures and resonate throughout an entire generation. They were unaware that new candidates were set to replace old ones and restore confidence in Democratic Party leadership and social policies that sustained the country through the worse years of the Depression and the Second World War. They had no way of knowing how fortunate they were to grow up in the peaceful interregnum from the end of humanity's bloodiest conflict to the gruesome public beheading of a popular president.

* *

With some help from their parents and hastily drawn maps, they embarked on the Red Car Trollies along Whittier Boulevard to downtown LA. It is hard to believe, but an efficient modern urban transportation system connected all regions of greater Los Angeles in the 1960s. The demolition of this dependable urban mass transit rail system destroyed viable neighborhoods, created monstrous jammed 'freeways,' and resulted in fetid air.[2] The three intrepid young road warriors were even less certain of the purpose of a 'convention' than the route to get downtown, but they nonetheless made their way from the endless bedroom communities of Eastern Los Angeles Country to the venue in the City of Angeles.

Upon arriving at their destination, Mark noticed large crowds gathered in a park in front of the hotel. Television crews were unwinding miles of cables and remote trucks with large radar-like antenna parked nearby, but no visible security. Curiously, no one even asked who we were or why we were at the convention.

"We just walked up the front steps of the hotel and blended into the crowd," recalls McGinnis.

"No uniformed police, undercover security or registration desks for reporters, or anybody else for that matter."

"Delegates were wearing ID badges, but flashing our hastily forged learner's permits allowed us to gain entry," he remembered.

"We walked up the stairs into the ornate hotel lobby and recognized a youthful and tanned Bobby Kennedy in animated conversations with others."

"What do think they were talking about?" asked friend Bill.

"I donno, maybe something about a speech? Politicians make lots of speeches, ya know."

"So many of them, wonder where they all came from? Look, there's one from Illinoice. [mispronounce] I wonder where that is?"

"They are from all over the country, dummy, can't you see from their nametags," Mark responded to the stupid question in a know-it-all voice.

"Oh, is that what those things around their necks are?" responded his friend.

The interlopers were unaware that the New Deal coalition of big city bosses, intellectuals and Southerners, which has held the nation together during the depression and war years, was beginning to fray at its edges. Following the 20-year Roosevelt-Truman dynasty from 1933-1953, the Democratic Party was shut out of national political power for eight of the most prosperous years in U.S. history. After losing two presidential elections to Republicans in 1952 and 1956, convention delegates were anxious and eager to return to national power. Party bosses from large cities were desperate for victory and urgently seeking new faces to restore luster to Thomas Jefferson's once dominant Democratic-Republican Party, the oldest surviving entity of its kind in the world.

In most large cities, Democratic mayors still controlled elections using organized labor, political machines and strong-armed tactics. Economic inequality, discrimination, partisan politics and restricted social mobility accompanied segregation and racism. Welfare recipients in Chicago were (and probably still are) compensated for voting "early and often." They participated in the "graveyard vote" using the voter cards of those deceased since the last election to vote as often as they could before someone noticed. Absolute political control was an accepted reality imposed to overcome the First Great Depression and to promote national unity and personal sacrifices necessary to defeat Hitler and Tojo.

After the war, political alliances shifted with rapid industrial growth and population changes— enabled by new interstate highways connecting cities and suburbs in rural Southern and Western states—helping to revive Republicanism and threatening the Democratic Party's political power base and future survival. These halcyon days were best exemplified by the rock-solid "Ike and Dick" years from 1953-1961. Under the steadfast leadership of Army general and President Dwight David Eisenhower, the post-war economy prospered and produced full employment opportunities for nearly all White working class Americans.

We eliminated global competition and American products dominated world markets: General Motors produced half the world's automobiles, jobs were plentiful, and the country was on the move. Advertising men thrived by creating 'hidden persuaders' to entice middle class consumers with cash to spare to purchase more goods. Taxes were low and corporate capitalism was triumphant and thriving. The middle class was expanding and, for most of those who had survived the First Great Depression and the rationing of the war years, the go-go economy of the 50s was a welcome relief. America was in harmony as the incomes of wealthier Americans grew at the same pace as middle and lower-income families.

Today, in sharp contrast, CEOs of large corporations make over 350 times the average hourly pay of workers; Detroit is bankrupt and decaying; well-paying manufacturing jobs outsourced to Mexico, China and other Asian countries; wages for American workers have stagnated; and factions within the country fight bitterly among themselves for political power rather than focusing on a common foe. Not only have corporations succeeded in dominating political parties, but they also now control large portions of the United States Government. If we only knew then what we know now, maybe our catastrophic trust meltdown could have been avoided...perhaps?

Adlai, Dick, Jack, and Eleanor

Adlai Ewing Stevenson was an eloquent orator from a prominent Illinois political family whose rhetorical style impressed many liberal political leaders, intellectuals and academics. His 'dovish' attitude toward international conflict belied a tough rock-solid opposition to government interference in our private lives. His pivotal role as United Nations Ambassador during the Cuban Missile Crisis would reveal his true metal. In the pre-internet era, he prophesized that:

> *"If I were asked what the greatest danger is today in the conduct of democracy's affairs I suppose I would think first of war—but second, and important—we in America are becoming so big, so diversified, so organized, so institutionalized that there is increasing danger that the individual and his precious diversity will be squeezed out completely."* [3]

Those qualities alone were not quite enough to defeat the Supreme Allied Commander and his much-less-supreme running mate, Vice President "Tricky Dick" Nixon. The Eisenhower-Nixon ticket fit the boom times and won both elections handily.

Before declaring his loyalty to the Republican Party, both political parties wanted him as their candidate. Prior to the 1952 presidential nomination process, many conservative Republicans viewed Ike as just a little too moderate. Since many of General Eisenhower's political views were unknown, the always-suspicious right wing of the Republican Party supported the reliable conservative Sen. Robert Taft of Ohio for the nomination. The Supreme Allied Commander was suspect because of his support for the United Nations, NATO and the Marshall Plan as well as his wartime friendships with Roosevelt, Stalin and Russian generals. Maybe those commies got to him? To secure the conservative faction of the Republican Party, Ike chose Nixon as his running mate. Nixon may have reminded Ike of one of his Russian comrades.

Besides being politically astute, Tricky Dick was favorite son of the precursor to Tea Party wing of the Republican Party, the John Birch Society. Birchers were similar to today's radical right wing, but without its deep-pocket support from the Koch brothers and other billionaire oligarchs. What was the big difference? In addition to being a reliable conservative, his connection with a generally liberal and rapidly growing state enhanced Nixon's broader electoral appeal.

By all accounts, Dick did not have a warm relationship with Ike. Nixon's confidence might also have been just a little shaken by the realization that Eisenhower was so popular that he probably would have won whomever he chose for vice-president. Even with that insight, their backgrounds could not have been any different: Ike the warrior was from Mars and Dick was the dog from Pluto, the only dwarf planet investigated and expelled from the Solar System.

Nixon was not a dwarf, but a self-made hometown hero from Whittier, California, a cloistered and inward-looking Southern California (SoCal) bedroom community nestled in the Puente Hills about 30 miles east of Los Angeles. As Vice-President under Eisenhower, Nixon upheld a strict conservative image, despite the occasional gaffe such as the so-called "Checkers" incident, which nearly cost him his political career. Turning that gifted little dog into a political asset was simultaneously one of the most brilliant and sleaziest moves of the 20th century.[4]

With the exception of his younger brother Donald, a lanky good-natured local restaurateur enmeshed in a petty-scandal with the infamous Howard Hughes, members of his family were respected locally as humble, law-abiding hard-working Quakers.

As the heir-apparent to the presidency, Nixon was practically a shoe-in to carry on the Eisenhower legacy, believed the good folks of Whittier. The economy was growing and, aside from the occasional dustup with the Russians and the Korean "police action" known today as the Forgotten War, the U.S. was at peace. Japan and Germany were under reconstruction, and few Americans had the stomach for a nuclear World War III with the Soviets and its powerful allies, China and North Korea. Nixon reinforced his hawkish button-down conservative middle-class image as the staunch WASP who had turned down a full scholarship at Harvard to attend Whittier College and continue working in his family's grocery store. (Hard to swallow, but this actually *is* a true story.) This noble and unselfish act helped cement his pseudo-image as a rabid anticommunist, dog lover, and fiscal conservative and self-made man.

Nixon's image did little to help his alma mater, which before (and after) his vice-presidencies and presidencies was a little-known private Quaker institution located somewhere in Eastern Los Angeles County. The City of Whittier was far less forgiving. After Nixon disgraced himself, the nation and his party with the Watergate scandal and resignation in August 1974, the city renounced the hometown hero by purging his name from one of its main streets: Nixon Boulevard was renamed Bewley Street. The politics of street naming can be brutal.

****

Prior to the convention, the Democratic frontrunner and party leader Adlai E. Stevenson announced curiously that he would not again run for president, but he would accept the nomination, if drafted by the convention delegates. Miraculously, thousands of "Stevenson for President" lapel buttons appeared at the convention. His supporters were enthusiastic, but others leery about a candidate who had already lost twice to Eisenhower and Nixon.

Democratic Party leaders were equally suspicious of Kennedy's ultra-wealthy family (a distinction usually reserved for Republicans), his infamous ne're-do-well father Joseph P. Kennedy Sr. and, most of all, his Catholicism. The anti-Catholic stereotype of 'Rum, Romance, and Romanism' still prevailed in many regions of the country, especially in the Deep South where Democratic support was essential for victory and eroding quickly as the party moved further left on social issues such as civil rights and school desegregation.

Ironically, the stage was set for 60 more years of 'culture wars' by conservative Republicans Eisenhower and Chief Justice of the Supreme Court Earl Warren of California with *Brown v. Board of Education* in 1954, the case which overturned the 'separate but equal' doctrine of institutionalized racism which had stood as law of the land for the previous 60 years. Most voters viewed Jack Kennedy as the more socially liberal of the two candidates; he fought hard in the primary elections to overcome his social status and over-Privileged-Bostonian-Elitist-Catholic roots while appealing to working-class Americans.

Prior to the convention, JFK was still short of a majority of delegates needed to clinch the nomination. Southern white 'Dixiecrat' support was vital for any Democrat to run successfully against an entrenched and popular Republican incumbent and his apparent successor to the White House. Few could have predicted that future events would make this the last open convention in American history. Three naïve teenagers were about to witness history.

From Smoke Filled Rooms to Super-Pacs

Prior the 1960 presidential campaign, Kennedy was little known outside the Northeast. He had served less than two-terms in the U.S. Senate and garnered national exposure at the 1956 Democratic convention, finishing behind the bland Senator Estes Kefauver of Tennessee in the convention balloting for vice-president. Polls in the late summer of 1960 following the conventions showed that Republican incumbent Vice-President Richard M. Nixon had a solid 6-point edge.

In those days, political party bosses, local elected officials, and convention delegates tightly controlled campaign funds and candidate selection processes. Newspaper syndicates acted as surrogate cheerleaders for the major party candidates and helped political parties disseminate their messages to potential voters. Attitudes as well as populations were shifting, expanding westward and seeking new beginnings in open geographic and political spaces.

Unlike today's made-for-television "debates" among ideologues, misfits and warped personalities bankrolled by reclusive billionaires, political campaigns and elections in the day were amateurish, old-fashioned and often comedic events motivated by local 'grass-roots' enthusiasm and flag-waving patriotism. Information travelled more slowly without Internet or social media and most literate citizens still read newspapers and magazines for detailed coverage of economic and political events. Political advertisements were limited to a few million dollars' worth of billboards, bumper stickers, campaign buttons, newspapers ads and radio spots. Direct communication between candidate and citizen was still decades away.

Despite its flaws, most participants preferred clumsy 'press the flesh' democracy with direct contact between citizens and politicians at all levels in the affairs of government. This was especially important in local governments where economic elites controlled city hall, police, schools and zoning laws. Those who wanted to be involved with local politics were encouraged to join, so long as were respectable upper-middle class Whites, Rotary Club members and military veterans—preferably all three.

New technologies such as targeted radio advertising and random-access telephone dialing were just beginning to influence political attitudes and weaken the king-making power of party bosses and local newspaper editors. Young boys still played war games and worshipped combat heroes.

The all-seeing eye of the television camera would soon replace traditional ways of selecting nominees for higher political office. These changes would make many voters yearn for the 'good old days" of apple pie, motherhood, hometown newspapers, and one-party dominance in the 1940s.[5]

Unlike his Democratic predecessor Harry S Truman, Republican Dwight D. Eisenhower managed a steady hand on the wheels of government during the 1950s, without alienating his political opponents. Eisenhower's Democratic opponents during presidential elections of 1952 and 1956 were gentlemanly U.S. Senators from Illinois, Alabama and Tennessee. They were also losers.

In this era before big media and money determined the outcome of party conventions, much the so-called 'horse-trading' for votes was rumored to take place in 'smoke-filled rooms' among state delegates promoting individual regional interests and districts. The three boys were unaware of lobbying efforts taking place around them among the principal players as they nervously drifted from one conference room to another.

Mark McGinnis thought to himself as they strolled confidently through the ornate hotel hallways on thick oriental carpets: "We hardly looked like those baggy-eyed, bourbon-belching, cigar-chomping, pot-bellied Midwestern politicians."

"Nonetheless, we had free run of the hotel and took elevators to upper floors and witnessed these "caucuses" first hand. They were indeed held in smoke-filled rooms occupied by paunchy grey-haired old men in white shirts and suspenders smoking stinky cigars!"

The ease droppers listened to arcane discussions about a party platform, electoral reform, and delegate counts—strange subjects of which they knew nothing. They recognized familiar faces such at Lyndon Baines Johnson of Texas, a towering man with a hangdog face whom they later learned was Speaker of the House of Representatives—wherever that was?

On that day, none of the boys or the glad-handing politicians could have envisioned Johnson's destiny and how their lives would become intertwined with his presidency.

McGinnis remembers that: "After a few hours of listening to boring discussions about issues we knew nothing of and cared less about, we meandered into a large conference room. Our eyes were immediately fixed upon television cameras set up at both ends of the room."

"Friend Bill was a techie, so we all slipped on the earphones and began pretending to 'direct' the proceedings. After a few minutes, the room began to fill with reporters, many of whom were asking *us* where to sit. We diligently obliged the requests, chuckling to themselves about the reporter's pipes and funny hats, stuffed with bits of paper stuffed in their brims."

"Another set of cameras across the room was manned by real professionals, so we thought it might be best to drift into the unfilled seats with the 'other' newspaper and television reporters.

To our shock and amazement, in the room walked Eleanor Roosevelt followed by Adlai Stevenson and their entourages. Even lackadaisical SoCal teenagers realized that a presidential candidate and a former president's widow had just entered the room. The whole experience was becoming surreal.

Mrs. Roosevelt, a tall and gangly grey-haired woman, now in her late-70s, whose distinctive high-pitched voice was immediately recognizable, even to naïve teenagers. In a short speech, Mrs. Roosevelt endorsed Stevenson as her preferred choice for the Democratic Party nomination, which set off a cacophony of questions by the assembled *Paparazzi.*

On that eventful day in Los Angeles, they were unaware of any of the backroom deals or political drama surrounding this or any other announcements made at the convention.

"We didn't know then that she was a leading feminist and friend of the civil rights movement who had been under constant surveillance by the FBI since her husband's death in 1945," McGinnis discovered years later.

Mrs. Roosevelt remained on J. Edgar Hoover's black list for the rest of her life simply because of her sympathy for the poor, minorities and the civil rights movement. Obviously, Hoover believed, she had Communist leanings.

They still wondered later in life how many of J. Edgar's henchmen were in that room on that day, listening and watching.

****

McGinnis and the others were unaware of efforts by civil rights activists to distance themselves from anything or anyone remotely associated with communism. Hoover was convinced that Reds had infiltrated civil rights organizations and that Blacks were preparing join them in revolt against the United States. The FBI investigated civil rights leaders, including Martin Luther King, and labeled them "communist" or "subversive." (Racist Southerners referred to Rev. King in the most bestial terms as Martin Luther Coon.) The moderate elements of the movement, such as the Student Nonviolent Coordinating Committee (SNCC), the Southern Christian Leadership Conference (SCLC), and the Congress of Racial Equality (CORE) were careful to separate their organizations from anti-war and militant civil rights groups. The Black Panthers and the Nation of Islam, better known as Black Muslims, accepted assistance and encouraged participation from anyone, regardless of political affiliation. Conservative politicians would play off the fear of Whites who were scared shitless by the prospect of armed Black revolutionaries assaulting their suburban enclaves.

After promising political party bosses that he would select the dog-faced Texan as his running mate, Jack Kennedy's nomination for president was all but assured. His acceptance speech on July 15, 1960 before a massive crowd and television audience in the Los Angeles Coliseum articulated an ambitious domestic and international agenda. The ground breaking New Frontier speech inspired a new generation to meet lofty domestic and international public policy challenges and civil obligations.

> *...I stand here tonight facing west on what was once the last frontier. From the lands that stretch three thousand miles behind us, the pioneers gave up their safety, their comfort and sometimes their lives to build our new West. They were not the captives of their own doubts, nor the prisoners of their own price tags. They were determined to make the new world strong and free -- an example to the world, to overcome its hazards and its hardships, to conquer the enemies that threatened from within and without.*
>
> *Some would say that those struggles are all over, that all the horizons have been explored, that all the battles have been won, that there is no longer an American frontier. But I trust that no one in this assemblage would agree with that sentiment; for the problems are not all solved and the battles are not all won; and we stand today on the edge of a New Frontier... the frontier of unfilled hopes and unfilled threats... The New Frontier is here whether we seek it or not.*
>
> *Beyond that frontier are uncharted areas of science and space, unsolved problems of peace and war, unconquered problems of ignorance and prejudice, unanswered questions of poverty and surplus. It would be easier to shrink from that new frontier, to look to the safe mediocrity of the past, to be lulled by good intentions and high rhetoric...That is the choice our nation must make -- a choice that lies between the public interest and private comfort, between national greatness and national decline, between the fresh air of progress and the stale, dank atmosphere of "normalcy," between dedication or mediocrity.*
>
> *All mankind waits upon our decision. A whole world looks to see what we shall do. And we cannot fail that trust. And we cannot fail to try..."*

Source: Public Domain

No one in the Los Angeles Coliseum on that warm night filled with hope and optimism about the future could have remotely imagined the violent death of this young president or the end of an era of open participatory democracy. Television and other electronic media had not diminished democratic electoral traditions such as open primary elections, stump speeches, and stuffing ballot boxes. Strict security precautions at conventions following Kennedy's assassination would all but end the American tradition of bottom-up representative democracy. Few realized just how vulnerable our leaders and our political system had become as the Closed National Security State replaced the Open Democratic State.

The door opened for ultra-right wing super-wealthy demagogues to self-fund campaigns and pay for their own Pretorian Guard security detachments without constitutional checks or democratic balances. Support from grass-roots organizations and local political parties disappeared quickly with the advent of electronic media campaigns. Most Americans were unaware that the electronic mind fucking of the electorate had begun.

The emerging convergence of political movements and technological innovations since the turn of the 21st century might have bridged generational differences and restored trust in electoral and governmental processes. Alternatively, these centrally controlled devises could entrap untold future generations in a multi-media web of deceit, fraud, manipulation and surveillance. Questions about modern campaigns remain unanswered: has digital technology become the once-heralded substitute for the press-the-flesh political campaigning? Has its promise for communicating political information been blunted by unlimited contributions from ruthless right-wing billionaires targeting vulnerable semi-literate groups with negative political ads?

Future trends are clearer: those of all ages use personal data devices to communicate with others, seek information, connect with friends, conduct business and maybe even govern. Corporate and political operatives monitor data generated by these same devices to extract vital and once privileged information stored in our innermost previously unreachable imaginations. Citizens feel bitter about big government's perceived intrusion in their private space, especially when its paranoia, policies and regulations affect us directly.

****

After his humiliating defeat in the 1960, most pundits hoped that they had seen the last of Tricky Dick Nixon. They were wrong. By shear fortune and fortitude, Nixon recovered from narrowly losing the presidency and soundly trounced two years later in the race for the governorship of California by Edwin G. 'Pat' Brown (the current Governor's father) to finally achieve his ultimate quest by capitalizing on widespread opposition to the Democrats, LBJ and the Vietnam War. Just six years later, the "New Nixon" would capture the rightward turn in American politics and sense the widespread negativism among voters. He would master the cool mass medium of television and concoct a 'secret plan' to end the War. (The plan was so secret that the Master of Deceit failed to share even its basic details or expected consequences with the American people.

After twice winning the presidency in 1968 and 1972, Nixon abruptly resigned during the Watergate investigation in 1974 following the House Judiciary Committee vote to impeach him. This cowardly act confirmed that his ambition recognized no limits to achieving his personal goals. Baby boomers would suffer from one man's perverse aspirations.

If nothing else, Nixon, like the Italian Prince Niccolò di Bernardo dei Machiavelli, received some credit for his cunningness, political realism, and raw staying power. He foresaw China's emergence as a formidable economic, military and political power and perhaps avoided a potential nuclear confrontation.

Forty years after the scrawny second-stringer failed to make the 1932 Whittier College football squad, he would conquer the NFL of politics—but he would never exorcise his own personal demons.

CHAPTER 5: Godless Communists and Cuban Nukes

The world changed suddenly on October 4, 1957 when the Soviet Union (Russia) hurled a beeping basketball-sized spy satellite into space. It heightened the Red Scare, reinforced fears of a communist invasion, and initiated an applied science and technological revolution that would forever alter the history of the United States.

The frightening extent of the Soviet threat became even more apparent shortly after Kennedy's inauguration on April 12, 1961 when the Russians launched the first human into space. Cosmonaut Yuri Gagarin orbited the earth and American politicians went ape-shit. The Space Race was on. Rumors spread that the Soviets were building a huge rocket aimed at the United States carrying paratroopers. Future techno-boomers Bill Gates and Steve Jobs were 2-years old when 'Sputnik' was launched.

Televised Debates and Machiavellian Politics

Technology was beginning to force permanent changes in family values, political campaigns and society, but television had still not yet replaced newspapers or radio as the primary sources of political information, as it would a few decades later. At the beginning of the Eisenhower-Nixon administration in 1953, only 10% of American households owned television sets: by the 1960 presidential campaign, nearly 90% of all households had at least one TV. In less than a decade, talking heads in black and white had penetrated nearly everyone's living room.

The first prime-time evening news broadcast was the CBS Evening News with Walter Cronkite a decade later. Families clustered around the new medium in much the same way they had listened to radio broadcasts during the war years. Bedrooms were off-limits for the new medium, but that would soon change with the advent of cable networks, color, smaller screens and pornography.

Few campaign consultants and even fewer so-called "average" citizens foresaw the immense worldwide persuasive power of electronic media and its negative impact on civic values and democratic participation.

During campaign speeches and press conferences before the first televised debates in American history, Nixon portrayed Kennedy as inexperienced and unprepared to be commander-in-chief, despite his distinguished war record and heroism in the South Pacific. Nixon emphasized

his own non-combat naval service during World War II and his 'presence' during top-sec
discussions with the Eisenhower foreign policy team. Although his leadership role during the
Korean War was questionable, he was at least 'in the loop' during many of the tense negotiations
leading to commitment of U.S. forces and peace talks with North Korea and Red China.

Kennedy fought to overcome the stigma of his religion in a country that had never before
elected a Roman Catholic president. His thoughtful speeches on the separation of personal beliefs
from politics and policy-making helped partially dispel some aspects of this divisive campaign
issue. Kennedy shrewdly finessed the issue of his Catholicism with glib platitudes about
separation of church and state. Most Americans had more important worries than the Pope
influencing elections. Rather they were obsessed with threat of 'creeping communism' spreading
across Eastern Europe, Asia and perhaps even the Americas.

Apart from his religious convictions, Kennedy was just as much of an ideological anti-
communist as Nixon was. He took full advantage of his earlier associations with the infamous
Sen. Joseph McCarthy of Wisconsin, a friend of the Kennedys. Bobby Kennedy, the Senator's
brother and future Attorney General, was Special Counsel to the House Un-American Activities
Committee (HUAC), the shameful inquisition established in the late 1930s to identify and
eliminate alleged fascist and communist sympathizers in the federal government.

After the war, HUAC turned its attention to the world of the arts and entertainment and
'blacklisted' several Hollywood actors, screenwriters, musicians and directors for their leftist
political views. Among those refused to take a "loyalty oath" and whose careers were destroyed
were academy award winners such as Dalton Trumbo and the Hollywood 10, some of whom
spent time in federal prison for contempt of Congress. Big name conservative Hollywood stars
and producers such as Gary Cooper, Ronald Reagan, John Wayne, and Walt Disney lent their
fame and 'friendly persuasion' to the HUAC cause and helped reinforce the Red Scare. Other
geopolitical forces deeply concerned Americans.

In the pre-electronic news media era, candidates gave many stump speeches and held
unscripted interviews with newspaper reporters. They appeared on radio and television, including
nascent network news shows like *Meet the Press* and *Face the Nation*. For the first time ever,
presidential candidates agreed to debate each other on national television. Nixon, hoping for a
single "knockout blow," negotiated for just one debate; Kennedy wanted five. They settled on
four.

prepared for the first debate with aides who acted like young Ivy League college ...ming for final exam. This is probably because his coaches *were* young Harvard College ...ds. During prep sessions, he went over policy issues in detail with his aides, drafted an opening statement and practiced rebuttals to Nixon's rejoinders. Kennedy had a nap in the afternoon prior to the first debate, after which his "brain trust" met again, peppering JFK with questions from prepared note cards. Nixon spent the day alone pacing back and forth in his hotel room, with barely a visitor or phone call. He was nursing a knee injury, which he inflamed again by hitting a car door on his way to the studio in Chicago.

For the first time on September 26, 1960, presidential debates pre-empted the Andy Griffith Show and attracted an audience of over 65 million viewers. Three other barely-remembered debates followed in October and the cumulative results were widely credited with erasing incumbent Vice President Richard M. Nixon's lead over John F. Kennedy in the race to succeed Dwight D. Eisenhower.

Kennedy won in November by a razor-thin margin in one of the most controversial elections in American history. Kennedy historian Theodore White wrote naively and nostalgically that the debates "revived face-to-face political processes that disappeared centuries ago." He further opined that the "personal choice of a leader was missing for centuries from modern civilization- or less limited to such conclaves of deputized spokesmen of the whole as...a gathering of Communist barons in the Kremlin." What the TV debates supposedly did was to generalize this tribal sense of participation, this emotional judgment of the leader, from the few to the multitude. Whom was Teddy kidding? Those Communist barons in the Kremlin and Beijing were just waiting for a patsy like Kennedy so they could bury us.

Ironically, as things turned out, it was not Kennedy, but Nixon who became the ultimate communist tool. Nixon made the conventional party choice for vice president, Boston blue blood Brahman Henry Cabot Lodge who, it is said, descended from families so rich and so powerful that, in proper Bostonian circles "the Cabot's speak only to the Lodges and the Lodges speak only to God." After seeing Nixon's performance and consulting with God, Cabot Lodge was much less forgiving in his condemnation of the outcome of the debate: "That son of a bitch just lost the election." God had apparently spoken, but Nixon helped the Republicans snatch defeat from the jaws of victory. Of course, the losers objected.

Rumors circulated that Kennedy men had bribed the Chicago television station to turn up the temperature in the studio to make Nixon sweat more profusely. This was plausible because Chicago was a Democratic machine-run city under the firm control of Mayor Richard J. Daley, a staunch Kennedy alley. Daley maintained control over the local television stations as well. Ever since Kennedy won the historic televised debates with Richard M. Nixon in 1960, relationships among citizens, corporations, and governments have become increasingly distant, fragmented and controlled. The mass media blindly support corporate capitalism, but conveniently ignore the sequestering of our political processes and suppression of the middle and lower classes. The myth of American democracy is still lauded—even as millions languish in minimum wage jobs and standby helplessly as deep pockets have replaced votes in determining the outcome of elections.

In the end, Kennedy looked presidential. Nixon just looked tired. The fact that Kennedy stood on the same stage with Vice President Nixon improved his personal appeal and stature. The debates erased Nixon's main argument against his opponent: that he was not up to the task of being president. Some viewed the head-to-head confrontation as nothing more than a triumph of Kennedy style over Nixon's substance. After the other three other debates in October, Kennedy and his style were well ahead in the polls and never relinquished the lead.

Although most voters did not realize the significance at the time, the Kennedy-Nixon debates ushered in the transition to the modern era of big money, manicured candidates, *Moneyball* politics and media-driven campaigns. The decade also witnessed a stunning transformation in candidate-to-citizen communication technologies, precursor to the Internet revolution that would signal the final victory of elites and the end of direct participatory democracy in the late 20th century.

Kennedy capitalized on the mid-century electronic media revolution and, like President Obama in the 2008 campaign, probably would not have been elected without the image-shaping power of the new visual media. Indeed, as Marshall McLuhan observed several decades ago "the medium is the message" and politicians a half-century apart successfully deployed new and compelling technologies to reach a broader audience.

Three Crises

After winning a close election and competing with the Russians for dominance in space, newly elected President John F. Kennedy would confront three major global crises during his much too brief tenure in office: the first was an ill-fated and poorly-executed CIA backed invasion by Cuban exiles at the Bay of Pigs, near Cienfuegos in Southern Cuba; the second, a tense eyeball-to-eyeball standoff with the Russians over access to occupied Berlin; and last, the Cuban Missile Crisis, a perilous standoff between the U.S. and the Russian which brought the world to the brink of nuclear war.

The Russians provoked the young president; he had to apologize to the American people for his inept meddling in Cuban affairs, and adroitly managed one of the world's first nuclear standoffs—all in less than three years. Repercussions or backlash from any of these foreign policy misadventures could, and probably did, provoke deadly retaliation by one or more of Kennedy's growing list of powerful enemies.

The Cold War with the Soviet Union was in full swing. Communist Dictator Fidel Castro was in power for over a year in Cuba just 90 miles away from Key West. Many were still angry that the U.S. had "lost" China and Cuba to the communists and convinced that the United States faced an even greater danger, a "missile gap" with the Soviet Union. Despite the reality that the U.S. had enough firepower to annihilate Russia ten times over, Americans feared the Godless Communist menace and were again prepared to shed blood and treasure to protect apple pie, capitalism, democracy, and motherhood. The era of communist witch-hunts to root out Reds in the federal government, led by Senator Joe McCarthy, was still a fresh memory. His latter-day clone, Fox News hatchet man and sex harasser Bill O'Reilly uses his media pulpit and the same communist smear tactics to root out liberal academics and politicians who oppose right-wing politics.

Global confrontations fundamentally changed the power of the presidency and constitutional authority of the executive branch. Modern presidents learned from Kennedy's mistakes that they exert power less by brute force than by diplomacy and control of information; presidents who can decisively influence the shape of internal deliberations, media reports, negotiations and public debate through the manipulation of trusted sources of information usually emerge victorious. The classic failure involved President Kennedy's explanations of what was promised to anti-Castro Cubans who tried and failed to overthrow Fidel Castro at the Bay of Pigs in April 1961.

Although the Eisenhower administration authorized and funded the covert operation, Kennedy launched the invasion less than three months after he assumed the presidency. After its failure, Kennedy claimed that he was unaware of the details of the operation. He would later confide in his chief advisors that he felt betrayed and misled by the intelligence community, especially the CIA.

In all respects, the invasion was a fiasco for the United States. The air cover allegedly promised for the amphibious landings never materialized and Kennedy's spokesmen—a Pentagon press officer with years of experience on the job—lied about American involvement, denying any connection with either the planning or the execution of the abortive invasion. Pentagon officials followed up their denials with claims that national security justified their lying to the press and the American people. (Does that sound familiar?) Unfortunately, this big lie technique has become standard practice for presidential responses ever since.

Castro knew of the invasion in advance from his spy network in Miami. The Cuban armed forces, well trained and equipped by the Russians, easily defeated the rag-tag invading exile combatants within a few days. President Kennedy cancelled airstrikes to establish plausible deniability that the U.S. was directly involved. This, too, became a familiar theme for isolating presidents from the consequences of future misadventures, including other high crimes and misdemeanors such as Lyndon Johnson's Gulf of Tonkin resolution, Nixon's ill-fated Watergate break-in, the Reagan-Bush administration Iran-Contra scandal, and George W. Bush's blatant lies about the existence of Weapons of Mass Destruction (WMDs) to justify invading Iraq.

Recriminations followed the abortive Bay of Pigs invasion. Kennedy learned a bitter lesson: never trust the established bureaucracy to provide anything except self-serving information. The CIA was less than forthcoming in sharing with the president what air support they had promised the Cuban invasion forces. This placed the President in an impossible position—either he escalates the conflict and admits that U.S. was involved in the planning and execution phases, or withdraws air support and blames others for the fiasco. Kennedy chose the latter course and fired high-level administration officials, including CIA Director Allen Dulles. This was also a turning point for Cuban-American relations with the Democratic Party.

The 1959 Cuban Revolution brought Fidel Castro to power and forced thousands of Cubans from their homeland seeking freedom and refuge in the United States. Exiles were welcomed to the United States and received special treatment because they were fleeing a communist regime. Many immigrants hoped the U.S. would overthrow Castro so they could return to Cuba. Many blamed the President for hesitating to provide air support allegedly promised the Cuban invaders.

Kennedy's support among Cubans plummeted and Cuban-Americans who fled Castro's repressive regime realigned with the Republican Party.

Among the other consequences of the disastrous Bay of Pigs operation, Cuba entered into a mutual defense pact with the Soviets. The Russians viewed the failed invasion as a ham-handed attempt by an inexperienced young president to meddle in military matters, just as Nixon had predicted. If presidents cannot acquire accurate information readily under the most extraordinary circumstances, even potential nuclear crises, then they surely distrust internal flows of information from subordinates in routine situations. The Soviets quickly tested the new president by asserting their military dominance over a divided Europe. Access to Berlin would revert to Russia's puppet state of East Germany. Despite the blustering rhetoric, neither side wanted to relive the horrors of Second World War. Hardline Soviet Premier Nikita Khrushchev hinted that a deal with Kennedy or Nixon might be possible over Berlin, but a summit with the Big Four powers was cancelled after a CIA U-2 spy plane was shot down over the Ural region of Southern Russia on May 1, 1960. (Remember Tom Hanks in *Bridge of Spies*?) The Soviet Union retaliated by constructing the infamous Berlin Wall in 1961 to stop Eastern Bloc emigration westward, preventing escape across the divided city sector border from East to West Berlin. Checkpoint Charlie became a symbol of the Cold War, representing the 'Iron Curtain" separating Communist East from Democratic West Europe.

As the confrontation over Berlin escalated, Kennedy spoke to the nation on national television, reiterating that the United States sought peace and recognized historical Soviet concerns about German aggression. Kennedy said he was willing to renew talks so long as the Soviets did not try to impose pre-conditions, but subsequent actions did not match his diplomatic words. Acting upon recommendations of his military advisers in a risky countermove, Kennedy announced that he would ask Congress for additional billions for military spending, mostly for heavy weapons such as tanks for a land war in Europe. The Soviets were convinced the military build-up threatened war. Echoing Winston Churchill, Kennedy boldly proclaimed, *"We seek peace, but we shall not surrender."*

Soviet and American tanks faced each other muzzle to muzzle in the fall 1961 near Checkpoint Charlie separating East and West Berlin. Despite provocations on both sides, cooler heads prevailed to deescalate the crisis. Memories of the horrors of World War II were still too fresh and the prospects for a nuclear war were all too real. Americans and Europeans had seen the devastation caused by the atomic bombs dropped on Hiroshima and Nagasaki and were afraid of a war with the Soviets. As bad as these confrontations may have appeared at the time, conventional war was still the preferred option for political leaders.

The last stanza of Alan Ginsberg's beatnik era poem *America* captured the nation's fixation with television, fear of nuclear war, fervent anti-communism, homophobia, and racism which pervaded politics and society in the late 1950s (Full poem is in Appendix).

> *America you don't really want to go to war.*
> *America it's them bad Russians.*
> *Them Russians them Russians and them Chinamen. And them Russians. The*
> *Russia wants to eat us alive. The Russia's power mad. She wants to take our*
> *cars from out our garages.*
> *Her wants to grab Chicago. Her needs a Red Reader's Digest. Her wants our auto*
> *plants in Siberia. Him big bureaucracy running our filling stations.*
> *That no good. Ugh. Him makes Indians learn read. Him need big black niggers.*
> *Hah. Her make us all work sixteen hours a day. Help. America this is quite serious.*
> *America this is the impression I get from looking in the television set.*
> *America is this correct?*
> *I'd better get right down to the job.*
> *It's true I don't want to join the Army or turn lathes in precision parts factories,*
> *I'm nearsighted and psychopathic anyway.*
> *America I'm putting my queer shoulder to the wheel.*

The British, French and Americans distrusted "them Nazis" almost as much as they feared "them Russians and them Chinamen." Ideological conflict often boiled over and the Soviets would further tighten the Iron Curtain separating Communist East from Capitalist West Europe. The inexperienced Kennedy undercut his own bargaining position by acknowledging Russian territorial claims to Eastern Europe, suggesting agreement to a permanent division of Berlin and Germany. Even under the best circumstances, presidents find themselves forced to react to crises without critical information vital to an impending decision.

Partially because of miscommunication between the Americans and Russians, the Cuban Missile Crisis brought the world's super powers to a precipice of nuclear holocaust in October 1962.

Repeated attempts by the CIA to overthrow the Castro regime provided an excuse for the Russians to export intermediate-range Intercontinental Ballistic Missile (ICBMs) to Cuba. Several years earlier, the United States had established ICBM bases in Turkey as part of its NATO alliance. Kennedy was badly misled by his closest advisors in two previous encounters and needed to establish beyond any doubt that Soviet missiles existed before deciding what actions to take— actions that could quickly escalate into mutually assured destruction (MAD)—nuclear war with the Soviets. Despite the terrible urgency, Kennedy could not obtain the necessary photographic evidence of missile placement in Cuba. Once aerial photographs confirmed their existence, Ambassador Adlai E. Stevenson confronted the Russians at a tense UN Security Council meeting. This was high drama with the lives of the 300-500 million people dependent on the outcome.

After displaying the U-2 photographs at the United Nations, Russians could not deny the presence of Intercontinental Ballistic Missiles (ICBMs) capable of hitting cities in the continental United States. Unbeknownst to most Americans at the time, the Cuban Missile Crisis had begun.

Events in Cuba, Germany and Russia were far too remote to have any bearing on the daily lives of youngest Isla Vistans. Their only ideologies were self-imposed isolationism and hedonism. How wrong they were.

One of those who thought little of global events at the time was 18-year old Richard Pierpont Morgan. During a late afternoon visit to the Red House, one of Rick's friends, Dennis Finch, was tossing his duffle bag into the back of his car dressed in full Marine Corps fatigues. Dennis had recently enlisted in the Marine Corps Reserves to avoid being drafted.

"Where the hell are you going?" Rick asked, naively.

"Florida, man." Dennis answered, "someplace called Tampa somewhere back east."

"Bitchin,' man. Why are you goin' down there?"

"I am not sure, but they are serious, this time. It's not a drill. We're not even supposed to talk about it." Their conversation ended abruptly.

Dennis was called up along with thousands of other reservists in a massive deployment of troops at Southern Command Headquarters in anticipation of a D-Day style amphibious invasion of Cuba, should high-level negotiations with the Russians fail. This was one of several unpleasant options that the young president was considering to resolve the missile crisis. Some of his most trusted advisors and cabinet members argued forcefully for a 'preemptive tactical nuclear strike,' a little nuke, against Cuba. This would certainly have prompted retaliation by the Russians with bigger nukes against Miami, New York or Washington. Among the proponents of this apocalyptic solution was none other than General Curtis LeMay, former Commander of the U.S. 8th Air Force in Europe during WW II and Chairman of Kennedy's Joint Chiefs-of-Staff. Remember George C. Scott's eerie portrayal of General Buck Turgitson in Stanley Kubrick's brilliant black comedy, *Dr. Strangelove: How I Learned to Stop Worrying and Love the Bomb:* that was LeMay. The land invasion, even though it would have cost the lives of many young Americans, possibly including Dennis, considered a moderately risky choice.

Fortunately, a naval blockade of Soviet ships carrying missiles to Cuba was chosen instead. This was still a risky option involving the forcible interdiction of Russian transport ships on the high seas. Any contact between U.S. and Russian vessels, accidental or incidental, would have been viewed as a hostile act of war and prompted retaliation.

For 10 tense days in October 1962, the world's nuclear powers were 'eyeball-to-eyeball' in an escalating conflict with the Russians. After intricate back-channel negotiations, Kennedy agreed to remove obsolete American missiles from Turkey in exchange for the Russian removal of the ICBMs from Cuba. The rest of the story became Cold War history. Robert F. Kennedy, a participant in war rooms where the high drama unfolded, estimated a 50:50 chance of nuclear war with the Russians. Cooler heads prevailed, Dennis stayed in California and the entire nation breathed a little easier.

That night, Rick Morgan had an apocalyptic premonition of historic events to follow. He awoke at 4:15 AM after just 4 hours sleep. In the dream, he was at a baseball game when he noticed that some of the players were women. Hair began falling out of their caps. They chased large soft balls in wet marshy grass on an uneven playing field at night. The game was played in a fog on a weird shaped field where he could not see the batters or the outfielders. The bases seemed to be moving erratically in three dimensions. He talked to some broadcast guys and tried to impress them with his knowledge of the game, but couldn't remember their names. Sitting near a chain-link fence on a grassy hill, he did something wrong with a round gooey object, a ball or something, and tried to pay for it at an office. Dennis was in the dream and tried to short-change him, so he fumbled with change, a few coins and Kennedy half-dollars. As he rushed to car to escape, the women chased after him with baseball bats. Youngish Hispanic women in a dark green suit, probably Cuban but he was not sure, stuck her finger in his eye socket. It hurt like hell, so he bit her finger; it made a God-awful crunching noise in his mouth. Blood and cracking finger bones tore as she pulled away. She disappeared into the night sky as he spits out cracked bone fragments and blood and woke up afraid and sweating.

November 22, 1963

Our confidence and hope for the future disappeared on one fateful day in fall, 1963. At 12:30 PM, Dallas time, President Kennedy was smiling broadly with his wife sitting next him in a motorcade on the way to the Trade Mart to give a speech. In an image that is now forever frozen in our memories, he was stuck first by a bullet in his upper back, then the fatal shot (or shots) to his head. It all happened in just five seconds. Oliver Stone's 1991 film *JFK* immortalized the 8 millimeter Abraham Zapruder film of the moment the bullets struck and, raised the ominous possibility that Kennedy was killed as a result of a conspiracy.

At about the same time that morning in Isla Vista, after cramming all night for exams, we received the news from a history professor that Kennedy had been assassinated in Dallas. The President, dead, how could that have happened? Classes were cancelled, people wept openly. For most of us, this was the first time (but not the last) that we experienced real collective grief. Our perfect little enclave of beautiful beaches and pristine views of the Channel Islands violated and our lives changed forever.

Most of us didn't know him well, but Kennedy affected us in so many positive ways: his youth, vigor, energy and boldness contrasted so starkly with the dour politicians of the 1950s. Perhaps our parents' generation was the greatest, but for us hope for a New Frontier ended on that day.

Conspiracies, so Many Conspiracies

Who killed Kennedy and why have obsessed historians, investigators, journalists, and filmmakers for over 50 years. The most likely suspects included the CIA, the Mafia, military industrial complex, the Secret Service, or Cuban exiles. Others implicated included Lyndon Johnson, George H. W. Bush, Allen Dulles, Mafia bosses Sam Giancana and Johnny Roselli, J. Edgar Hoover, Earl Warren, Frank Sinatra, the United States Secret Service, the John Birch Society, and far-right oversexed wealthy Texans. Foreign suspects included Fidel Castro, Muammar Gaddafi, the KGB and Nikita Khrushchev, Aristotle Onassis, the *entire* government of South Vietnam, and international drug lords including an Indochinese heroin syndicate. The Mafia, the CIA and anti-Castro Cubans were the most likely groups to carry out a *coup d'état*.

These three groups were all in bed together at the time and several years earlier had attempted unsuccessfully to assassinate Fidel Castro.

The Warren Commission finding that a lone gunman assassinated Kennedy has been widely discredited, but no plausible alternative has been established. Soon after the assassination, allegations surfaced of a conspiracy between Oswald and a group of prominent New Orleanians. The U.S. House Select Committee on Assassinations found no evidence in Harvey Lee Oswald's file that he had ever contacted the CIA or any other agency. Big surprise. It would be highly *unlikely* that the Agency would keep a file on one of its own hired killers and Congressional investigators would not to look too closely at Oswald's connections with the CIA.

Kennedy's plan to deescalate U.S. involvement in Vietnam made him a target for groups within the United States who benefitted from sustaining military conflict, especially the Pentagon and defense contractors. In 1991, Former Texas Senator Ralph Yarborough stated that:

"Had Kennedy lived, I think we would have had no Vietnam War, with all of its traumatic and divisive influences in America. I think we would have escaped that."

JFK could have been killed because he was turning away from the Cold War Hawks and seeking a negotiated peace with the Soviet Union. He was not the kind of jingoist macho-leader the CIA, the Joint Chiefs of Staff, and the military-industrial complex wanted in the White House.

The Secret Service was excoriated upon for its failure to protect the president. Unconfirmed rumors persisted that Kennedy himself had asked that the Secret Service to become less visible during the Dallas visit. Agents in the motorcade were unprepared to protect the president against a crossfire or sniper and plots against the president were never fully investigated. The Secret Service agent who drove the president's limousine told investigators that the decision to remove the bubble top from the limo was not made by Kennedy. If this was true, who made those decisions? Definitive answers remain a mystery to this day.

Militant Cuban exiles and mobsters had ample motives to kill the President. Many Miami-based exiles worked closely with CIA operatives in violent activities against Castro's Cuba and other unfriendly Latin American governments. After the Bay of Pigs, the CIA was desperate to eliminate Castro, so they sought out a partner equally angry with him—the Mafia, which had lucrative investments in Cuban casinos before the Revolution. Organized crime figures hated Kennedy and his younger brother, Attorney General Robert F. Kennedy, who had conducted a legal assault against the mob years earlier as special counsel to the McCarthy committee. Both the Mafia and the anti-Castro Cubans were experienced killers and the Cubans trained by the CIA. Jack Ruby, who killed Oswald on national television, was a known associate of Chicago mobster, and Kennedy nemesis, Sam Giancana.

Critics of the Warren Commission's lone-gunman theory accused LBJ of plotting the assassination because he hated the Kennedys and feared that they would drop him from the Democratic ticket for the 1964 election. In 1997, a woman claiming to be Johnson's mistress also fingered Johnson in a conspiracy to kill Kennedy. She said that Johnson, in cahoots with Texas Oilman H. L. Hunt, began planning Kennedy's elimination as early as 1960. The conspiracy allegedly involved a wide network of persons, including the leadership of the FBI and the Mafia, as well as prominent unnamed politicians and journalists. On the contrary, Johnson himself believed that Fidel Castro ordered the assassination because the Cuban dictator feared that retaliatory measures against Cuba might escalate to nuclear war with the Soviet Union. On separate occasions, Johnson stated that JFK's assassination was orchestrated by Castro in retaliation for the CIA's efforts to kill Castro and that Oswald acted alone.

****

For most war boomers, idealism vanished with Kennedy's death. Feelings of helplessness and isolation replaced optimism about our ability to change the future. We began to question our parents' faith in government and civic lessons that taught us to accept government actions with which we disagreed, but were obligated as loyal citizens to support. Lofty ideals about individualism, freedom, and social responsibility were replaced with deep concerns about collective security:

Where is the section in American government books that tells us what to do when a beloved leader is cut down before our eyes?

How much of what is taught in those books is actually true? And who is in charge when chaos erupts?

What if the United States had taken a more realistic stance against the Cuban government earlier, much like President Obama's initiative to open diplomatic relations with the communist nation in late 2014?

Would Kennedy have lived to finish out his term?

Can foreign government hack our antiquated Electoral College vote and alter the outcome of elections?

Unanswered questions haunted generations: questions that frustrated then and repeatedly revisited in the future.

****

It was against this dark background—escalating political violence, rabid anti-Communism, threats of nuclear war, sharpening social divisions, repressive politics, continued social injustice and dashed optimism for the future—that intrepid young boys and girls becoming men and women traveled to live and learn in a cloistered Southern California coastal community known as Isla Vista.

Before Kennedy's death, we enjoyed our own version of Camelot, albeit without the formal state dinners, palace intrigue or nuclear brinksmanship. The Isla Vista version consisted of endless beach parties, freedom to roam open spaces, host toga parties, perform strange initiation rites, worship farm animals, engage in bizarre dating rituals, and consume alcohol...lots of alcohol...all to drown out our doubts and fears about the future.

CHAPTER 6: Reborn in Isla Vista

Eager to leave high school boredom and crowded SoCal behind, Mark McGinnis tooled his customized '57 Chevy Bel Air (lowered, tuck-n-roll upholstery, B&M Hydro transmission, Edelbrock heads and full race motor) from the vast suburban wasteland to remote Isla Vista to check out the beaches, girls and fraternity houses. He soon learned that his classic Boulevard Cruiser, the one that had been such a chick magnet at school and annoyance to his mother at home, was of little value among the upper crust brain trust of high school graduates admitted to the University of California. He quickly realized that IQ, physique and personality were more important than gearshift knobs or horsepower. Within a year, he had traded that priceless gas-guzzler for a status-appropriate Volkswagen Beetle, a bitchin' '57 ragtop convertible no less.

The 120-mile trip from SoCal to Isla Vista would become a welcome respite after laundry trips home, summer jobs, oppressive heat, and parental enslavement. Cruising up Ventura Highway on U.S.101 from the beach cities, through the lush valleys and the dry rolling hills of Thousand Oaks was a welcome ritual several times a year. Once escaping the concrete jungle and cruising through the Ventura Hills, U.S. Highway 101 flattened out along the coast through the rich farmlands of Oxnard, Carpentaria, Port Hueneme, Camarillo and Ventura. Along a narrow spit of highway hugging the coast, past wetsuit-clad surfers shooting the curl at Rincon; up the rolling hills to Summerland, past the polo fields, through filthy-rich Montecito, dipping briefly by the manicured green lawns of Montecito Country Club into downtown Santa Barbara, past State Street, by the airport and…finally…to the campus and IV. Relief at last.

McGinnis recalls his first trip along this soon-to-be familiar route to campus, I.V., and freedom:

"I was in such a hurry to escape the smog and stifling summer heat of LA that I arrived a week before Frosh Camp began and had to find a place to stay. I rented a room at the Ocean Breeze Motel for $15 a day, scored some beer using my excellent fake ID and set off to reconnoiter." His first impressions were more than a little disappointing.

"From pictures I had seen of Big Ten and Ivy League campuses, I imagined fraternity houses with long stairs, ornate columns and manicured lawns with cool-looking guys in white button-down shirts and Ivy-league ties smoking pipes outside. Admiring them from the base of the stairs were bleach-blond chicks in cheerleaders' skirts and tight tit-hugger sweaters holding pom-poms and gazing up at these BMOCs with awe."

"I had visited Berkeley and UCLA and was expecting a similar fantasy. It wasn't happening in I.V."

Isla Vista was not exactly the image of Dartmouth or Princeton's fraternity row: one paved road six blocks long surrounded by acres of dusty dirt roads and open fields. The new UCSB campus was under construction somewhere among the old WWII Marine barracks that temporarily served as student housing. The on-going campus construction was far less interesting to a wide-eyed freshman than the social life on Isla Vista, then a barren plateau of ram-shackle apartments, weathered beach cottages and the occasional fraternity or sorority house. Most fraternities were located in shoddy apartment buildings and looked like firetraps ready to explode.

****

McGinnis barely qualified for the Tier 1 University of California, just making the cut "with considerable help from his mother forcing me to earn a 'B' in a painful biology course, dissecting dead frogs reeking of formaldehyde, and putting up with a jerk of a science teacher."

Berkeley was too far away and, according to his father, UCLA was too Jewish, so he happily settled for UCSB.

The campus remains one of the only universities in the world with its own beaches surrounded by miles of shoreline as well as a synthetic lagoon between San Rafael and San Miguel Residence Halls. The picturesque inlet was a former tidal salt marsh fed by ocean water and the run-off of water used by the Marine Science Building's aquatic life tanks; it is an artificial estuary, created by a combination of fresh and salt water.

Isla Vista in those days was a barren spit of rock sitting adjacent to the county club campus surrounded by unspoiled beaches, old-growth eucalyptus trees and (at that time) wide open spaces on a promontory overlooking the Pacific Ocean (cover). The closest city of any size was Goleta "that dirty, hot, little town,[1]" a sleepy agricultural village of about 4,000 residents 10 miles west of Santa Barbara. The 30 miles of coastline north from Goleta to Gaviota Pass remain today the longest stretch of undeveloped and unspoiled beachfront in California. (Developers have been fighting with anti-growth groups, country officials and environmentalists for decades to open this pristine section of California coastline for highways, infrastructure and new housing.)

On clear days, you can see the Channel Islands (Anacapa, San Miguel, and Santa Cruz, and Santa Rosa), a large and uninhabited ecological wonderland only about 20 miles away from the beaches of Santa Barbara and Ventura counties. With binoculars, wild goats could be seen running on the disserted beaches. On warm summer days in Goleta, you could smell cow dung from the agricultural fields near town. On cold winter evenings, the dank odor of oil-fuel burning smudge pots hung in the night air above acres of avocado, lemon and orange groves. Goleta consisted of only one main street three blocks long anchored by the 101 Ranch Market at one end and a cool bar at the other end called *The Spigot*, where folk legends Joe and Eddy played. In between was Bernie's Liquor that would sell to anyone with a passing facsimile of an adult ID, Sam and Verna Hensen's Goleta Strip bar and café (a scrumptious pastrami sandwich, buck a pitcher beer and pool tables—anyone could drink with or without IDs).

At the end of the only paved road on I.V. was Tebi's Café—then the gold standard for the best hamburger—and around the corner was the Omatae coffee house. Omatae was a student enterprise and THE destination for the "coffee date" i.e. opening gambit for trying to get into some girl's pants. Everyone loved the Omatae and Tebi's. The art-house movie theater Magic Lantern and the Unicorn Book Store were about the only other IV hangouts. The Magic Lantern was the place to go see surf flicks, foreign films and cult films like *The Rocky Horror Picture Show*. The Unicorn Book Shop and its community press published a number of noted poets, many of whom were "noted" for their unconventional lifestyles and heavy drug use.

Hippies would migrate through on their way to San Francisco, but had to vacate quickly when observed loitering too long in Isla Vista. No love lost between the dope smoking 'beatniks' and the Earl Warren conservatives of Santa Barbara, aka Santa Barbarians. The smug Santa Barbara community was disdainful of counterculture 'couch surfers' who were pausing in Isla Vista during their Discover America road trips, often for months. In addition to IV, the Haight Ashbury district of San Francisco and East Village of New York City became home to two of the largest hippie communities later in the decade. As the 1960's progressed, alternative lifestyles spread to Canada and many large cities in Western Europe, especially London, Amsterdam, Paris, Berlin and Rome. How conservative and repressive were the Santa Barbarians in those days? The

County District Attorney raided the Magic Lantern in the early Sixties for showing a French film containing full frontal female nudity. Male genitalia were still considered off-limits, even by French standards. The theater operators were charged with obscenity, lost financing, and had to close. The theater was subsequently purchased by the university and reopened in the 1980s.

Santa Barbara County Sheriff's Deputies were even less enamored of open marijuana use and drug dealing on the streets. Rumors that Jim Morrison of *The Doors* wrote the song "The Crystal Ship" one night while on an LSD trip with a group of hippies camped out on the cliffs overlooking Del Playa Beach, watching the bright lights of an oil platform a few miles off the southwest tip of Isla Vista. Several new businesses were created in Isla Vista including the original Kinko's Copy Center. (Paul Orfalea should thank me for the plug, as if he needs one.) Many established businesses, including dentists, jewelers, and hairdressers later fled I.V. during the decade, as it became increasingly estranged from the surrounding suburban communities. Eventually, most of the eclectic businesses disappeared and students became even further isolated from the stayed Santa Barbarians.

According to a recent description in the student newspaper:

> "I.V. has always been a mysterious misfit, a jagged appendage that surrounding cities would love to hack off and send adrift in the Pacific Ocean. But despite the inherent sense of uncertainty and transience, there is an abundance of culture in this pressure cooker. Spring quarter alone features the park concerts Earth Day, Chilla Vista, Surfrider and Wordstock; there's the Reel Loud film festival, Shakespeare in the Park, Theater and Dance productions and constant exhibitions of students' visual art. Each Wednesday music echoes from Storke Plaza and the Music bowl; every weekend live bands rock house parties while comedy lights up Embarcadero Hall. The Catalyst and WORD magazines bring a definitive flair in both visual-literary arts and journalism, respectively. The various Co-Ops provide their own distinct art and flavor, and undocumented work is being done by thousands of residents every day." [2]

Sporadic efforts to incorporate Isla Vista and form a local government actually representative of its residents repeatedly failed, in each case due to the Local Agency Formation Commission (appropriately named LAFCO), a wholly controlled subsidiary of wealthy elites, voting down incorporation. The five Santa Barbara families who owned most of the property on the mesa (and controlled LAFCO) became richer and richer from student growth projections in the UCSB Master Plan. Although a fully incorporated Isla Vista was supposed to be part of the UC Regents Master Plan for campus growth, pressure from wealthy landowners, contractors and local officials repeatedly killed the idea. They were not then, nor are they now, willing to relinquish local control to a bunch of beatniks, freaks and potheads. Profits trumped infrastructure, police protection, and security.

Isla Vista residents did wield some influence in the Goleta Water District that covered a large area of the Valley. The Isla Vista vote helped usher in the era of no-growth policies in the greater Goleta Valley area, over the more growth-oriented blocs of voters in Goleta, who at that time favored expanded boundaries. The entire Valley, of which IV was a part, grew from 20,000 in 1960 to 70,000 in 1970. With such growth, came calls for more stringent regulations and enforcement of zoning codes everywhere except IV. With the growing population, Goleta residents soon converted to the no-growth stance, but they simultaneously shunned transient IV residents. No zoning enforcement and minimal services in the student ghetto inevitably contributed to political and social instability and greater vulnerability to outside influences.

Despite modest development, most of Isla Vista in the early Sixties was a huge dusty open field all the way from the Pacific beaches to Storke Road where married students' housing was located—somewhere you didn't want to live—apprehensively known as 'sperm village'.

McGinnis remembers that:

"The only building with any apparent human habitation was a crooked scruffy looking wooden red barn-like structure with an oversized black and white heart on its front."

More like a social club than a fraternity, its members were reasonably law-abiding, perhaps with the exception of the occasional goat parties, kidnappings, police pursuits, or underage Toga parties. All were drawn to this venue to enjoy each other's company and camaraderie. The house had 22 residents, including a resident cook who made breakfast and dinner for everyone while reserving special privileged for himself.

In coming years, he and a few other fortunate inductees would bond with this dwelling and its assorted inhabitants. For most, these years would form and mold adult personalities and sustain lifetime friendships. Who knew?

Order of the Blue Orbs

According to early county records, the red-painted wooden structure built as a dormitory for monks, believed to be Buddhist, but no one was quite sure, who inhabited this isolated region of Santa Barbara County in the early 1930s. Due to financial reversals during the 20th Century depression, as well as a general lack of enthusiasm for monastic traditions such as celibacy, the

Order of the Blue Orbs disbanded shortly after the beginning of WWII. (Most of the monks-in-residence had heard something about Pearl Harbor and the draft and wanted to move farther north, Canada perhaps?)

These fears were real, as the area was an active war zone, a Japanese invasion expected along the West Coast at any time after Pearl Harbor.[3]

Most of the area then encompassing Isla Vista was considered unfit for economic development or human habitation due to lack of a reliable water supply and limited transportation. The mesa was loosely connected to the mainland with dirt roads separated by a wide seawater marsh, referred to locally as "the slew."

During the Big War, the Marine Corps built a barracks in Goleta and U.S. Army Air Corps constructed an airfield and flight training facility on the flatlands just below the barren frontier outpost not-yet-known as Isla Vista. The Army later built a large prison for captured German soldiers just north of Goleta on Collister Ranch. Locals tell stories about German prisoners who were so comfortable at the facility that many hesitated to return to their frigid native land after the war. This partially explains the large number of defections as well as the origins of several small 'Danish' (read German) communities such as Solvang (German for salvation) in the San Ynez Valley in succeeding years.

After the war, the Marine Corps deeded the surplus base to the University of California, which moved its downtown Santa Barbara Riviera College campus to the much larger property by the sea.

At about the same time, an enterprising group of former Santa Barbara City College students acquired the land with plans to build an apartment house after delinquent taxes were paid. Their intent was to tear it down and build cheap student housing, referred to locally as 'planned obsolescence." Financing for the project fell through and several of the partners reluctantly decided to keep the house open. The rush for new members was on.

McGinnis remembers his first view of the Red House on Isla Vista:

"Out front were two guys tossing a Frisbee—I recognized Rich Tull and later got to know John Sabor. Ironically, Rich and I were from the same hometown, but he was a year older and went to the "other" high school. We drank some beers and hit it off."

He ended up hanging around the house and met a few more interesting guys. After a boring semester in the dorms, he went through fraternity rush but elected not to pledge mainly because Canalino Hall in Anacapa Residence Hall on campus was a serious party venue and a kick-in-the-ass place to live.

In the spring of 1962, Mike Fowler convinced him to pledge. Fraternity boys were always subjectively stereotyped, especially by those who were "bonged" as "turkeys" during rush week and failed to gain admittance to the amnesiac IV party scene. The SEAs were all plastic, Betas were jocks, Delts were animals, Lambdy Pi's were just that; the only other real choice was the Gamma Sigs who were just fuckin' crazy. Among other memories from that first year:

Wild intramural touch football games between rival houses played at maximum intensity for bragging rights. The Reds were intramural champion three straight years from 1964-1966.

Skateboard surfing while towed behind Omar Khalifa's (a Kuwaiti Prince's son) Vespa on the wide curving sidewalks between the dorms and the dining commons with students screaming out their windows at us to stop. Skateboards in those days were made with steel roller skate wheels nailed on a piece of scrap wood. Those fuckers were really loud on cement and it was usually after midnight when we skated.

Shopping the roadside off Las Cositas Road for bags of low hanging avocados and lemons to make guacamole—a local friend Alan Palmer's family owned those avocados and boy did we enjoy them.

TGIFs, joints with the dorm girls, the 101 Drive-in theater—a buck a car, Louis Hensen's pastrami sandwiches, life as a pledge, actually having sex, coffee dates at The Mote, surfing, lying in the sun slathered in coconut oil, Brew 102, Vino Toro burgundy.

Nubile blond young surfer girls roaming the streets walking their dogs in the cool late afternoon. Rolling down the window and asking if she would like a lift. No, she replied, but "would you like to come over to my house for some tea?" Following her and pulling into the driveway. Idle chatter about her boyfriend, a fisherman away at sea. Accepting a reciprocal invitation to visit my apartment. Making out on the couch for what seemed like hours and finally saying "Maybe you should go home." Her unforgettable reply: "Why aren't you trying harder?" After having every type of sex imaginable to a 20-old, lying exhausted in bed, and her whispering in his ear: "Would you like some more?

Girls inviting us to their apartments cook for us with the mutual expectation of sex afterwards. Going to a different apartment each night for a nice meal and an even nicer fuck. Everyone seemed happy with the arrangement until someone talked to someone else. Unfortunately, the girls knew each other and, after they talked, no more food or sex.

Jerry having sex with Jeannie every night after dinner and putting her in the hospital with a torn pussy. Not only was Jerry himself an oversized dick, but he had one too.

Who could forget John Hodger's "blue dart" from the back seat of a car and his "dump in the purse" trick—a real co-ed turn on!

Alan Harrison's "flaming dick" trick, which was painful to watch and even more difficult to describe. Al poured lighter fluid on his penis and carelessly lit it with a cigarette lighter. The trick was not to over dip or under dip the organ in lighter fluid as this could cause a lifetime of celibacy. Not surprisingly, Harrison never married.

After being busted for a major goat party, watching with amazement as future lawyer Sam Cormack attempted to organize our defense. We were at Refugio Beach on a TGIF and Sam was briefing all of us on what (and what not) to say to Dean. After too much beer at the function, we chased Sam off the podium and decided to organize another goat party.

Homecoming Parade Fall '62 (aka Scene from Animal House)

The Homecoming Parade down State Street to La Playa Stadium at the Santa Barbara Marina was a colorful college town ritual, which did not last much beyond the late 1960s—for good reason. Indeed, the Santa Barbarians had just about enough of the raunchy production by 1963. As depicted in the infamous scene from the movie *Animal House*, it was a raucous affair, replete with broken down floats, half-full beer cans flung at spectators, and the brassy sounds of high school marching bands. Nonetheless, the spirit of intermural competition combined with a full day's supply of beer enticed many to participate.

Jim Colegate, our star lineman and chief float engineer, recalls detailed planning that went into float construction.

"After escaping the threat of probation by the just-in-time removal of a trailer in front of the house, the brothers laid plans to stun the UCSB community with a magnificent float entry in the Homecoming Parade."

First, of course, we had to have a great party with all sorts of food and drinks.

71

"We then set about to organize and prepare to build the float: a splendid pirate ship. Float trailer, check. Nails to build float, check. Sails for the ship, check. Wood to build the ship? Wood, anybody? We used the money for the wood to have the party. Can you give us some more? No problem. There was quite a bit of construction going on at the time in I.V. so a plan for some midnight requisition of wood was hatched."

Only one site had all the wood we needed and it was hastily removed to House area, and stored in the open for float construction.

"Unfortunately, the contractor soon noticed that a big stack of wood was missing and quickly discovered it two blocks away from the site at the house. He called the police who called the Dean who again put the house on probation."

Amid all the revelry, world events were changing—more rapidly than any of us realized or cared much about.

Where the Hell is Vietnam?

One fine spring day, several brothers were wandering around the lagoon headed for coffee at the Student Union. Someone called out:

"Guys, Mario Savio, leader of something called the 'Free Speech Movement' at Cal-Berkeley, was speaking outside the building."

"Who is this Hippie Wop?" someone asked, vaguely aware of the nascent anti-war protest movements that were starting at Berkeley and several other college campuses around the country.

"Some long-hair trying to rile up the students," echoed another.

"Are you shittin' me? Why bother? Nobody around here gives a shit about hippie free speech and all that crap," chimed another.

Straight-laced Rick Morgan suddenly became agitated and defensive.

"Hey, asshole, this bullshit is not about hippies or free speech, it's about the war in Vietnam and these fuckers are Commies! If we don't kill 'em, they're gonna get us on the beaches of San Diego. My Dad said so and he was in the Navy. He calls 'em the 'Yellow Peril' and says they kill their own girl babies. I don't want any of those chinks killin' my baby," said super-straight Rick 'Dildoe' Morgan.

"Far out, somebody probably took a bite outta your brain, shit-for-brains," said David Eggert, whose opposing personal convictions about politics and war had been firmly shaped by family experiences as well. During the course of his studies, he befriended student radicals, including the future leaders of the <u>Symbionese Liberation Army (SLA)</u>, the kidnappers of heiress Patty Hearst.

'Fuck you, you pinko bastard. The best part of your brain dribbled down your father's leg. Let's go and listen to the long-hair freak," Morgan responded.

"Bitchin, let's go, shit-for-brains," chimed friend Mark McGinnis.

Out of morbid curiosity, we listened to his rant against the corrupt UC administration, the Johnson war machine, and the innocent victims in Vietnam. We and most of the others halfheartedly listened while basking in the late afternoon sun as Savio tried in vain to stir students to some form of political action. He failed to motivate anyone to do much of anything.

We didn't know it then, but the Vietnam War would alienate allies and divert the nation's energies and resources for another decade before coming to a dismal end in 1975. No one even knew how many Vietnamese were slaughtered by a succession of presidents, Congresses, and militarists fed by the flames of greed, pride, and stupidity. Estimates ranged from one to two million in a country with then a population of 55 million. Even the alleged attack on American forces used by LBJ to justify starting the war, the <u>Gulf of Tonkin Resolution</u>, never actually happened. Vestiges of this suffocating quagmire remain today in the minds of 30 million boomer and Gen X males who served in the American Armed Forces from 1955 until 1975. Many of their brothers, fathers and friends sacrificed by Nixon's arrogance and treason.

The Vietnam War's anti-communist ideological foundation, the mantra cited to keep the slaughter going for five years after Nixon was elected on a promise to end the war, was discredited after we lost. No other Southeast Asian "dominos" fell to communism. To the contrary, the effect of the U.S. withdrawal actually helped stabilize the region. When genocide broke out in neighboring Cambodia in the late 1970s, it was not the U.S., but a unified Vietnamese Army–those evil Godless communists–who stopped it. Peace and stability in this region have helped promote economic development and trade with other nations.

The Vietnamese kind of converted to capitalism and now compete with the Chinese, offering cheaper manufactured products and services at lower prices on global markets. Americans, Europeans and Japanese hire and purchase goods from the Vietnamese instead, tacitly endorsing the tactics of the Red Menace that we shed blood against and swore to defeat a generation ago.

An American businessman seeking to start an Internet-based firm learned just how competitive the Vietnamese are when he interviewed U.S. graduates of West Coast universities—all of whom were software engineers expecting starting salaries in the $120,000 range. With limited resources, the globetrotting entrepreneur went to Vietnam instead. He was able to hire four fully trained graduate engineers for the same amount. Until Obama's diplomatic coup reopening commercial and diplomatic relations with those Godless Cubans, Right-wing Republicans still punish Communist Cuba for what...um ...Cuban? At the same time, they reward China with multi-billion dollar contracts for trade deals because...um...they are Chinese Communists?

The "duck and cover" generation had to defend democratic capitalism by fighting pajama-clad guerillas in Southeast Asian jungles. Behind our backs, corrupt political leaders conspired to sacrifice our generation to enrich themselves and fellow global economic elites. Statistics alone do not explain how and why the United States has permitted these corrupting developments to occur. Simply stated, this situation has occurred because of tax cuts for the rich, political gridlock, trillions wasted on two unpaid for wars, and an arrogant distain toward minorities' efforts to achieve.

We secretly dread that our government may be incapable of providing answers or even asking the right questions, but we have yet to find an alternative. In the meantime, fully indoctrinated Communist Chinese students, many of whom will doubtless become their country's leaders, flock to elite American universities to learn our secrets and systems. Multi-national companies continue to outsource jobs to these same countries that ideologically despise us: millions of millennials shut out of the workforce and millions of boomers, who should be retiring, continue to work out of financial necessity.

We were unaware that an incendiary fuse lit on our tranquil campus-by-sea (back cover) would explode just a few years later The climate on campus was changing as news reports began to trickle back about the 'democratic struggle for freedom' and high casualties occurring in some place called Vietnam. Where the hell was Vietnam?

United States' involvement in this protracted "little war" produced only mild opposition until the mid-1960s, when combat deaths increased dramatically and Americans began questioning the war's justification and rationale. After all, we were the loyal sons and daughters of the Greatest

G.I. Generation who had sworn to defend our country from those evil hungry communists lurking in them Southeast Asian jungles.

"The only good commie was a dead one" went the off-repeated refrain, and we were ready to kill them bad Viet Cong in order to protect the good capitalist Vietnamese rice crops from the marauding Chinese. Unfortunately, for those called to duty, it was impossible to tell the good gooks from the bad ones cuz' they all looked alike!

We were just too naïve to realize that right-wing politicians like Goldwater, Nixon, Ford, Reagan, the Bushes, and now Trump labels anyone who opposed their idiotic domino theories or hair-brained neo-conservative plots as 'communist sympathizers,' enemies of America, or subversives, to preserve and protect their own narrow global economic interests. In time, the Bushes would substitute aggressive commies with Godless Foreign Dictators as our sworn enemies and the justification for once again sheading blood to remove the "yoke of oppression" from other mineral-rich nations: this time to protect U.S. petro-dictators who controlled the oil supply in the Middle East. Few of us realized that we were to become pawns in a "Cold War" with the Chinese and the Soviets.

The entire country was caught off-guard by Vietnam because it was a portrayed as a "different kind of conflict" than previous foreign wars, justified as part of a 'containment' strategy to block the spread of communism in Southeast Asia. If it weren't stopped, the 'Red Menace' would soon infest the rest of Southeast Asia, swimming across the Pacific Ocean like Godzilla sloshing into our backyards. Who needs a communist at a barbeque?

Political history is subject to continuous revision. Our history and political science professors failed to mention that the United States exercised its military muscle 70 times in covert and overt actions against perceived threats to capitalist interests between 1946 and 1989. These were also *different* types of conflicts than WW II, guerilla wars without huge land armies locked in bitter life-and-death battles fighting for territory, democracy, capitalism and freedom until defeat or retreat. With the exception of the United Nations Korean "police action," post-WW II conflicts were "asymmetrical" wars often carried out to protect U.S. economic interests in emerging nations with valued resources. You can spell those shared values O-I-L.

The ideological justifications for Vietnam could not have been more obscure. We believed we were fighting to contain communism; local partisans knew they had to oppose foreign invaders to protect their families and homeland. They had learned from reading Mao and Cho-En-Lai that only viable strategy to resist superior forces was guerilla conflict, aka terrorism, rather than conventional warfare. Their strategy worked because they believed in their cause. We didn't.

In the end, no victory for Americans to celebrate, no ticker tape parades for downtrodden vets, only disillusionment with an ambiguous cause lost in vague political rhetoric. If we only knew then what we know now, would anything have actually changed?

ROTY and Military Service

Unless you "voluntarily" enlisted in one of the armed services (and nobody was crazy enough to do that) every male was subject to the draft. When males turned eighteen, they had to register and issued a 'draft card' from the Selective Service System, an independent federal agency that still exists, just in case the Viet Cong or some other enemy attacked San Francisco. This reliable method of conscription sustained 'cannon fodder" for warfare from the Civil War through Vietnam—the 'citizen soldier' drafted into service as needed by his country. A decade later, the draft was replaced by an all-volunteer military force, too late for thousands of patriotic draftees who were already on the front lines.

Male Sixties survivors coped with the inevitability of public service in varied and often creative ways. Some preempted the certainty of the drafted by joining ROTC and becoming commissioned officers; others became federal officials; many hastily married and divorced even faster; and still others served in public service agencies such as the Peace Corps. Many tried to postpone the draft lottery by going to business, law or graduate school. This worked for some for a few years, but not for most others. In the end, many boomers fulfilled their obligation and faithfully served their country in various ways.

Eighteen-year old males were forced to fight, but could not vote. Because of the campus protests and discipline problems that accompanied opposition to U.S. involvement in Vietnam, compulsory ROTC was dropped in 1973, in favor of an all-volunteer Army. This happened two years after the passage of the 26th Amendment, granting 18 to 21-year olds the right to vote. At some schools, ROTC was expelled from campus altogether, although it was always possible to participate in off-campus ROTC or wait to voluntarily join and go to Officer Candidate School (OCS).

Today, it is necessary to enlist in order to endure the hardships of a military life. The Army now targets high schools and community colleges for so-called junior ROTC units. Apparently, 14 to 18-year olds are more malleable and less questioning of authority than the average college student is. Aggressive young males no longer forced to take 'Military Science' courses or compete in competitive sports choose instead choose the lonely life of the skateboard street surfer.

Prior to 1973, military service was neither a video game nor an optional choice along one's life 'passages.' It was a grim reality for every able-bodied straight male over 18 years of age. Rather than drafted into the Army as 'grunts' by locally-controlled draft boards, college males could instead take the 'safe road' and volunteer for duty as officers. All able-bodied males who turned age 18 prior to January 27, 1973 had to volunteer for military service or they be drafted. Laws exempted women from military service because they were women.

For many patriotic red-blooded American males, the Reserve Officer's Training Corps (ROTC) was the obvious and only choice to forestall the inevitability of the draft. Those who actually wanted to learn something in college could delay the decision and voluntarily enter Officer Candidate School (OCS) after graduating, but that would interfere with futures and lower grade point averages. Liberal Professors who had a hard-on for jocks and future military officers would never consider them better than "C' students, in effect kissing off their grad school or law school plans.

On certain days, we were required to wear our uniforms on campus. When left-wing professors learned we were "military science" students they openly berated us in class. The occasional tongue-lashing by an A-hole professor was far more tolerable than the treatment of those less privileged black and brown brothers who were unable to enroll in college or dropped out, and whose lottery number came up in the draft. They were ordered to Army intake processing centers as grunts. Colleges and universities cooperated with the local draft boards by providing the names of male students who dropped out of compulsory ROTC after their sophomore year. A few chose to migrate to Canada, while others pretended to be gay during Army physical examinations to avoid involuntary conscripted service. Planting a big sloppy kiss on the recruiting sergeant's lips would not qualify. As opposition to the war grew, an underground army of anti-war psychology graduate students sprang up on many campuses to advice 'draft dodgers' how to correctly answer which questions in order to be disqualified.

All you had to do to avoid service was to check 'yes' in the boxes on the Army Medical History Form which said: Are you attracted to other men? Do you have thoughts about having sex with men? Are you a homosexual? Check yes…yes…yes.., see the shrink, and you were out. This declaration would also constitute a permanent record of one's sexual preference at a time when such inclinations were illegal in most states and would permanently disqualify anyone from any future government employment. These were the pre-Reagan years when government jobs still had some degree of respect and homosexuality was still illegal and very much in the closet.

Ironically, the Obama's administration's 2012 political victory in repealing the 'don't ask, don't tell' policy of the Clinton administration stimulated a surge in the growth of ROTC programs at elite colleges and universities such as Columbia, Stanford and Yale where they were banned decades ago in protest to the Vietnam War. Columbia University reinstated Naval ROTC after a 42-year ban of the program. Stanford University voted unanimously to support ROTC's return to campus and the faculty senate voted to support the recommendations. Likewise, the Yale faculty committee on ROTC released its own report, recommending the repeal of four resolutions approved by the faculty in 1969, which led to the campus ban on ROTC.

Hippies and the Summer of Love(birds)

At the opposite end of the civic social responsibility scale, the hippie movement to may have been born in Isla Vista on October 12, 1962, give or take a decade or so. Here, with little fanfare, quiet groups of peace-loving 'flower children' camped out on the ice plant covered bluffs in tents overlooking the Pacific Ocean. Their numbers were small at first, but grew steadily larger as other students rejected the materialistic and militaristic environments enveloping college campuses. They were exploring inner-space and discovering new and stimulating chemical and herbal mind-expanding remedies to escape daily doldrums. Non-conformist "hippies" rejected the materialistic and militaristic environments prevalent on college campuses and explored inner-space, discovering new and stimulating mind-expanding chemical and herbal remedies to escape daily doldrums. Not surprisingly, many were also bored with school and wanted to avoid the obligations of traditional marriage while practicing "free love."

The hippie counterculture began as an anti-establishment movement in United States culture and society during the late 1950s and 1960s. The proximate causes were drugs, beatnik poetry, the Vietnam War and advances in reproductive science. Many hippie-converts were wounded souls whose fathers, friends and brothers had been drafted, wounded or killed in Vietnam. They wanted to make their anti-war views heard, hoping that they could bring peace and harmony to the world at a time of such great disruption in family values. The liberal ideals of hippie culture were also influenced by sexual liberation resulting from access to birth control, allowing guys to get more sex and women to avoid unwanted pregnancies. What could possibly go wrong?

One of the major consequences of safer pre-marital sex was that women gained greater control over their bodies, without necessarily embracing the conservative values espoused by their parents. Other factors were the increasing popularity of psychedelic drugs and rock and roll music, a groundbreaking new art form that encouraged peaceful expression, while also bringing people together in large and unruly groups.

The jarring unity of rock music connected diverse individuals and allowed them to identify with each other through a means that all could share and understand. Many hippies developed their own cultural unity through communal musical concerts and gatherings, the most famous of which were Woodstock in Bethel New York and the Summer of Love in Northern California from 1968-1970. One of our members observed that:

"These were tumultuous years and the art, music and culture of the time reflected campus unrest radiating out opposition to militancy and support for civil rights. The feminist assertion and the cultural movements of pop, minimalism, earth, and conceptual expression were both frightening and liberating."[4]

Although countercultures existed in urban areas and large cities, many hippie movements began on suburban college campuses such as UCSB. Liberal students rejected the social privilege they had been born with because they didn't agree with the conservative values and political ideals which accompanied it. The hippie movement also spread through communes, cafes and bars, which increasingly became centers of anti-social political gatherings at the time. In many ways, this was the origin of racial homogenization and misogynistic rap music favored by today's millennial techno-hippies.

As the natural counter reaction to the materialistic culture and conservative society of the 1950's, the original hippie movement gained strength from the paranoia of the Cold War and the televised violence in Vietnam. Rebellion against older more conservative lifestyles flourished as young people opposed societal restrictions and values forced upon them by the GG. Hippie counterculture was a way to express personal views for peace, freedom, and non-conformity, creating new lifestyles and having voices heard and opinions respected as a group.

In addition to weed, which has practically become a sacrament for today's techno-hippies, boomers had access to mind-altering drugs (hallucinogens), many of which (such as LSD) were compounded in university chemistry labs. This contributed to counterculture lifestyles as drug use became more accepted by mainstream culture. Today, most of the thrill-seekers avoid chemicals, and prefer "natural" highs from marijuana, cocaine or heroin. Besides, recipes for acid are widely available on the Internet and dangerous hallucinogens sold at street corner head shops.

Sophomore transfer student David Eggert first observed the tribal gatherings on Isla Vista from the second story of his apartment on Sabado Tarde Road. He was curious and just happened to be one of those whose brain receptors were pre-programmed for the THC in cannabis, encouraging him to become a founding member of the IV hippie movement. When he decided to move into a tent on the cliff occupied by two friends, Norm Cedrick and Dennis O'Malley, he joined the joyful group of free-spirited sex-addicts, frequent marijuana users, and occasional LSD cubers.

They were also avid sand beach volleyball players, a sport born on the West Coast destined to grow in popularity and become an Olympic event. Eggert quickly joined in the sport little known outside Santa Barbara. He had no way of knowing at the time that he would later become world famous as a U.S. Olympic Volleyball coach. Sometimes, prophesies do come true.

The hippie movement began when O'Malley and Alexander noticed unused property on a cliff overlooking the Pacific hidden behind some bushes. Being fair-minded individuals, Jason went to the local hall of records and got the name of the property owners. He then wrote Signal Oil, owners of the vacant land/campground, carefully explaining the need to occupy the property for an important graduate biology project. The letter stated that Norm was a biology major planning to do a study on the nocturnal habits of the Snowy Plover, a rare bird that just happened to nest only in Isla Vista and often in the bushes on Signal Oil property. They wanted to set up a study camp in the bushes and observe the nocturnal habits of this rare bird. Was that all right? When no response came from the owner, an attorney in San Francisco, they called his office.

"I have no plans for the property at this time, so I don't care if you live out there and conduct your experiments," said the obliging attorney.

Eureka. That answer could not have better suited their camping, drinking, toking, fucking and other biological and substance abuse urges which were soon to be satisfied. O'Malley printed up some official looking "Experiment in Progress. Do Not Disturb" signs stating that this was a scientific study area, rented a roto-tiller, dug up the ice plant and moved in. They and numerous others, male and female, were able to occupy this tent city for 3 months before being busted by the Santa Barbara County Health Department. Several held hashing jobs at nearby sororities to provide food and other benefits. Study rooms in the library on campus were open at night to study in, so all they needed was a place to bathe, sleep and party. And party they did.

After three months, they became good friends with one of the Gough sisters (Leigh and Sara) who lived one street over and offered them a place to hide out for a few days when she saw a sheriff's car nosing around. But as fate would have it, one afternoon they needed some class notes and had to return to the tent city. Sitting down enjoying the view was the law. Officer squarepants said that they needed to be out of there by Friday or they would be arrested on three counts of squatting, to which Norman replied,

"You mean a challenge to forget about the birds and meet you on Del Playa with guns drawn or get out of dodge before Friday?"

The cop responded "yep, you got it son."

Norm Cedrick still wonders,

"How any of our brain cells survive after all the Red Mountain wine and various other chemical and organic substances we consumed?"

The tents came down and another of the young boomer generation's feeble attempts to undermine authority went down the tubes.

The Glorious Isla Vista Summer of 1964

It was a perfectly idyll and gloriously unproductive summer. Only five brothers lived in the Red House: Bill Richardson, Rich Tull, Beto Negrial, John Sabor and Art Carlton. Bill lived in the little trailer behind the volleyball court. Beto was a pledge brother and classmate and the son of a wealthy Mexican hotel owner. John Sabor was a senior and a complete wild man who held nearly mythical status among the younger Red House brothers. He was killed in a freak car accident just before school restarted. Art Carlton—a junior, was a surfer, but we didn't hold that against him. Only a few hundred students stayed on IV that summer.

Plenty of work for day laborers and nail pounders from contractors who were building cheap apartment buildings in Isla Vista, slipshod buildings later labelled as "planned obsolescence." All you had to do was show up at 8 am at a site and you were hired for the day. One day a week or five...up to you. The $25 cash paid at the end of the day was big bucks in those days. When adjusted for inflation, day laborers receive about the same amount today, the difference being that basic commodities, housing, and transportation have not remained the same! Those who worked probably averaged 3 days a week, had plenty of money for Brew 102, and almost saved enough for the fall tuition. Our goal for the summer was to cover the side yard with Brew 102 cans and we got close.

Other hazy memories of that perfect summer include beach volleyball every afternoon, endless bowls of guacamole, surfing, tanning in the "ray box," visits with high school girlfriends, beach parties with Isla Vista summer residents. We didn't know what *carpe diem* meant, but we indeed seized the days.

Mark McGinnis remembers that, in so many ways,

"We were all reborn in Isla Vista, learning how to trade on our creative abilities, instincts, imagination, written words and story-telling skills. In one way or another, we have been honing those skills throughout our entire lives."

Those abilities centered on the totality of the story and the relational skills needed to communicate its essence to others.

One of his most memorable experiences with a Red House legend was the first meeting with Mike Fowler (a truly gifted scholar-athlete) telling an incredible story in the third person using his hands as gestures to punctuate his message. His animation, enthusiasm, and sense of wonder at the dramatic moment while narrating was a talent held in great esteem within this group of characters that made up this club, this house, this brotherhood. Whatever our personal choices or interests, passions or professions, we have all, in one form or another, been duplicating, extending, and replicating that experience ever since.

Today, Isla Vista has one of the country's highest urban population concentrations with over 22,000 students jammed into a square mile space.

CHAPTER 7: Life in the Red House

Ballad of the Old Red House (P.T. Jameson)

*I had an off day at the reunion and ducked out of the
chapter to skip holy communion.
Despite our founders' devotion to the Christian religion
I had flown far from grace, like a carrier pigeon.*

*So I decided to take a walk on the campus, a
Nacho set loose once again on the pampas.
Chancellor Bellin has been a bit of a builder and
for me his design just left me bewildered.*

*I lurched from one blank structure to another;
I'd never felt more in need of a brother.
I wandered alone through the grass and the hedges
when I chanced to encounter one of our pledges.*

*He asked me to tell him of the Red House's history.
I told him that much was still shrouded in mystery,
but that there were some things it would be better to
master if he wanted to go active a little bit faster.*

*I asked if he knew that we'd pledged Dick Gozinya,
who was really a Jew unknown to Charlottesville, Virginia.
He had no idea of the trail that we blazed
and pretended at first to be sorely amazed.*

*After a while he had the nerve to inquire if it
was true that to go active they would set him on fire. I
said I had no recollection of the path of the mystics but
that maiming was rare as I recalled the statistics.*

*He asked my advice about how to succeed, said
he hoped we'd never engaged in the smoking of weed.
I said we got in top shape and drank lots of water,
that this was our path to the Red House imprimatur.*

*At that his tone changed, he became a bit pointed; he
said he'd heard stories, which were somewhat disjointed,
of drinking and goat parties and a few peccadilloes,
which included opposite sexes hitting the pillows.*

I said I was shocked to hear of these rumors,
especially of young women losing their bloomers.
He said it was disgusting that I got so defensive, that
he had studied our scrapbook, which was truly offensive.

From his glance I could tell he'd become deeply skeptical,
that he found our behavior nothing short of contemptible.
I sharply admonished him to respect our generation. We
established tradition, we are due veneration.

Perhaps there were occasions of a few moral lapses,
which in college are inevitable, just like death and
taxes, and if in some instances we fell off the wagon
it wasn't his place our reputation to blacken.

That's when he rose up and shouted a lecture
that for our behavior there was no conjecture.
There is right, there is wrong, there is no middle way,
that sin will be punished forever one day.

Time at the chapter should be spent reading the Bible,
the pledge manual points us to spiritual revival.
There was no justification for the acts I defended;
it was clear that my morals were only pretended.

Refusing to be treated like a debauched ancient geezer
I railed that he couldn't find his dick with a tweezer.
He seemed quite unfazed by this clever rejoinder:
could he have heard of the woman who claimed that I'd loined her?

I was tired of this youngster who judged our morality;
most of our actions were within the bounds of legality.
Some of my memories might be a little unpleasant,
but for most of my sins I remain unrepentant.

So I left him behind, with a twinge of regret.
I did understand him. There's a pledge in me yet.
There are things he can't know. He just got to college.
It isn't the skills. It isn't the knowledge.

We're all growing old. It's getting hard to remember.
He can't know what it's like to face another December.
It wasn't the college. It's really the brothers.
It's their memories we share, above all the others.

Our square mile retreat sheltered us from a dangerous and uncertain world, especially after the Kennedy assassination in November 1963. Among the more memorable experiences during the years spent on our cloistered playground were chapter meetings, fraternity rush, hell week, keg parties on the beach, dining clubs, Red Death Punch, farm animals, and the Sunday afternoon meals.

The Sunday dinner proceeded chapter meetings, which were light-hearted male-bonding affairs which no one took too seriously except during fraternity rush. This was the time necessary to replenish our ranks.

Our favorite cook, 'Tog' (short for "tub of guts") prepared meals. He got this peculiar nickname during the spring semester of his sophomore year. Like so many other Red House legends, the nickname stuck with him for the rest of his life.

Like most college students, lots of beer and extra food had taken its toll on Tog's gut and he had a nice beer belly going. One night, a bunch of guys went down to the 101 Drive-In in Goleta to take advantage of buck-a-car night to see Marlon Brando's new movie *One Eyed Jacks*. In one unforgettable scene, Karl Malden's character, the mean Sheriff Dad Longworth, ties Brando's hands to a hitching post and smashes his fingers with the butt of a shotgun. Before the Sheriff breaks his hand, Brando guns down a ruffian beating up a women and utters the classic line "you scum suckin' pig, you tub of guts." Someone in the car exclaimed: "tub of guts, holy shit, that name fits the cook!" Within a few days, tub of guts was shortened to Tog and all the brothers jumped on it.

Oh, to have been a frat house cook in the Sixties. The rewards were spectacular, by the standards of the day. Because Tog had to cook breakfast and couldn't take early morning classes, he got up early. Breakfast was served at 7:30 and by 8:00, nearly the entire house was vacant, giving him a solid 2 hours to study. The cook only prepared meals, the 'hashers' were indentured busboys who set and cleared the table and washed the dishes. Hashers were the only others in the house and got reduced room and board for doing that thankless job—they also chowed down food that the others never saw. Gary 'Ranger' Jones was a hasher for a year and enjoyed every minute of the job. Jones was small in stature but the undisputed house eating champion. He won the Great

French Toast Chow Down twice easily besting Bubblebutt Bob McGrath (he doesn't want to be called that anymore) and our star lineman Jim 'Big Chuey" Colegate. Ranger Jones got his money's worth in the food department.

The cook's lifestyle also affected our health and probably contributed to chronic intestinal illnesses in later life.

After drinking beer and sweating profusely on the volleyball court in late afternoon, the now-inebriated, grumpy and sunburned Tog would go directly into the kitchen shirtless and sandy to make dinner—not too sanitary. The brothers would rag him about this and just about everything else.

"This food tastes like shit, where did you get it from, the toilet?'

"Fuck you, asshole, if you don't like it, go cook your own food," Tog would reply in an aggressive yet pimpy tone.

In retaliation to the constant complaining, he would spend many of his waking hours concocting payback schemes. One of the more creative ones was to 'season' the raw hamburger for the evening post-volleyball meal by slapping the meat under his sandy and stinky underarms, giving it a spicy, if somewhat gritty, salty and hairy taste after being cooked on the grill. Only Tog and a few of the hashers were aware of this grisly practice.

The cook also got first dibs on the little room downstairs that had a private entrance and only one other roommate. Most of the rooms upstairs in the house bunked three or four and were interconnected and always chaotic. There was only one bathroom/shower upstairs. Tog had that semi-private room downstairs for three semesters, the only room in the house where it was possible to study.

Tog recalls that: "With no room and board cost and a case of beer a week as a perk, I had almost no expenses and could save most of the $267 a month stipend. That financed entire summers of travel in '62 and '63 and meant that I only had to take out student loans of a couple of thousand dollars to finish a $10,000 four-year University of California education."

At one of the special Sunday evening gatherings, Tog prepared his now infamous Isla Vista meat loaf, better known as "Polish Hash."

Polish Hash: Sunday Dinner at the House

During the elaborate preparations for the Sunday feast, Tog was inclined to finish off a jug of Red Mountain wine left over from the night before. Especially drunk and jolly this day, he offered everyone at the table extra milk and second helpings of his Polish Hash. Needless to say, the brothers were devouring their meals and exclaiming the wonders of Tog's cooking:

"The best ever", "Magnificent", "Give me some more of this shit," exclaimed many. They wolfed it down and asked for seconds.

During seconds, Tog entered the room bare-footed, eyes glowing red and sweating profusely, with a trashcan full of empty cans which he proceeded to scatter on the floor—dozens of cans of Skippy Premium Dog food.

"Rat fuck you all," he shrieked, "I am glad you enjoyed your fucking dog food."

He immediately ran from the dining room and the chase was on. You can run, but you can't hide from 40 pissed-off brothers stuffed with premium dog food.

They finally captured him a few blocks away, stripped him naked, tied him up, and coated his entire body with Mayo, Catsup, and Mustard. Today, this punishment would be prosecuted as flagrant hazing and sexual abuse. Next, they delivered this sorry piece-of-shit to the front door of the Delta Phi Sorority house next door, rang the bell, and left. Screams filled the streets of I.V. for the rest of the evening.

Eventually feeling sorry for him, a few of the brothers without intestinal cramps rescued him from throng of horrified, but strangely curious Delta Phi's.

"We felt so sorry for him," said one of the sorority princesses.

"He was bound and gagged and had all this gooey stuff…ya know…down there. We didn't know what to do. But all the time he seemed to be … just laughing." That was Tog, knowing he had won the food wars.

A few days later, as if to gloat and declare complete victory, Tog posted his "Recipe of the Year," Polish Hash with Mushroom Gravy, the Galloping Goleta Gourmet.

Hellweek

From the moment a pledge gets his pin, his ultimate goal is to go active. Before that, each pledge must face, endure and survive Hell Week, a series of hazing rituals, physical activities, and arcane traditions designed to build unity, forge permanent bonds, demonstrate incredible endurance and show how much each pledge really wants to become a full-fledged member of the

House. On the other hand, perhaps Hell Week was just a sadistic ritual perpetuated by the actives to ensure that the new guys suffered just as much as they had. Among the poignant memories:

Holding a hand-painted brick outstretched at a 90° angle for seemingly endless hours. Because McGinnis could outlast just about everyone else holding the brink, he received the nickname 'Iron Man.' This feat was achieved by focusing all his anger towards our sadistic pledge trainer and on that ugly piece of concrete. Teaching us patience.

Having been strengthened by holding the brink, remembering his right arm being restrained by another pledge as he was about to take a swing at our sadistic pledge trainer…a sure way to get bonged. Teaching us restraint.

Eating meals as a pledge class while seated at a long row of benches with right hands tied to the long unity bar (of about 15 feet) so that everyone had to take their food, lift it and put it into their mouths at the same time. Teaching us teamwork and pledge unity.

Sore knees from doing the quack walk (waddling in a squatting position) through the sand volleyball court with our bricks held behind our necks with both hands, building character, weak knees and strong necks.

Running (with brick in hand) seemingly hundreds of times up to the corner of Embarcadero del Norte street just to say "hello" to the stop sign. The sign never responded. Pure harassment, teaching us nothing.

Ordered to do 500 jumping jacks after four or five days of hard work, virtually no sleep and near total exhaustion. The jumping jacks had to be done in unison and, of course, with bricks in hand. The toughest part was stopping after exactly (no more and no less) 500 jumping jacks. This was not an easy task since everyone was to remain completely silent and thus keep track of the count in his own now-exhausted memory. Clearly remembering the killer looks on pledge brothers faces when I stopped once at 499 and, just as clearly recalling the pain and anger when one did 501. The penalty, of course, imposed without mercy, was another 500 jumping jacks. Sadistic bastards.

The Apple Relay was another disgusting and humiliating hazing ritual designed to break us. All pledges had their hands tied behind their backs and the first was required to wiggle to the bottom of a zipped up sleeping bag where he had to find and retrieve, with his teeth, the "apple" (really an onion). After he snagged it with his teeth, he had to wiggle his way back out of the sleeping bag and pass it from his teeth to the teeth of the next waiting pledge. The second pledge was required to crawl to the bottom of the bag, leave the "apple" at the bottom for retrieval by the next pledge and then crawl out. This was repeated until all members of the pledge class had taken their turn with the increasingly soggy, tooth-marked and rancid "apple." While being first wasn't good, it was far better than last one to bite the apple dripping with saliva and smelling like the inside of a used sleeping bag.

Hell Week took place prior to the beginning of each semester and its stated purpose, apart from torturing pledges, was to clean the house. One of the actives had a title like pledge "ombudsman" with the task of secretly supplying pledges with as much beer as he could smuggle in without being caught. This part of the Hell Week ritual was a hide and seek game played between the pledges and the actives. The pledges, with the help of the designated active, tried to drink as much beer as they could during the day. If caught, there was usually hell to pay, often in the form of a long run with bricks in hand. On one particular occasion, the pledges had obviously been drinking lots of beer but the actives could never find out how. It turns out that the pledges had empty cans of their cleaning products i.e. Ajax or Comet, with the bottoms cut out and the beer cans cleverly concealed inside them. This lesson in subterfuge would become useful in other future life endeavors as well.

Segregation, Racism and Campus Dining Clubs

Segregation and racism were widely practiced in nearly every neighborhood and commercial enterprise during the pre-civil rights era. For millions of Americans, condescending efforts to provide equal opportunities and partial human rights were still decades away. Not unlike the rest of society, discrimination among frat boys and sorority girls was rampant, usually based on superficial criteria such as looks or physical ability. During rush week, eager young 'rushees" would visit fraternity and sorority houses in search of new identities with particular Greek-letter societies. Those already anointed acted like young old geezers who wanted to associate only with their own self-selected fellow Klansman. Those who did not make the cut would often suffer a lifetime of identity crises, personality disorders and self-doubt. Worse yet, selection was limited to the upper class of already privileged Whites, many of whom viewed country county clubs and private clubs as bastions of white superiority.

Despite token rulings by federal courts, Blacks and Hispanics were segregated by white majorities who controlled city hall, local boards of education, police departments, and selective service boards. Inter-racial marriage was illegal in most states and minorities were ghettoized in low-income neighborhoods with limited opportunities to escape. In the pre-civil rights enforcement era, public opinion reflected deeply held racist attitudes. All Black railroad porters were called "George" and all minorities were forbidden from riding in the front of public buses or trains. Movie stars like John Wayne would sarcastically defend their racism with comments such as:

"When those Blacks are smart enough to play quarterback, I will believe they are equal to Whites."

Too bad old Duke is not alive today to eat his words.

How Jackie Robinson endured these racial epithets when he was first to cross the color line in major league baseball in the late 1940s was painfully depicted in the both the Ken Burns' documentary and the film "42." Although racist attitudes are more covert than a generation ago, the dark musings of Donald Sterling's world still echo in the halls of private clubs and exclusive billionaire refuges. Legislative actions such as the repeal of Obamacare further re-segregate those dependent of government subsidies for healthcare.

Despite the forced integration of the armed forces in the late 1940s by Harry S Truman and Black competence demonstrated during World War II fighter pilot training in Tuskegee Alabama, private clubs rife with racism continued to prevail, especially—but not only—in the Deep South. Institutional racism and *de facto* segregation prevailed in most regions of the country despite early efforts to desegregate schools and apply civil rights protections to all Americans, regardless of age, race, creed, color or national origin.

Although many far less affluent countries had previously abolished segregation and enforced equal access to opportunities for all citizens, many Americans view race as a permanent condition. Religious leaders even quote biblical verse to justify racism and too many Americans equate dark skins with poverty.

Other equally absurd rationalizations perpetuated racial segregation and its resulting income inequality. Some excused racism because it was beyond their control, pointing to global market forces and the resurrection of Japan, Germany and other rapidly developing economic competitors as a justification for not granting full rights to all citizens and raising wages for workers. Others believed that doing something about it would make us all worse off by opening our domestic economic markets to cheap foreign competitors such as Japan and China. Imagine that? These justifications were nothing more than excuses that thinly masked the real reason: distain for those with darker skins and inferior souls.

Racism took of many forms, from the segregated ghettos of South Central LA to the 'separate but equal" classrooms of Little Rock, to the visible dividing line between the Upper East Side and the squalor of Harlem. Intimidation and threats of violence were always present for anyone who dared cross over these *de facto* and *de jure* lines. Even well intentioned Whites bemoaned the forced integration first imposed by Eisenhower and later by Kennedy's 'liberal' Eastern establishment following the *Brown v. Board of Education* decision in 1954, a landmark case brought before the Supreme Court by the NAACP's legal arm to challenge segregation in public schools. It began after several black families in Topeka, Kansas, tried to enroll their children in white schools near their homes. Oliver Brown's daughter Linda was among those barred from a white elementary school. The lawsuit was joined with cases from Delaware, South Carolina, Virginia and the District of Columbia.

On May 17, 1954, the Supreme Court ruled unanimously that separate facilities for black and white children were unconstitutional, because black children were denied their 14th Amendment's guarantee of equal protection under the law. The Court's historic dictum:

"In the field of public education, the doctrine of `separate but equal' has no place."

The decision overturned the court's blatantly discriminatory *Plessy v. Ferguson* decision that, since May 18, 1896, established a "separate but equal" doctrine for blacks and whites in public facilities. Chief Justice Earl Warren further wrote:

"Separate educational facilities are inherently unequal."

Although numerous efforts tried to undermine its scope, *Brown v. Board of Education* has never been overruled. The Justice Department still actively enforces the law as co-plaintiff to more than 180 desegregation orders against school districts. Sadly, Justice Department Attorneys must now devote more time to investigating police shootings of Black men, undercutting efforts to enforce school desegregation efforts.

The Supreme Court did not immediately order enforcement of its *Brown* decision, an action viewed as too dangerous for minorities and too disruptive for whites. In 1955, Chief Justice Earl Warren ordered lower courts to tell states and school districts to admit students "to public schools on a racially nondiscriminatory basis *with all deliberate speed*." What does that mean? Lawyers still quibble about these four words.

In the South, white parents removed their children from public schools and officials resisted enrolling black children into integrated schools. In 1968, the justices ruled in *Green vs. School Board of New Kent County* that states operating segregated schools had to come up with a system that eliminates racial discrimination "root and branch." In *Swann v. Charlotte-Mecklenburg Board of Education* in 1971, the Supreme Court endorsed sending students from different neighborhoods to the same school to promote integration, leading to the widespread use of busing to end segregation. Many of the desegregation and busing orders have since been dissolved and re-segregation is occurring at a troubling pace.[1] Re-segregation also affects Latino students, the largest minority group in the public schools. Many advocates blame this delay on the federal courts for removing school districts from Brown-inspired desegregation orders. The changing demographics of the school system, so-called "White Flight" of parents withdrawing their students from the public systems and the booming Latino population also contribute to the changing colors of the schools.

Ernest Greenly, one of the original "Little Rock Nine" and one of the first Black students to graduate from Little Rock High School, remembers the hatred in the eyes of white students, male and female, as he and the eight others were spat upon as they were escorted into school by armed members of the Army's 101st Airborne Division. The Little Rock Nine were turned away the day before by Governor Orval Faubus who deployed the Arkansas National Guard troops to support the segregationists. Attitudes change far more slowly than laws.

Southern Whites condoned unspeakable crimes against 'uppity' Negros and Northern civil rights workers before begrudgingly accepting federal court-ordered desegregation years, and sometimes decades, later.

Civil rights leader Medgar Evers was cut down by a bullet from a high-powered rifle in front of his family at his home in Jackson, Mississippi on June 12, 1963. Evers was an NAACP field secretary, civil rights activist, and a retired United States Army Sergeant buried in Arlington National Cemetery in Washington, DC. His killers were Klansmen who, with the help of the local courts, escaped justice in the Mississippi for over 30 years. His widow, Myrlie Evers-Williams spent three decades fighting to win a conviction for her late husband's shooter. In an overdue and fitting tribute, she spoke at President Obama's second inaugural in 2013.

Civil Rights Wars in the 1960s produced countless other less visible casualties. Prosecutions by state authorities were rare until the passage of Civil Rights and Voting Rights Acts in the mid-1960s when the federal courts assumed jurisdiction in those states with histories of ignoring segregation. In the meantime, the slaughter of innocents continued.

On September 17, 1963, four small black girls attending Sunday school were killed in a Birmingham, Alabama church bombing. Three civil rights workers were murdered after traveling to Neshoba County, Mississippi to investigate the burning of a black church. No one was ever charged, although Federal agents identified a group of Klansmen as the killers. The bodies of civil rights workers were discovered by FBI agents' months later buried near the town of Philadelphia, Mississippi. Years later, a federal case against 19 conspirators was brought to trial. In October 1967 a jury returned guilty verdicts against only seven conspirators, nine were acquitted, and the jury could not reach a verdict on three of the men charged. The film *Mississippi Burning* depicted these and other gruesome details of such travesties of justice. The recent Charleston, South Carolina church massacre shows just how far radical right-wing hate groups are still willing to go to maintain white supremacy.

The Birmingham church bombing was the worst domestic terrorist attack on Blacks in modern history until the AME Church massacre on June 19, 2015. Numerous groups still hate Blacks and will kill for White supremacy. Dylann Roof, a 21-year old White Southern racist assassin wanted to start a race war by murdering 9 innocent people during a Bible Study class. His racist rants blamed Blacks for the miseries and indignities allegedly suffered by Whites since the Civil Rights era. This heinous act may have ripped open an only partially healed wound on the American psyche and reversed much of the progress in race relations made in the past 50 years. Apartheid was deep-seated and violently enforced, even in Western states where skin color was less of a determinant of social class than income.

David Eggert remembers a professor in a Mormon religion class at Brigham Young University explaining the difference between blacks and whites. With a pompous tone in his voice, the professor said:

"Non-whites were given their dark complexions as a punishment for their sins of their ancestors and, as a result, they cannot hold high office in the Mormon Church."[2]

Lower income Asian, Black, Native-American and Mexican families were concentrated in urban 'ghettos' or reservations with names like Little San Salvador, Koreatown, South Central, and Watts. None of this seemed to bother most whites who, in Mohamed Ali's prophetic words, "had the complexion and the connections to get protection."

The Legendary Red House-Dining Club

Like all private clubs, fraternities and sororities selected their own members, subject to racist Southern traditions and rituals which barred Asians, Blacks, Hispanics, Jews and other 'undesirables' from mingling with pure White Christians. The fraternity was founded in Charlottesville, Virginia, at the heart of the Old Confederacy.

During initiation ceremonies, we sometimes wondered why we needed to wear those black hoods, robes and masks. At the end of the ceremony, we used lighter fluid to burn a cross on the initiate's chest. A brother always stood by with a bucket of water just in case the initiate panicked or the fire spread. This part of the ritual was viewed humorously because of the rank smell created when those with hairy chests were set on fire. In another instance, the fire burned too long on a pledge with a sunken chest and he had to be dosed with water. Denial about the true meaning of those 'traditions' kept us from thinking too deeply about the sorted history of rape, racism and lynching hidden beneath such garb.

One of the more hilarious moments of Red House rituals occurred during one of these pseudo inaugurations. Most of the active members looked upon these ceremonies as nothing more than humorous diversions, so keeping order under such circumstances was always difficult. We were all getting antsy listening to Pete Fowler, then president of the Red House, trying to guide the brothers through a training session on how to welcome new members into the House. One segment of the ceremony required that each of us place our hand on the holy book and repeat the words. For some reason, the brothers were having a tough time with this task so Pete cut loose with an impatient plea.

"Jesus Christ, you fucking assholes, put your hand on the God Damn Bible and get on with it!"
****

Our own version of elite selectivity and secrecy led to the creation of the soon-to-be infamous Red House Dining Club.[3] Perhaps the last names of its members—Berkman, Rubin, Gozinya, Kwock, Jaffe, Nakita, Negrial, and Rosenbloom—offer a bit of a clue?

All fraternities and sororities were White, all-Christian private clubs governed by strict covenants dating from the late 19th Century. When the local Santa Barbara renegades decided to pledge a bunch of distinctly non-Christian ethnic, racial and religious inferiors, this immediately created a huge problem. What was to become of the infidels when representatives from the national office came around to inspect the pledge rolls?

The national rep or, as we called him, the Travelling Fuck (TF), would overnight at the House and we were expected to provide dinner and chitchat about the great work of our national KKK leaders. The TF's pathetic job was to visit the local chapters, inspect the membership rolls, protect their racial purity and ensure that the locals measured up to the lofty segregationist standards of the National Headquarters. As with most dilemmas, lots of creative thought went into designing what turned out to be a win-win solution.

On those Gestapo inspection evenings, the House gave the infidels enough money to go out and have a nice dinner so that they did not have to eat (or be seen) at the House or at the following chapter meeting. The House won because National never knew these racial inferiors existed, the TF won because he never saw or heard of them, and the infidels won most of all because they got a great dinner (far better than was ever served at the House), avoided the TF and didn't have to sit through the long, boring chapter meeting.

At one point during one of the pledge roll inspections, the TF saw the name "Kadji Nakita" on the membership roll, and asked about his ethnicity. Thinking quickly, Mark McGinnis explained:

"Oh, this was a typographic error. Sorry about that. His name is actually Conrad Nachman, a nice German kid from Sacramento. We were lucky to pledge him." The TF swallowed hard and nodded.

The Blackballing of Juan Esperanza

Social rejection can have lifelong negative consequences for post-adolescents. Unfortunately, not everyone qualifies for fraternity or sorority life: life is subjective, especially men and women of color. At least that is what many still believed in the segregated Sixties. Although no 'formal barriers' prevented minorities applying for admission to the University of California or participating in fraternity rush, the high standards for high school grades in certain college prep subjects excluded all but the brightest and whitest. Athletic ability helped, but race did not. The *de facto* racism was subtle, just below the surface but part of nearly everyone's geographic home and upbringing.

Most of the members had attended all-White Catholic, private or suburban high schools supported and often *over*-supported by attentive parents in well-funded public school districts in affluent communities. Most just didn't know many Blacks and Hispanics who lived in less affluent segregated neighborhoods. A few other non-Christian Whites qualified for admission, but some of the members from rural areas held hardline attitudes about attending classes or socializing with minorities.

John Esperanza was a polite lad of Mexican descent from Chula Vista, a suburb of San Diego near the border. He was good storyteller and after rush was invited to join the fall pledge class. He was outgoing, personable and had all the personality characteristics that were desirable for full membership. During Hell Week, his hot temper began to boil.

What other pledges took as 'just another hazing ritual,' John took personally. Even though other more-seasoned members advised him to keep quiet and take the shit being thrown at him, he spoke up. This was a mistake.

Any member could call a conclave to vote on any pledge during hell week. That evening at a secret meeting, John's name was called. Each active was given two marbles, one white and the other black. After the small wooden box was passed around the room and opened by the Pledge Master, a single black ball huddled among the dozens of white ones. Some demanded that the black-baller speak up and give a reason for his vote, but no one spoke. It was over in 15 minutes. We never knew who bonged him or why.

The Pledge Leader was ordered to inform John that he was out. He did not take it well, screaming at the top of his lungs that we were all a bunch of bigots and racist assholes. He packed up his stuff in his car and screamed out of the parking lot, burning rubber all the way up the street. This cruel and arbitrary selection process might affect some for their entire lives. The fact that so few cared exemplified the inbred conceited attitude of ethnic superiority. We would soon encounter an immovable object that cared not about our superior attitudes.

Confronting the Dreaded Cyclops

Although generally apathetic about the more radical elements of the civil rights and anti-war movements, most of the Red House members were keenly aware of the penalties for breaking rules. They had experienced harsh forms of military justice from their coaches, fathers and teachers. Some had also felt the sting of buckle end of the belt, heavy punishment for relative minor offences. Most had suffered painful sports injuries and, rather than seeking medical treatment, were told by coaches to "walk it off" risking permanent ankle, leg and knee injuries. Intercollegiate sports had two sets of separate *in loco parentis* regulations applied to both sexes. This arrangement was common in institutions with antiquated enforcement arms such as Deans of Men and Women.

Most respected research universities (mini-Iveys) had long ago eliminated *en loco parentis* positions such as these to comply with student demands for the new moral relativist society of coed dorms, sleepovers, and condom machines in campus restrooms. Not so at prudish Santa Barbara in the 1960s. Even though most the 18-22-year-old residents of I.V. were fucking their brains out on a regular basis, the UC system still maintained some disciplinary figureheads, probably to reassure tuition-paying parents that Johnny or Joanie coed were actually attending college to study.

The enforcement arm of this puritanical policy for raucous males and curious females was a former Army Major who had lost an eye in combat. Not only did "Cyclops," as he was affectionately known, have a scared face and empty eye socket, but also his mere presence scared the shit out of us. He was an impressive figure: tall, dark and disfigured. The black patch covering his face concealed what we could only imagine was a horribly scared face. Some said it was a result of a Japanese bayonet; others were convinced the wound resulted from a German hand grenade. Whatever the reason for being summonsed to meet with him, 'Dean of Mean' Bob Jones was not to be trifled with. This did not stop one of our friends, George Jenkins, from relentlessly taunting him.

He and others hosted gotcha parties for the obvious purpose of luring innocent young coeds into playing board games and disrobing items of clothing if they landed on the wrong square. It was cleaver combination of monopoly and strip poker. The game was harmless at best and experimental at worst for all players. Anyone who objected was free to leave. Nonetheless, George felt the Wrath of Cyclops after being ratted out by one of his embarrassed invitees who doubtless landed on the wrong square. Of course, the Dean of Mean would have none of this tomfoolery on his campus.

Those who attended the party were interrogated by Cyclops and threatened with expulsion if they didn't 'name names.' Someone eventually squealed on poor George who confessed under duress and begrudgingly accepted his fate. He did not go down without a fight. After being singledout, he provoked Cyclops relentlessly, running for class president under the slogan:

"I know what's under the patch." He did not win.

Dean Jones suspended him for a semester for lurking at innocent young coeds and holding the immoral gotcha party.

Institutional morality enforcement went even further in the authoritarian efforts to control our alcohol consumption and testosterone urges as well as clean-up our collective 'spirits.'

Drunken Cheerleaders and other Spiritual "Crises"

The headline from the November 22, 1963 school newspaper *El Nacho*, revealed just how isolated we were: "Cheerleaders Ousted in Student Association 'Spirit' Cleanup." Hide the children and the pets: here come the drunken UCSB Cheerleaders. HEADLINES: "Yell leaders fired in Council action; drunkenness cited."

The accompanying article highlighted the despicable details: "Two UCSB cheerleaders who allegedly put on a drunken display before packed stands at Saturday's Cal State game were fired Tuesday by Legislative Council. A third yell leader, who passed out in front of the crowd according to witnesses, resigned."

Compared to the recent binge drinking street riots and homicidal violence which has occurred in I.V. recently, the so-called Spirit Cleanup looked like a minor infraction: but one with deadly consequences for one of its alleged participants and a close friend.

The deposed yell leaders were of course Red House members David Eggert and Mark Rubin. The Student Council also accepted a remorseful resignation from a third yell leader, Kevin Moore, who so embarrassed by the incident that he withdrew prematurely from the University to join the Marine Corps.

Eggert and Rubin were dismissed by an 8-3 vote with one Council member abstaining. The three disgraced cheerleaders, who were not present to answer charges, confessed to "drinking quite heavily," explained Associated Student Body President Andrew Bobbs solemnly, as if he were prosecuting Nazi war defendants at Nuremburg. Eggert and Rubin pled guilty to drinking and were soulfully apologetic.

"It would never happen again," they said, chuckling.

The other two cheerleaders, Dave Johnson and Ted Gold, were cleared of charges. "They did a fine job of handling the crowd…and behaved admirably," reported AS Secretary Alice Webster, an informant who attended the game.

The Council acted swiftly and showed no mercy. In unanimous votes, Johnson was appointed new head yell leader and authorized to appoint three assistants, subject to Council's approval. From varying stories reported by at least 10 students—often distorted and exaggerated according to Bobbs—the AS President said he had managed after extensive probing to pin down these facts:

The three arrived at the game a few minutes before halftime in a bus chartered by the Campus Group for Student Body Spirit (CGSBS). Johnson and Gold arrived on time and led cheers alone during the first half. According to other witnesses, Moore was "visibly inebriated—so much so that when he walked in front of the stands he passed out."

Eggert and Rubin were "not as bad," but were "obviously under the influence of alcohol."

One of the witnesses said a Cal State photographer snapped one shot of the fiasco. He was asked to leave by Eggert.

Dennis Foss, CGSB President, gave this concocted story:

"The bus arrived late, around 11:30. Somebody asked if the cheerleaders could go with us. They were drinking quite heavily when we picked them up."

Questioned by *El Nacho*, Foss, who attended the meeting to defend the CGSBs against student body charges, admitted drinking on the bus by both the cheerleaders and the CGSB members. He also alleged that the yell leaders took four or five quarts of Country Club whiskey aboard the bus, enough to kill several elephants. Eggert denied that they were drinking heavily before boarding the bus. "We each had one beer," he said. "Most of the drinking was done aboard the bus and we drank CGSBs beer after finishing off the three or four bottles of beer that we had." In a letter of resignation addressed to the Council, Moore wrote:

> *"With reference to the football game, as a cheerleader representing the student body, I wish to submit my resignation and apology for the complete lack of discretion on my behalf. It was a display along with others which convinced me that it is high time I grabbed hold of myself. I have petitioned for an honorable withdrawal from school and have enlisted for a three-year term in the Marine Corps effective this date (Nov. 17). It is with a mind filled with regret that I look back over this semester, and also a mind filled with determination to return and serve myself and the University in a new light.*

Kevin never got the chance to redeem himself. A year later, after completing boot camp at Camp Pendleton, he was killed in a head-on collision caused by a drunk driver on a 2-lane stretch of unfinished Interstate 5 north of San Diego between and the Orange County line known as "blood alley." He was on his way back to visit his girlfriend. We always wondered if his thoughts were clouded with self-doubt that night on the highway. We will never know. Although our 'spirits' were apparently cleansed, we all again felt the profound loss.

Sully's Dogs and Muff the Goat

If you stop and think about it, farm animals and frat boys have much in common: both are always hungry, sleep a lot, smell bad, and leave huge messes behind. This explains why so many adopted various pets, or vice versa, with which to share living quarters. One of the early Red House occupants, Mike O'Sullivan, would dump sand and seaweed all over the floor of his room so that his dog would have a place to piss and defecate. He later moved out of his room after many stench driven protests from fellow residents. However, he did not go far. He parked his truck (the old grey Navy delivery van) on the front lawn of the House, hooked up an extension cord, and lived that way (with his dog) until evicted by local authorities. Not only was Sully an ardent dog lover, but he was also a gifted Flamenco guitarist, someone who adapted creatively to a changing environment.

Several other domestic pets and farm animals would roam in and out of the Red House, but by far the most memorable was Muff the Goat. No one really knew where Muff came from. She just appeared one day. She was a loyal companion who presented us with a catalogue of some of the funniest experiences of our entire college years. She would insist on eating with us at the dinner table by affectionately butting us with her horns. We enjoyed wrestling with her and in time, she became territorial and protective of her little corner of the dining hall. She would nibble on the grass in front of the house and relieve us from the arduous task of mowing the lawn.

One day, Muff was doubtless feeling frisky as a brother walked inside the dining hall with his date. Naturally, Muff wanted to protect her turf and came after the girl. As she ran out of the room screaming, the goat butted her in the rear. She failed to see the humor in this, but we laughed our asses off. Why not teach Muff to butt our dates so they would fall into our arms? Whoever thought of this anthropomorphic perversion was obviously sick, but Muff seemed amenable.

The gag worked something like this: when the unsuspecting date arrived at the house for coffee, tea or whatever she wished, another brother would hold Muff until just the right moment.

When she turned her back, he would release the animal and, seeing the foreigner, she [Muff] would head directly for her buttocks. The unsuspecting girl would scream and fall into the waiting arms of the brother who would comfort her and offer protection from the wild beast.

"Where did that monster come from?" would be the phony question.

"Aren't you glad that I was here to protect you?"

This sounds hokey, but girls ate it up and goat also seemed to enjoy the exercise as well.

All this was good fun until Joe "Knifeman' Leishman brought his 9-year old sister to visit the house. Why he did this was incomprehensible and the consequences were swift and brutal.

The little girl, who was about the same height as Muff, heard the charging goat hooves on the tile floor, turned too quickly and received the full impact of sharp horns with a head butt directly to her ribs, knocking her several feet in the air. Muff thought this was just another heroic act for which she would be rewarded with food. It wasn't. The little girl received serious injuries and would likely never visit a petting zoo again for the rest of her life.

Knifeman sawed off Muff's horns and released her in an open field on Isla Vista that night. Wild dogs made of quick meal of poor Muff, but the owners of the House avoided a nasty lawsuit.

Red Death Punch

John Lambright remembers when he lived in the Animal House wing of the Red House in the last year before it was bulldozed into oblivion.

"What a contrast when we moved into the new red brick building with the snazzy red door. I missed the old house and the sand and sea weed spread over the chapter room floor for parties, Muff the goat, and sully's dogs."

He further recalled a favorite bathtub concoction referred to as "Red Death Punch." Famously, Red Death Punch (Boxed insert below) was a sacrament and essential part of Red House rituals.

RECIPE FOR RED DEATH

5 gallons of Red Mountain
1 jar of lime juice
Assorted citrus fruit
2 liters of Vodka
Fill with new Garbage Car
Stir with broom handle

Lambright remembers:

"I'm not sure who the victim was, but I think we almost left one of the brother's dates to drown in a bathtub full of the stuff."

John was close. Actually, it was Eggert's date who passed out in the bathtub after consuming too much Red Death.

According to eyewitnesses,

"Nearing the end of one of Tog's masterpiece toga parties I found someone's date passed out in a bath tub still half full of our famous brew, better known as the Red Death. Brothers were pausing nonchalantly as they walked by, stooping to scoop another cup of Red Death despite her unconscious soaked presence in the tub."

Alcohol, Drugs, and the Border Guards

It did not take long for drug dealers to figure out how to market their products on university campuses throughout California: Isla Vista was a ripe target with thousands of 18-24 year-olds willing to tempt the law without risking being found hung over, naked, rolled, or dead on a Mexican Beach. This is precisely what happened to one the brothers who lost perspective by consuming too much of the illegal substance he was trying to sell.

Dave Eggert was dating Norma Palideros who, in addition to having a killer body and difficulty achieving organisms, hung out with some suspicious looking characters. Outward appearances would tag them as 'lodos,' frequent marijuana users who enjoyed the long afternoons toking joints and drinking beer, but little else. They were probably local junior college dropouts, but no one cared enough to ask. Work was not in their vocabulary, but they always seemed to have lots of beer money. Some were probably trust-fund babies, others posers, scavengers, wannabes or just hangers-on. Although David and the rest of those who were acquainted with them never saw them acting particularly violent, they did seem reticent to socialize with others.

One afternoon at work, Norma called him in a hysterical panic: in a high-pitched voice, she shrieked:

"David, you have to come over, they are here and want me to hide it. I am scared. Please help me."

She lived in a small mother-in-law cottage tucked away behind a larger house in Montecito. When David arrived, he found her in her nightgown huddled on the floor, crying hysterically and babbling about 'the stuff.'

"What stuff?" he asked, now more sheepishly.

She babbled, "Let me show you, under the planting box outside the window. They were here and said they needed to hide the stuff quickly...I didn't want to be mean so I let them do it. I couldn't talk them out of it, even if I tried."

"What the hell are you talking about?" he asked.

She pointed under the flower box at two large suitcases, more like duffle bags, stuffed with smaller heavy cellophane bags. Eggert pulled out one to the large bags and it weighed maybe 3040 pounds. He opened it and found at least 20 kilos (2.2 pounds each) of tightly packed marijuana stuffed into thick red plastic squares. This was the first time he had seen this much pot, so tightly packed and moist to the touch. It felt like chewing tobacco, but smelled much more pungent. Highgrade stuff.

"What the hell are you doing with all of this?" he screamed.

She responded meekly that they were 'friends' and said they only needed to store the bags for a few days.

"They said they will be back to get it," she mumbled naively.

"Are you fucking crazy?' he yelled at her.

"Do you know where this came from?"

She muttered something about Mexico and some friends of hers, but didn't know any more details.

The 'details' were alarming. Earlier that morning, he had heard radio broadcasts and all-pointbulletins (APBs) about two U.S. Border Patrol Agents who were killed in Mexicali when a drug deal went bad. The APBs described two white guys who were suspects in the shooting.

"Holy shit" he said, "We have got to get this shit out of here. You have to tell these guys to get rid of it."

She babbled some more phony excuses about why she couldn't leave or "they" would become even more suspicious, whereupon Eggert left as fast as he could. Unbeknownst to Eggert, one of "them" was Scott Peters who, by all outward appearances, was a successful entrepreneur living the good life in Santa Barbara.

Bad dreams would haunt Eggert for several nights after this encounter. One was about an apocalyptic trip on the twisted freeways to Los Angeles with Norma talking endlessly in a car, seeing bridges overturned, buildings blown-up, and stuck in train station looking at an old ledger book. Because of his fruitless search of this useless book, they missed a train back to Whittier and just looked at each other with hazy astonishment. Another encounter included a violent surfer fight dream, swimming toward a buoy in the water, and hearing loud voices asking to contribute to the Salt Water Gods. Feeling free in the rough surf and people "jeering" from a balcony on top of the buoy, cheerfully led by a leering old women in slinky black dress who closely resembled Norma's mother, whom he had met on a few painful occasions. He went into a violent rampage using a large knife to slay his roommates in bottom story of apartment. He could not escape. A large container blocked the entrance to another room. He was stuck.

In the ensuing days, no news of arrests or suspects. Most of that hashish doubtless made its way in small bags to Isla Vista, into the innocent lungs of unsuspecting college students, eager for a quick high, but unaware of the real price.

Scott Peters was one who journeyed too far in the opposite direction—internally. He became a victim to easy access to mind-altering drugs, herbs and compounds designed to lessen the mental burden of external forces, but ultimately weakening his internal coping mechanisms. Peters used his own drugs to relieve migraine headaches. He mistakenly trusted one of his informants after crossing the Mexican border too many times with his VW Kombi loaded with heroin. Unaware that DEA had turned his man, Peters walked into a death trap.

****

Today's college students continue the revered I.V. traditions of abusing their bodies and brains by consuming too much alcohol and weed, yet without the moral calling, tension and urgency produced by causes such as the civil rights struggle or the anti-Vietnam war movements. Years of recession, underemployment and tight job markets for college graduates have focused students' attention on more practical matters, such as getting decent jobs and paying back student loans. Escapism is still the major cause of drug use, and the sluggish economic recovery has taken its toll on millennials' brain cells.

It now takes twice as long as it did a generation ago for college graduates to reach the median salary level for their chosen professions; increasing numbers forced to live with parents and delay marriage, home purchases and parenthood. Many feel their lives stalled, even before they have the opportunity to take-off.

Voters' approval of leisure and medical marijuana outlets and the slackening of possession laws in several states has doubtless increased drug use. The falloff in voting among the under 30s in the 2016 Election reaffirmed the fact that many are so apathetic and downtrodden that they don't even bother with politics or voting anymore.[4]

Hardline conservative attitudes have not changed—if anything, they have become even bolder and less compromising. Republicans have been out of the White House for eight years and are fighting bitterly among themselves to find direction and leadership. Trump's victory was assisted by states such as North Carolina and Texas that previously enacted tougher voter ID laws disenfranchising 'radical' students, minorities and women with their Democratic Party affiliations and left-leaning political views.

The agenda for change initiated in the Sixties remains incomplete. Senseless mass shootings at schools and other group venues have replaced armed revolutionaries, with Isla Vista again becoming one of a lengthening list of targets. Semi-constitutional anti-terrorist actions and massive homeland security bureaucracies created since the 9/11 attacks have affected society in less-thansubtle ways. Active 'suspect" organizations on campus have raised FBI suspicions including the Green Party, Libertarians, Log Cabin Republicans, the Pink Panther Party, NORML, and the Queer Student Union.

****

In recent decades, public policies have ceased to function as they once did in the mid-20th century to ameliorate inequality in college going. This policy failure is manifest in three areas: federal aid no longer promotes educational opportunity because policy makers have not raised the maximum amount for Pell Grants ($5730) in decades; state and federal assistance covers only a fraction of the expanding cost of higher education; and, as tuition escalates and financial aid declines, students left with no option except borrowing more.[5] The upward redistributive tilt of these policies has grown; since 2009, the largest benefits accrue to upper-income households with annual incomes of $100,000 to $180,000. States have also cut back support for higher education, with students and parents forced to borrow more at usurious commercial interest rates.[6]

Predictably, Republicans in Congress have introduced mean-spirited legislation to cut funding to students even further.

As a result of higher levels of education and two-parent upbringing, boomers were far less dependent on student debt, more openly sociable, less reliant on technology such as *Facebook,* 'texting,' and other so-called social media relationships. They value their privacy, families and friendships in much the same way that younger generations continue to seek lasting, albeit pseudo, relationships online. Such troves of distracting infotainment simply were not available in the 1960s when we ventured to Isla Vista. Nevertheless, that did not mean that we lacked either diversions or enthusiasm for learning. On the contrary, the campus was a rich environment in which to explore and participate in live theatre, music, television, and film productions.

Untethered by internet devices, we had to depend on local friends, colleagues, and acquaintances for entertainment. "Old media" turns out to have been a rich supplement to our formal and informal educations. Interacting with friends is how we learned about the protest music of Dylan, Country Joe, Joan Baez, Woody Guthrie, and the depth and history of social and political issues underlying their lyrics.

CHAPTER 8: ARTS, ENTERTAINMENT AND SEX

Impossible to describe or even imagine in today's ultra-connected e-world, but there were no cell phones, no digital cameras, no *Buzz Feed, Facebook, Twitter, Face Time* nor *LinkedIn*; no Google, Amazon, Wikipedia, Starbucks, computers, I-phones, I-pods or I-pads; no reverse marketing software, Ed Snowden, broadband access, emotional IQ or spyware. The intrusive presence of the Internet was still decades away. This may sound boring to most millennials and GenZers, but we were free to think and act on our own, without pre-programmed IOS internet operating systems. God forbid, we actually had to interact face-to-face with other human beings…gasp!

We learned how to converse, live, love and think independently, without pre-programmed robots and no way to plagiarize words from websites. Rather than cutting and pasting passages from books or Internet sites like Google, Moodle and Wikipedia, college-bound boomers actually had to read published articles and even books available only in libraries. Remember them? They are actual places with chairs and desks and bookshelves where other live people read, think and sometimes sleep.

Conducting research for term papers required actually reading original copies of articles and books. Some misfits did rip pages out of books and journals, but librarians would protect reading materials like wolf mothers guarding their cubs. Librarians actually counted the number of pages copied and billed the students a nickel or dime *per page*, thereby enriching IBM stockholders. It was more difficult to "upload" our work to anonymous pirate websites because we used arcane unconnected devises like typewriters rather than word processors to write term papers, carbon paper to make duplicates, and mimeograph machines with inky stincles to make copies. Professors read them and graded papers by hand with red pencils!

It is impossible to overstate the depth and scope of change—positive and negative—wrought by the spread and saturation of electronic information and communication technologies since the beginning of the so-called knowledge revolution. We are now tethered to the Internet for many of the same relationships we used to expect from other people, live people, real people who would cheat, betray, love and disappoint us as we searched for some permanency in our lives. What were once private conversations, accomplishments and disappointments have now become public via the Internet. Imagine the horror that parents, relatives and friends felt upon seeing a beloved daughter and friend killed on *Instagram* at the 2016 Orlando nightclub massacre.

Trade-offs certain as traditional knowledge-transfer methods and socialization rituals delegated to the I-Pad or other devises, replete with voice activated lessons for attentive children. Parents read less to their children and we are all becoming less interested in conversing each other; e-books already outsell traditional hardcover and paperbacks; classroom teachers rapidly becoming obsolete; internet 'virtual' learning and "on-demand" teaching preferred modes of instruction for many budget-starved school districts.

Like so many other technological advancements, the origin of such intrusive technology was a fear-inducted innovation funded by the Department of Defense (DoD) to decentralize access to information in the then-likely event of a Soviet nuclear attack on Washington, D.C. Damn those Cubans and those Ruskies! The Soviet Union's launch of Sputnik spy satellite spurred paranoid American government to expand applied research in advanced technology in much the same way that the 9/11/01 attacks spurred the creation of the bloated Orwellian intelligence-industrial-complex that wealds so much intrusive political power today.

UCSB was one of the first to receive DoD funding from the Advanced Research Projects Agency (ARPA) to design the world's first electronic computer network. ARPANET was initialized on October 29, 1969 between UCLA and the Stanford Research Institute (SRI), in Menlo Park. In addition to SRI and UCLA, UCSB and the University of Utah composed the original 4-node network. By December 5, 1969 the entire network was connected. The rest soon became Internet technological history. ARPENET was designed to give individuals in remote locations the same level of computing power as central command, thereby forever changing how channels and users connected and communicated. Access to central command records also allowed 'WikiLeakers' like Edward Snowden to hack into once secure commercial and national security mega-databases and probe our innermost secrets. Subsequent innovations such as Internet browsers, cell phone towers, HTML, mobile phones, personal computers, search engines, micro devices, SKYPE and social networking sites would further redistribute access to knowledge, power and technology, spreading access to nearly the entire world's population. Only utopian philosophers imagined the reach of such a global village at the time.

George Orwell prophesized the emergence of dominant techno-elites, but also foresaw the consequences of structured inequality in *Animal Farm*. Referring to dominant elites: "all animals are created equal but some are more equal than others." Everyone ate but the master pigs were "well fed." Most of us suspected nothing of such dystopian horrors disguised as *Facebook* wonders and relied instead on dial-up telephones and local sources of entertainment—our own.

Commercial entertainment that was available spanned the transition from the late-1950s beatnik folk era to mid-1960s hard rock revolution: hidden messages in much of the creative work of the era still resonate today. Bob Dylan's *Freewheelin'* album was released on May 27, 1963. Songs included classics such as: *'Blowin' In The Wind,' 'Girl from The North Country, 'Masters of War,' 'A Hard Rain's A-Gonna Fall,'* and *'Don't Think Twice, It's All Right.'* Robert Zimmerman (aka Dylan) was born in Duluth, Minnesota in 1941, and became the leading voice of social protest among folk and rock artists of the era. Dylan first tried out his songwriting and found his voice in Dinkytown coffeehouses and the Triangle Bar near the University of Minnesota campus in Minneapolis. *Blowin' in the Wind* was also recorded by Peter, Paul and Mary and became the anthem for supporters of the civil rights movement and those opposed to the war. These songs and many others still speak to millennials today, just as they did to us a half-century ago.

Among the trade-offs for not living in LA or San Francisco was a dearth of live entertainment. In those days, we did have the ROTC auxiliary 'Colonel's Coeds', the 'Honey Bears' (yum those Honey Bears), Spring Sing, and the Galloping Gaucho Review. The latter two were full-scale student choral and theatrical productions in which several students had the opportunity to participate, regardless of their talent. Because there were no personal data assistants, no *iTunes,* no *Facebook* or *Instagram*, we had to create our own assistants, songs, faces, books and spaces. Thus, we had to become more creative and entertain ourselves rather than rely on trashy recycled reality shows and vulgar hip-hopping rap lyrics. We had our own versions of folk-rock classics, raunchy story-songs reflecting our father's conquering WWII dominant male mentality combined with our own chauvinistic paternalistic humor and lack of maturity.

The Pryed of Cleveland

Although many of the Red House legends lacked both musical knowledge and talent, this did not deter them in the least from composing or performing. (Remember, not much else to do in those days.) Among the lasting tributes to the pre-women's liberation and chauvinistic mind-set of the day was "The Pryed of Cleveland," still rumored to be heard in some of the seedier corners of IV.

"The Pryed of Cleveland"

It happened one bright sunny day, last August I believe
We hadn't had no lovin' since Goleta we did leave
We'd been turnin' rocks in this fine town, searchin' all the while When
we came upon an ugly goat who offered us a smile.

Chorus: We pryed her up in Cleveland, down by the Erie shore, And
when this lass revealed her ass, we could ask no more.

We marveled at her long black hair, dangling from her pits
We marveled at her gorgeous face, adorned with juicy zits,
We looked at one another and said to this lovely wench, Oh
what is there about you dear, that creates such a stench.
Chorus
We knew this goat could trim our horns, of this we were quite sure
We were suffering from an ailment that this slut could surely cure
But first we felt it only fair that she should have the chance To
push away the rock before we dived into her pants.
Chorus
"Oh don't you find me ugly," she snorted through her nose
"NO" we echoed quickly, as we leaped out of our clothes.
We placed a bay around her head, so her face we could not see
And we sprayed her smelly body with a can of DDT.
Chorus
We wallowed in the mud with this gruesome piece of shit
We search for half an hour but could only find one tit We
screwed her and we screwed her till on our backs we lay,
Then she crawled back underneath her rock and sent us on our way.
Chorus
We hurried out of Cleveland with fond memories
Of the night that we had spent with this rancid sleeze
We smelled our scussy bodies and laughed so merrily To
think we had chaulked one up for dear ole RBT.
Chorus

Source: Original from Songbook.

Most women enjoyed the earthy humor, while others were repulsed. Not unlike rap music today, other 'drinking songs' were slightly less offensive, far less insulting to the women of Cleveland, and much more forgettable. Entertainment was cheap and you got what you paid for. NOTE: As an historical reference, the picture below demonstrates the technique used by some of the brothers to actually 'pry' women out from under rocks. Not all good-humored I.V. women were looking for husbands—at least not just yet.

Viking Beach Party

Beach parties were hallowed and revered events. Some were themed, others just happened as an excuse for spending a day at the beach playing V-ball and drinking beer rather than going to class. Gathering driftwood and empty 50-gallon oil drums from behind the Chemistry Building were also requisite activities, with enough of large wooden planks left over to build a fence in the backyard of the Red House (which still exists today as a memorial to beach frolic and grand theft).

During the late summer, a few of the enterprising brothers collected purloined lumber and construction materials for future parties. Haphazardly, we decided that a worthy event would be a Viking Party and an appropriate destination would be the Channel Islands, 20 miles across the cold, open and shark-infested waters of the Pacific Ocean. Carloads of lumber and empty oil drums were dispatched free fall over the cliffs of College Beach and construction of the vessel commenced. Many bothers and a cluster of adventurous females, including Katrina 'Kat' Cressida, Norma Palideros and Valerie Gordon, participated in the festivities. And festive they were, at least for a short cruise.

After consuming several kegs of beer, the leaky and overloaded rafts left the shores of Isla Vista covered by some four inches of water, a maritime disaster in the making. Captain Morgan commanded the vessel, assisted by first officer Gordon, first-to-be mated Cressida, and several shit-faced brothers hanging for dear life as the pontoon raft launching into the Pacific.

This drunken marine disaster-to-be was observed though binoculars in route to the Channel Islands by one off-duty Sports Information Director Bernie Donald, who was having a cocktail on the deck of his beach house. At first, Donald could not believe his eyes: a floating armada of makeshift rafts with nubile young bodies flailing against the currents and tide? Local authorities were summoned, a flotilla of Coast Guard rescue boats launched and disaster averted. The Viking Raft flag of convenience "Beaver" was courtesy of Brother Tyson who borrowed it from the north end of the town of Beaver, Oregon on a 1963 road trip around the country. Remnants of this tradition remain to this day among the playful masses of Isla Vista students who, for many years, have engaged in a much larger and potentially more hazardous water world function.

Youthful exuberance raised its uncontrollable head again in the chaotic and now infamous contemporary Spring Break affair known as "Deltopia" (a street party held on Del Playa Streets in

I.V.). This event became so dangerous that University officials have repeatedly, and unsuccessfully, tried to ban it. Masses of partiers erupted into riots on I.V., most recently during Spring Break in March 2014.

Deltopia began in much the same way as its predecessors—copious amounts of alcohol, drugs and thousands of students roaming the streets. The daytime partying was held in warm weather, and even without the pulsing beat of DJs lining Del Playa, the unmistakable presence of unbridled enthusiasm often morphed into violent civil unrest. The most recent manifestation of this street scene began with huge crowd of UCSB students, junior college wannabes, and out of town 'guests' in beach gear—bikinis, board shorts, and costumes.

In 2015, the annual event drew an estimated 15,000 people, with over 100 people arrested throughout the day, including 18 during the unrest, and 44 others transported to the hospital with injuries. As in previous years, all involved were seriously committed to a day of partying. Deltopia activities turned violent after an unknown partygoer attacked a UCSB Police Department officer with a backpack containing bottles of alcohol, causing a crowd to form and prompting law enforcement to declare an unlawful assembly and use tear gas to clear the streets. Once the smoke cleared after the riots that night, social media outlets were flooded with students expressing discontent with the behavior of the rioters, the role of out-of-town visitors, and the tactics employed by law enforcement officials.

The dialogue on the *Deltopia Civil Unrest* blog became even more expansive after receiving national coverage and an Associated Press story about the gathering made the rounds on news sites from *Yahoo News* to the *Huffington Post*. The story was also covered by the *Los Angeles Times* and international media. Deltopia and its offspring in other regions of the country are part of a larger youth rebellion coupled with alcoholic escapism and fueled by social media. Despite efforts to ban the event, an even larger "Flotopia" has become a social media happening and migrated to other coastal venture such as Miami Beach, Florida with similar opposition from civic leaders.

The Glass Ceiling and Sex without Consequences

Career opportunities for nearly all women and minorities of both genders were restricted prior to the feminist movement of the Seventies; professional careers in academia, business, law, medicine and sports were rarely accessible to women or non-whites. Athletic scholarships were reserved for white males only: no Blacks or women need apply. The prevailing male attitude: they couldn't jump and probably would get married anyway, so why waste the money?

Although their mothers had worked long hours as "Rosy the Riveters" in factories to support the World War II effort, boomer women were denigrated and reprogrammed to be co-dependent on heroic male bread-winners. Rosy the riveter became Lucy the homemaker.

Differing explanations for social regression exist, but the sudden repatriation of victorious adrenaline and nicotine-filled conquering males figured prominently in post-war realties, politically and socially. Precisely why social policies regressed after the war is a matter of conjecture, but an obvious and explicit correlation exists between the eight years of Republican political leadership (1953-1961) and the denial of civil rights and gender equality.[1]

Prior to passage socially conscious policies, qualified women were routinely denied admission to prestigious Ivy League universities because they were 'of marriageable age' and thus more likely, in the minds of anointed members of the 'fair-haired boys' clubs, to marry, become pregnant, and assume their natural roles as housewives. Airline flight attendants (aka stewardesses) were summarily fired on their 32nd birthday and expected to marry and raise a family, just like all other women. Girls were routinely denied access to all-boy science clubs. That was the order of things, at least from a dominant male perspective.

The most viable options for all but a few ultra-smart and super-determined women were marriage, pregnancy and child rearing, in that order. Careers in nursing or teaching were open, so long as Mrs. Homemaker was back by 4:00 pm to fix dinner for the husband and kids. The glass ceiling prohibited access to nearly all professional careers except for the lowest-paying hospital and elementary school teaching jobs. Women were stuck at home and repressed anger built against the white male establishment. It was no coincidence or surprise that 'women's liberation' movements emerged during the Nixon administration in the early 1970s, shortly after the widespread introduction of birth control.

Civic duties, politics, sports and warfare were strictly man's work. Feminism did not yet extend to military careers for women, who were exempted from the draft because of their gender. The thought of women in military service or (God forbid) in combat was never even considered and, if it was, the subject was treated with utter contempt and ridicule. Most able-bodied males resentfully, but dutifully respected these discriminatory social mores. (It was not until January 23, 2013, that the Pentagon ended its policy of excluding women from combat positions.)

Women were summarily dismissed from other public service obligations by so-called 'protective' legislation that excluded most females from barefoot and pregnant in the kitchen. Download any pre-1970 Netflix courtroom drama such as *Twelve Angry Men* or *To Kill a Mockingbird* and you never see a female seated in the jury box. By law, a woman could not be called for jury duty unless she requested to be placed on the jury availability list. Few did, as the breadwinners (aka husbands) expected breakfast in the morning and dinner in the evening. Men wanted wives who could cook, take care of the kids, provide sex on demand and, above all, never have a job except childrearing and housework. Popular sit-coms of the day reinforced these sexist stereotypes. Remember the *I Love Lucy* episode where Desi and Fred ridiculed Lucy and Ethel's feeble attempts to work outside the house?

****

Although no one admitted the truth, most arrived in I.V. with raging hormones and vastly different sexual experiences. Some actually brought their high school boyfriends or girlfriends with them; a few were married (unhappily), but most were just trying to get laid. The best that horny guys to do was a drive-in quickie which left them with blue balls and sticky fingers. Big Obstacle: 'free love' was still a few years away and The Pill was just becoming commonly available. By mid-decade, only five million women nationwide were using the Pill and many states still banned its sale for unmarried women. The only birth control was abstinence or the "aspirin between your legs" method and most women feared pre-marital pregnancy as much as kids today fear STDs. Without a morning-after pill and only sure route to sexual satisfaction for most women was.... gulp.... marriage.

In the fall of 1964, the university decreed that any female student desiring birth control had only to go to the University Health Center on the appointed Saturday. The sexual revolution had begun. When this information leaked out, hundreds of horny males sat on the lawn across from the Health Center on the appointed day to survey the unbelievably long line of choice fruit waiting to be picked: notes were taken about the quality of fresh flesh exiting the building with prescriptions in hand.

About a month later, one had to be careful when walking through wooded areas of campus, near parked cars in dark areas or entering your room if you had roommates. Coeds were test driving the Pill with pent up vengeance. Fear of pregnancy was removed as an inhibitor to sexual experimentation. No one worried too much about getting syphilis, crabs or the clap, or other STDs, but getting pregnant could bring down the Wrath of God (i.e. parents), marriage, and seriously mess up your life.

When some of the early pioneers of the sexual revolution did get pregnant, choices were limited and highly correlated with economic status and family resources. Most were afraid to tell their parents and marriage under such circumstances was unacceptable: unwed mothers were still looked down upon with distain. If your family could not afford "summer school" in Switzerland, the only other method of aborting a fetus was the time-honored method: jumping on your pregnant girlfriend's stomach to induce a miscarriage.

The preferred location for performing this caveman ritual was on the beach as the sand provided somewhat of a buffer to cushion the blows and not injure the girl permanently. At least that's what guys thought. Without family money for trips to Europe, abortion was strictly forbidden—except in Mexico, where this service, and just about everything else forbidden in the U.S., was available for a price. The cost of these 'hanger-jobs" was exorbitant, over $200 in cash (about $1500 in current dollars), no IDs required, no forms to fill-out nor embarrassing questions to answer. The actual procedures were performed in shady medical clinics in the border towns of Tijuana, Mexicali, Agua Caliente, and Nogales.

Cuming of Age at the Blue Fox

America's late-1950s forbidden fruit was also accessible without long-term commitment in the Red Light Districts just below the Mexican border, a vestige of the Prohibition Era. Tijuana (rather than Vegas) was then known as Sin City, with a downtown full of bordellos, pimps, strip joints, and unbelievably raunchy floorshows. Besides, no one checked IDs and you could get what was generally unavailable from the UCSB coeds for about $5 without a long-term commitment. We quickly learned from the SoCal San Diego guys, especially those with older brothers in the military, what was available and how to access it. Some of the places such as the Long Bar, Fast Freddie's, Johnny Hot Nuts, Don Caesar's Restaurant, and the Blue Fox had already acquired world-class reputations among the notorious partiers of the area, most notably off-duty Navy and Marines from the San Diego area. Tijuana hotspots were officially off-limits to military as well as underage college-types, but we were just as mobile as anyone else and fully capable of falsifying our age and status. Besides, no one ever asked for IDs.

On the sidewalks outside these clubs, street hawkers tried to entice people in with promises of "F**king, sucking on stage and live donkeys..." The Blue Fox was particularly well known, having billboards, T-shirts, bumper stickers, and other memorabilia that those in the know proudly flaunted wherever they went; slogans like "Eat at the Blue Fox," "The Blue Fox Blue Plate Special," "Tijuana Pussy Posse," adorned T-shirts of the era.

The Blue Fox featured strippers who would take it all off, but the real show was not the strippers, but customers in the "restaurant" surrounding a large stage who had perfected what eventually became known as a "rail job" (not to be confused with Brother Rail). Whenever a particular stripper of their liking was performing, patrons would stand up (usually after many shots of Tequila) and put their heads upside down on the wooden rail surrounding the stage. The crowds of drunken partiers would scream with anticipation. The stripper, now nude, would sit on their face and, if they were so inclined, the customer would have the opportunity to partake of all they could eat. As they performed cuntalingus, the crowd roared and cheered them on. Rumor spread that one the strippers was a virgin, but each one was so heavily perfumed 'down there' that it was impossible to determine, even at close range.

On the second floor of these establishments were rooms where patrons could go with any of the entertainers of their choosing and do whatever they felt like doing inside those rooms, for a price...usually something less than $40. Bordellos around town hosted several social class structures, from the commonplace quickie joint to the extremely elaborate executive-type for wealthy businessmen. All staffed and priced according to what the traffic would allow.

On one such trip to TJ, we invited Jamie, a somewhat naïve lad whom we had regaled with stories about the forbidden fruit available a few hours away just south of the border. For some of the more naïve (i.e. Catholic) brothers, the first trip to TJ also constituted their first taste of beer and pussy. After several bottles of Tecate, we beckoned a "dancer" over and paid her to give Jamie a private lap dance. What happened next shocked even the most battle-hardened veterans of the Tijuana Bar Scene.

After stripping right in front of Jamie's eyes, she not only performed a lap dance, rubbing him on the front and back, but removed his glasses and slowly inserted them in her well-lubricated pussy. As we cheered her on to do more, she removed them slowly and returned his glasses. Flustered by all the unanticipated attention, he put the gooey glasses back on! Disgusting to watch and, at the same time, unforgettable. Not surprisingly, after that private tease, Jamie lost whatever

118

inhibitions were left and preceded to the rail, whereupon another *senorita* provided him the house special—a "hot box lunch." After that, she escorted him upstairs to the second floor for dessert.

The worse part about the trip was the 250-mile drive back to Isla Vista. Six of us had to squeeze into the car, and Jamie, now passed out, sat next to me. About the time we hit the Ventura Freeway, our drunken brother's head shifted, and the stench of barf, Mexican perfume, and stale pussy juice began to permeate the car. Not a pleasant trip up Highway 101.

****

Thanks to globalization, Nixon, and Chinese entrepreneurship, Mexico and especially Tijuana and its surroundings have now changed. As NAFTA and California entrepreneurs caught up with the location, places like the Blue Fox were either shut down or moved to an isolated "Zona Rosa" (red light district) further from the United States border. Twenty years ago, Twentieth-Century Fox built a huge production studio about three miles south of Ensenada, where the blockbuster film *Titanic* was filmed. Today, in what could only be considered a magnificent irony, the Chinese are building an automobile manufacturing plant in downtown Tijuana to produce their "Chery's" (no joke, that is the actual name of the car) for young American and Mexican drivers. Perhaps Jamie will buy one.

Another brother enthusiastically remembers even more sordid details of visits to TJ.

"I loved it. As a high school kid in SoCal, TJ was only a few hours away and we used to make regular forays for sex, booze and tuck and roll upholstery. The preferred sex was the licky, licky hand job... a $3 semi-blow job that took about 10 seconds! The Long Bar was mainly for drinking cheap beers while the Blue Fox and Johnny Hot Nuts actually did live sex and the infamous donkey fuck on stage. It is not a myth. I personally witnessed it at least three times. The most famous of the donkey girls could take about three quarters of that critter's considerable dong. Amazing, and at the same time disgusting."

For several years after UCSB was established, even with the favorable female to male coed ratio, getting laid was still not easy. Definitely possible—the Duck, Gleeper, Mouse, and Boom Boom and other goat party regulars did many—but the "highly desirables," who required a long-term commitment, were inaccessible.

Regulating Kidnappings

Sometimes, after 30 or 40 years, one's memory tends to play tricks. Not so when confronted with situations of utter fear or sheer terror. Memories of that night remain crystal clear in Mark McGinnis' mind.

It was early evening and he was sleeping. He heard a commotion at the front door of the apartment, and the next thing he knew, a black bag was thrown over his head and he was being panced and tied up.

A voice that he vaguely recognized told him:

"Don't resist, everything will be fine."

That was easy for him to say. Mark was not convinced.

Next, at least three hefty guys lifted him up, carried him off the bed and threw him in the back trunk of a car with roommate, Sam Cormack.

Sam was pledge trainer that semester, so it didn't take long for us to figure that we have been kidnapped. We had heard about and discussed the spat of kidnappings, and plane trips to LA and Chicago, and didn't relish the idea of trying to find our way back to SB from wherever we would end up. Besides, it was getting late and we wondered when our now several hour journey on a desolate winding road would end. Not soon enough. The car finally stopped and the trunk opened. We were still tightly bound and blindfolded, so we had no idea where we were.

As they lifted us up, they told us to be still and we would be fine. The car sped off and we were left alone in the dark. As we struggled to get loose from the ropes, we could hear other cars occasionally pass by. It was cold, so we knew we had been left somewhere in the mountains some 3-4 hours from campus. In order to loosen the ropes, the captives had to roll around on the dirty roadside. When they did finally get free and removed their hoods, they were on a shoulder of the road at the top of San Marco Pass Road on the precipice of a rather steep ravine. (YIKES!)

"No wonder they told us to stay still," McGinnis thought to himself.

"Things could have been worse. At least they left us with our underwear," Sam said.

Their minds are probably too embarrassed to remember much about hitchhiking back to campus, but seeing nearly naked guys on the side of the road was something that mellowed-out Santa Barbarians were used to. At least someone picked us up and took us to the nearest phone.

****

Imprecise as memories become, Rick Morgan clearly recalls leaving track practice one beautiful Santa Barbara Spring morning in 1965 on a Wednesday preceding the upcoming Modesto Relays. As he approached the Morgmobile (aka a 1959 Chevrolet Impala), he inquired of one of the pledges what he was doing sleeping in the backseat of the car whereupon he announced:

"You, pledge trainer, are kidnapped."

Carloads of additional pledges poured out of little cars parked nearby and the grab was on. Off to an apartment we went where I was placed in handcuffs and soon pinned to a large and immovable wooden bed frame.

"I believe that the entire pledge class was present and they were admittedly highly organized. Pledge Unity' was in full gear."

Telephones were ringing in the background and he soon realized that he was hogtied in a van and off for the Los Angeles airport where we were met by still other pledges and a wheelchair. As they wheeled him down the concourse, one of the pledges carefully explained to security personnel that:

"His medical condition required treatment in the Midwest." In addition, "He was bound and gagged for the safety of other passengers."

This was his first clue that it was going to be a long night. He was soon seated in the middle row of the coach section between two elderly women. Yes, Virginia, airport security in those days was *that* lax at LAX. (Just try to imagine that scene today in the uber-security conscious climate surrounding airports as a result of 9/11.)

Still wearing his shorts, tee shirt, socks and running shoes with no identification and no money, he learned from the elderly seatmates who helped remove the duct tape from his face that he was bound for Chicago and it was apparently on a prepaid one- way non-refundable ticket. Where was TSA when we needed them? Prior to takeoff, the aircraft doors were secured and a distinguished looking Captain approached with a greeting.

"Good evening, sir. I understand that you may be aboard this aircraft against your will," he stated officially.

"That is a mild understatement," he replied.

The Captain continued with his offer,

"I am prepared to manage your escape in a food cart if you would like."

Tempted as he was to beat the pledges home, he considered sacred fraternal responsibilities and informed the Captain of the concept of "pledge unity" and agreed to go. The pilot shook his head, gave him $2.00, and asked the flight attendants to get him a blanket and serve him a meal.

Upon arrival in snowy Chicago, he panhandled another couple of bucks from sympathetic passengers and called the Red House, whereupon brother Knifeman answered the phone. After relaying the kidnapping news, Knifeman soberly replied,

"Yeah, yeah great party," and hung up.

He redialed and insisted on speaking with roommate Adam Ross who somehow managed to rustle up $80 and wire it to Chicago in time for him to return, change clothes and make the bus trip to the Modesto Relays. During the following Sunday Chapter meeting a new rule was adopted: kidnappings were allowed, but only within the State of California.

CHAPTER 9: Road Trips

I was once the kind of traveler who always over-packed for a journey. I put in a suit that I would never wear, shoes I did not need, and books—always books—that, of course, I would never read. I returned home with the suit unpacked, the shoes unworn, and the books unread. I always picked up things along the way, clothes that differed from shops back home, a really comfortable pair of shoes unavailable elsewhere and other books—more interesting ones—than the ones I had brought with me. I was too conscious of the existing cultural boundaries to be open to new experiences.

In time, I realized why my travels were sometimes empty and painful: taking everything on a journey leaves no room to pick up anything new along the way. New experiences merely relegated to a sub-category of preexisting mental files. Like Kerouac, London and Steinbeck, I eventually learned to travel light and keep a sharp eye out for values and new experiences.

The more I travelled the greater the number of new and more interesting feelings I could catalogue mentally for future stories. As a result, I also found that many of my before-held truths became clouded with doubt. With each new journey, knowledge built upon and expanded on the past—ever increasing—until pre-categorized thoughts broke through to deeper understandings. These sometimes painful insights made the travel delays bearable and the time spent meaningful. After such experiences of unifying the inside with the out, balance lingered within me until it was time to move on. Bargains now appear at regular intervals.

I now recognize the traveler who carries too much baggage. He or she rejects anything that may threaten his neatly packaged bag of untested truths. An unexamined mass is draped about him in such a manner that he continuously depends upon it for support, even during new learning situations. This cloche always gives pseudo support, as does an after-dinner nap on a full stomach, an extramarital affair, or a promise of trust based on inexperience or future anticipation.

While on a journey, those travelling light and looking for lasting values/new experiences are easy to recognize. They are untarnished by prejudice, unshackled by convention, and unspoiled by need. They realize that while travelling there can be no closed system of beliefs, no unchanging set of principles, and no rigid pattern of responding to new situations. Their travels are guided by accepting change, understanding nature, and continuous reinterpretation of living events and experiences.

So now, as I plan my next journey, I think not of what to take or what to expect, but how to prepare myself with 'cleansed" spirit for the new ideas and values I know I will find. When someday the allure of travel begins to lose its luster, I shall look inside, filling the empty suitcase with memories complete and lasting, finding an ideal to travel for and not just things to travel with.

Marijuana: Medical or Otherwise

Among the positive side effects of enforcing outmoded laws is often the fear-induced preservation of lasting memories. Most of us remember the first time we smoked pot, so long as it was one of the last times we visited the 'choomwagen.' For those who became habituated to the weed, scant memory of that event or most others remain. For most the 99.9 percent who miraculously avoided the permanently addictive effects of the dreaded Gateway Drug, this occasion was especially memorable because of how and where it occurred.

In the 1960s, local police in most U.S. cities tended to frown on the sale or use of cannabis. Politicians had not yet discovered the revenue potential of legalizing its recreational use and violent drug gangs had not yet discovered the profit potential of dumping tons weed for widespread distribution and consumption on college campuses. Drug dealing was still a cottage industry with a fairly high risk/reward ratio. Scott Peters was able to avoid apprehension for many years by traveling directly to his suppliers in Afghanistan, stuffing his Kombi van with hash and shipping it back through France to Mexico. Others who pursued alternative paths to prosperity obtained their stashes from violent drug cartels. Naturally, this raised the stakes and, if you were caught and convicted by local or state authorities, penalties were severe. In states like Oklahoma and Texas, simple possession of a few ounces carried life sentences.

These heavy-handed enforcement policies resulted in part from the scare tactics that had been used since the 1930s, largely to protect U.S. alcohol, tobacco and pharmaceutical industries from competition from the homegrown product. Several exploitation films, such as *Reefer Madness* and *Weedoholics*, were produced to literally scare the shit out of anyone from even trying this superaddictive drug. Because it was illegal, many were even more encouraged to sample the reefer (hopefully without the madness) in safer surroundings: where else but Mexico, where it was treated as both an appetizer and after-dinner aperitif.

The San Diego-Tijuana border crossing was usually uneventful, with portly Mexican border guards nonchalantly waving narco-tourists through entry gates to devourer or be devoured by whatever temptations awaited. The first visit to TJ can be intimidating. Seeing the dirty barefoot children begging, the tittie bars, and the abject squalor within sight of the sedate and uber-rich San Diego touched a nerve, but didn't deter from the ultimate goal of reaching the coastal city of Rosarito, where a friend of a friend had a contact.

Secrecy was pretty much unnecessary, as all one had to do was hang out on almost any street corner in Baja California, wait a few minutes, and young Mexican boys would approach:

"Ola, muchacho, que quieres? My seester, she is a virgin," they would all say about the prostitutes.

When asked about marijuana, the answer was slightly more cautious. They would glance to the right and left and look behind to see if anyone was following.

"Si, hombre, pero lo que quieres? (what kind do you want) was often the answer.

At that point, they would escort you to a dark side street, settle on a price and walk to another location to purchase the goods to avoid being tailed. In the less urbanized areas, access was even easier. In some rural areas, plastic bags were sold by young boys darting onto streets giving cryptic hand signals. Being caught with one of these little *'bolcitas'* could cost hundreds of dollars in bribes with the threat of spending time in the Tijuana jail used as motivation to pay off local cops. That is why we decided it was wiser to move outside the glare of bright city lights to make our score. We headed for Rosarito beach resort, a small coastal town about 20 miles south of TJ.

After driving for several hours and getting lost on the mountainous dirt roads, we met our connection at a gas station. No cell phones or GPSs' in those days. We were told to look for a black lowered Chevy with chrome rims and a "We Love LA" vanity plate on the front. We had already purchased some Tequila and limes to wash down the taste of the weed and were looking forward to trying this forbidden pleasure under more relaxed circumstances. Jose, as he called himself, was the middle man who negotiated prices and made sure we were not *chivos* (goats) that would inform on him.

"Te cuento algo pero no te vayas de chivo" (I will tell you something, but you better not be an informant") they would say. We considered this a serious threat.

He told us to follow him to another location closer to the coast. As we drove down the now darkened dirt roads, we noticed that another car was following us. Again, making sure we were who we said we were, not *gingo chivatos* who had sold out to the local cops. At several gates along the route, mean-looking dudes checked us out each time as we passed through.

We arrived at what could only be described as a cluster of shacks, loosely teetering on cliffs overlooking the Pacific Ocean. After some quick gulps of tequila and further haggling over prices, one of the occupants of the 'house' bought in a 2-pound coffee can filled to the brim with the pungent grassy substance.

"Que bueno, no?" asked our host as he shoved the can under our noses. "Gud stuff. You like."

We had heard terms such as Acapulco Gold, China Doll, Maui Wowie, Juicy Lucy, Panama Red, Jalasco Juice, and Loredo Lid before, but most of us had never smoked, so we didn't know how much to consume to achieve what results. Senor Coffee Can gestured to us with his fingers on his lips, whatever that was supposed to mean? Our host then began rolling joints in something which look vaguely like dark cigarette paper, but much larger. The finished products looked more like big fat cigars than cigarettes, tightly packed and evenly rolled massive joints. In retrospect, smoking these lip-licking blunts was a huge mistake that we would soon regret.

The impact hit us almost immediately. Bright colors, heightened noises, strange paranoid sensations. That fucking mariachi music so damned loud! Who was that guy in the corner and what the hell was he carrying? Why is the damned room spinning? After several beers and more tequila shots, we were hungry and deathly afraid to drive, so we staggered back to a local seafood restaurant a few hundred yards up the deserted road on a main highway. The rest of the evening was a complete blur, replete with dancing senoritas, mariachi music and lots more beer and tequila. We found ourselves trapped by the walls of the noisy cantina which was spinning as we sank further into oblivion. It felt like a reverse replay of the tornado scene from *The Wizard of Oz*, without the crash landing, red shoes or munchkins.

Somehow we survived the evening's festivities and apparently crawled or fell down a narrow path and passed out on the beach below. The next morning, none of us had any memory of how we got down the steep cliff.

With a mouth full of sand and seaweed and waves crashing behind him, McGinnis felt something tapping him on his shoulder. Annoyed at first, he tried to fend off the sharp object, but soon became conscious enough to recognize the uniform of a Mexican police or military officer.

"He was nudging me with a bayonet on the tip of a rifle. Heavy surf was crashing behind me and his golden grills shinned much too brightly in the morning sun. His smile was deceptively dangerous but his harsh words were easy to understand, with or without knowledge of Spanish." I looked around, but my comrades were nowhere in sight.

I was stranded on a Mexican beach with some crazy cop sticking a bayonet in my gut. I thought quickly to remember my high school Spanish vocabulary.

"*Que pasa." Donde esta bano? Buen dias."*

He frowned and shook his head, not the least bit amused or interested in my responses.

He kept saying "*No va, No va*" whatever the fuck that meant.

I looked around for a small car, but none was visible on the isolated beach or on the bluff above. As I anticipated the cold steel piercing my ribs, I finally saw my compadres from last night staggering up the beach.

"Dios mio," I thought to myself, thank God they are here. He wouldn't dare kill all three of us, would he?

As we were escorted off the beach and back up the steep hill to the 'house" where we hoped our car was still parked, we finally figured out that "No-va" was not a small Chevrolet car, but he was saying "you can't go here," or something to that effect in Spanish.

When we introduced Officer Juan (I think he said his name was Juan) to our hosts in the shack atop the cliff, smiles of recognition, relief and laughter. They all seemed to be amused by our stupidity. We weren't amused at all. By then, "Juan" had shouldered his weapon, lite up a real cigarette and seemed to enjoy everyone's company on a gorgeous cliff house overlooking an otherwise desolate beach somewhere in Baja California. As they say in Mexico, "All is well the end's well."

The Mexico City Country Club

During 1967, someone got the bright idea to go to the 1968 Summer Olympics in Mexico City. Before long, brothers Rick Morgan, Tim Neckragel, Ross Rosenbloom, Rick Morgan and Bill Plant were also on board. They relied early on the superb administrative abilities of Brother Rosenbloom and put him in charge of securing tickets. A little man in house full of cubby holes doled them out, or perhaps we saw him in Mexico City, but that may have been a hallucination. This was the last Olympics Games that was remotely affordable to the average sports fan. We paid about $10 per event ticket.

Plant vaguely remembers the flight down (his first commercial flight) on Mexicana Airlines. We arrived at our hotel "El Fleabago Cheapo" where we all shared one room with two twin beds. The plan was to get so drunk every night that we could sleep on the floor.

Plant remembers that:

"This actually did work pretty well. Large political anti-government riots were going on in other parts of the city, but we missed them, or they missed us, I can't remember which."

During one of our first days at the track and field stadium, we saw Bob Beamon shatter the world record in the long jump. Later, many people saw the black and white video tape of the event but to have seen it happen live and in color was truly amazing.

The conversation was something like:

"Who do we like in the long jump?'

"The Russian-Terovernezian is tough, Ralph Boston should medal is well."

"What about this Beamon kid?" Lots of potential, who knows?"
Cut to Beamon's second or third try in the prelims:

"Here's Beamon."

"Holy shit! Did you see that?"

"He almost jumped out of the pit!"

Beamon actually landed more than a foot beyond the meter marks indicating the Olympic and World records. He moved out of the pit and looked at his jump, then sinks to his knees crying.

The entire experience was dominated by another up close and personal track memory. During the finals of the 200 meters, the performance of favorites Tommie Smith and John Carlos, teammates at San Jose State. Tommie and John were influenced by Harry Edwards, a world class discus thrower turned Black Panther sympathizer and later granted tenure at UC Berkley during the Mario Savio free speech era. Smith and Carlos have the top two times going into final race. Back at the stadium, gun goes off, and Smith blows everyone away—slows up at finish or world record would still stand. The surprise second was Peter Norman of Australia and John Carlos is third. The event finals and the medal presentations were often far apart and when Smith and

Carlos rose to the podia, they raised their fists and showed the now infamous "Black Power/Glove gesture" on the victory stand.

We all had the same thought:

"Hey man, what's with the black gloves?"

"I dunno"

Black athletes a generation ago showed their disdain for the White power structure by sponsoring dogfights and dropping their drawers to show their butt cracks. At least fists had some meaning. Fifty years have passed since Smith and Carlos ignited the sports world with their blackgloved fists raised on the victory stand at the 1968 Mexico City Olympics. In a recent book, Carlos says,

"I still feel the fire."

Police brutality and shootings of young Black men have again prompted Black sport stars to demonstrate their disgust for racism by wearing "Don't Shoot" and "I Can't Beathe" or "Black Lives Matter" on their jerseys.

Another part of our escapade involved sneaking into the Olympic Village. Perhaps that was overstated since we actually walked in claiming we were on the Estonian National Olympic Volleyball Team—at least three us, and that Ross was our manager. (Remember, this was the Olympics before Munich.) We had a great time talking to the real athletes and purchasing Onetsuka Tiger Track Shoes cut-rate in the Olympic Village. On the way out, we signed many autographs for adoring fans (t-shirts, arms, other body parts).

The final element of the trip involved one of Plant's classmates and an honorary brother, Beto Negrial who had family in Mexico City. Before leaving Isla Vista, he asked Beto if we might give his family a call and take anything down to them. He said something like:

"Beel, that is so kind; I do have a small package if it ez okay."

Reply: "No sweat, Beto. I will carry it home. Hasta la vista."

Flash forward to El Fleabago Cheapo:

Rube asked: "Bill, what's in the package?"

"Holy shit, I forgot that's for Beto's family!"

Brother Plant quickly called the Negrial residence and connected with his younger brother, Geraldo, the resident hell raiser. Beto had previously warned not to socialize with Geraldo, as he tended to go off on binges. Ignoring the advice, we arranged for a limo to pick us up outside the track and field stadium to bring the mystery package and meet the family. What a scene: Los quatro amigos in t-shirts and shorts in a limo on the way to meet one of the wealthiest families in Mexico. We feverishly practiced our poor Spanish as we roll through the Las Lomas district, the Beverly Hills of Mexico City. Upon arrival, Geraldo showed us into the study where the elder Negrial presides. Pidgeon Spanish gets us along, together with Papa's brandy. Jim appeared to have the best memory of Spanish, but we all blundered along. La Senora arrived after a suitable time and we babble and smile a little longer. Then Geraldo comes to the rescue and offers to show us around. Four days later we have been to the best and worst places in the Zona Rosa, fought baby bulls at some bull-breeding farm, sweated alcohol out at the high-end stream bath, and had brunch at the Mexico City Country Club.

The final night before departure, or deportation, and we are at an expensive nightclub. The gimmick here is that glasses of sherry that you pick up with your teeth and toss back, and "bode bags" (remember the cheap and unsanitary goatskin bags that you filled with red wine and got more on you than in you?). But these bota bags are crystal and you poured from the stem into your mouth. We agreed that we would pick up the tab for a change, and when the bill came, we pounced. Geraldo protested, but we were adamant. When we converted the peso amount into dollars, we knew we had a problem. After cobbling together all our dollars, pesos, and handouts for sympathetic Americans were still woefully short. Then brother Neckragel ponyed up his father's AMEX card and we were saved from whatever punishment befalls those who don't cover their expenses in Mexico. Never leave home without it!

We returned home with great stories, even better memories, and a commitment to attend the tragic 1972 Olympics in Munich. As it turned out, all of our careers were underway and that trip never took place. This was just as well, as we will always have memories of Mexico City.

Caribbean Misadventures

The travel magazine ad offered unlimited flights for 90 days to anywhere America Airlines flew to the Caribbean and the Virgin Islands for $300. This led to a serious adventure for brothers Tog Roberts and Jim McNabe in the summer of '70.

The first part of the trip was a drive across country to the Miami in Tog's Morris Minor convertible. It was a cheap trip at 40 mpg with gas at 27 cents a gallon. They stayed in fraternity houses along the way and avoided arrest as West Coast Hippie Agitators (with California license plates) in the Deep South. They had seen what happened to Jack Nicholson, Peter Fonda and Dennis Hopper in *Easy Rider* and were careful to observe speed limits and avoid pick-up trucks in Texas, Louisiana, Mississippi, and Alabama.

After the 3000-mile journey from IV to Southern Florida, they parked the car at the University of Miami Alpha Pi house and took off in a shaky DC-3 for the islands having no idea what they would find on the many islands that dotted the Caribbean. The deal was simple: show up at the airport and you could fly wherever they had space available, heavy duty planning optional.

Upon arrival in St. Thomas in the Virgin Islands, they were the only two passengers to deplane and the open air terminal was deserted. From the shadows emerged a hefty gregarious dude who said he owned the only Guest House on the island above a restaurant. He also owned a 1954 Pontiac with the roof cut off and hand painted bright yellow, the island's sole form of public transportation.

For $6-7 a day we shared a room and got three meals at the Fish House restaurant below; usually fresh caught snapper of amberjack. Virgin Isles Pale Ale mango beer was 25 cents a bottle. All through the Caribbean, the Guest Houses were under 10 bucks a day including meals so the paltry amount of money we had brought lasted for almost the whole trip.

Brother James had packed a boatload of Sano Seats and a .32 Cal pistol in his luggage. He was not going to get crabs or be mugged! Thankfully, the pistol stayed out of sight although he probably still carries it around with him, especially after two tours in Vietnam. After a couple of days into our week on the then totally undeveloped island, the dude invited us to a party in the jungle that night. Wow. We were two pale-faced frat boys among a couple of hundred Black locals—culture shock had immediate effects. They were unbelievably friendly, especially the girls, got us seriously drunk—would have got us laid if we weren't so drunk—and taught us a valuable lesson about alcohol, erections and prejudice.

To say the least, we were massively over our heads. We quickly accepted an invitation to go out on a boat in the pristine waters between St. Thomas and St. John and party with some others on fishing boats. We were supposed to cruise all day, drink and party at Trunk Bay on St. John. The prospect sounded inviting, especially because of the beautiful beaches and islands that popped up before our eyes at Red Hook Harbor and Megan's Bay. When we saw a larger boat steaming toward the smaller fleet, we were so plied with alcohol that we didn't hesitate to help unload the fresh catch of the day. Little did we know that we were drawn into a drug smuggling ring known as the "Wicked Tuna" gang which served as a conduit for illicit drugs making their way up from Columbia to Cuba, through the U.S. Virgin Islands, to Florida.

The drug ring worked something like this: pure cocaine would be shipped in waterproof bags from Cartegena to Costa Rica and on to Cuba, where the half-kilo bags would be stuffed in freshly caught fish and transferred to small fishing boats in the waters off the Virgin Islands. Extra hands were needed for to quickly off-load the fish catch from the Panama-registered trawler to the smaller boats belonging to local fishing companies in the islands. It was an ideal cover for drug smuggling, at least until one of the captains of the fishing ships spilled the beans to undercover ATF agents in St. Thomas.

Fortunately, our participation was limited to stuffing a few fish and signing a few blank checks, for which we received unlimited amounts of cocaine, enabling us to stay up all night and listen to Reggae bands during *Jouvet* festival. When we learned that some of our acquaintances and their fishing boats had been confiscated by the DEA, we decided that it was time to move on quickly to the next island, St. Croix.

On St. Croix, we met the granddaughter of Sir Charles Edwin (a famous rum maker) and his daughter RoseMarie. Her friend was the female golf champion of Jamaica and they invited us to go out marlin fishing on her own boat and. The day before the fishing trip, we met a couple of hotties from Ohio on the beach and ended up partying until nearly dawn. Promptly at 7am, Missy RoseMarie's man came to collect us. Still half in the bag, we agreed to go without checking on the weather. Oh God. The pitching and rolling of an old trawler with diesel fumes combined with chum and a hangover made for barf city. Needless to say, RoseMarie was disgusted and we probably blew a great opportunity. But, after we stumbled off the boat, we did re-connect with the Shaker Heights hotties on the return. We ended up having to pay a $100 police fine for lewd and lascivious behavior after being caught having sex in her father's station wagon.

We flew out of St. Croix on another ancient and shaky DC-3 in a driving rainstorm with the freaking door open and saw some truly beautiful places before they were wrecked by overdevelopment and too many tourists. Most of the islands were still under colonial rule and everything worked. With independence came offshore accounts and modern development. Old Grand Cayman is unrecognizable today, jammed with banks, condos, and motor scooters: only the French islands have stayed much the same, but that is the French way. On Martinique we drank *Tattinger* champagne for a couple of bucks a bottle and learned after we ate that *Tete de Veau* means head of the cow—surprise. In Trinidad, we were scammed by a local sharpie who we thought was setting us up with some airline stewardesses.

At the end of the trip in Puerto Rico, we stayed in a casino hotel and got lucky enough to be able to pay our bill before jetting back to Miami on a 707. On the trip back, we read stories about the Wicked Tuna gang busted for federal racqueteering and drug dealing. One of our hosts, the captain of the fishing boat we helped unload, was the ring leader. Apparently, our restaurant was a front for drug gangs who would purchase certain "tuna" at exorbitant prices and pocket the drugs stuffed in them. Nice scam while it lasted.

It rains in the summer in Miami and the back window on the Morris' top rotted out leaving 4 inches of water inside the car. Jim's gun was finally put to use shooting some drain holes though the floor.

Tijuana Long Bar Fight

Spring break provided an ideal opportunity for some of the more adventurous brothers to seek international cultural enrichment opportunities by again venturing to Mexico. Tijuana also provided unlimited opportunities to restock liquor supplies, frolic with the senioritas, and partake in local customs such as bar brawls.

On one such trip, the usual band of underage drinkers crossed the border, trunks stuffed with empty soda bottles and sanitized gas cans to store and smuggle the hooch, seeking whatever adventures awaited. This group included Fowler, McGinnis, Plant, Bill (he'll deny it) Roth, and a new member of the Mexico group, 'Oxnard Freddie' Navarone.

After visiting several liquor stores and stocking up on beer and tequila, hearing 'my seester, she es a virgin" hundreds of times, and sampling the local treats, we ended up in the notorious Long Bar, a well-known haven for cross-cultural exchanges.

We were seated in the middle of the noisy crowded bar, a long mirror to our left and an even longer wooden bar in front of the glass. Mariachi music blasted from speakers and we were getting hostile stares form a gang of non-so-friendly locals wearing and blue "National City Vatos" jackets leaning against the wall opposite the long bar. They had eyed us with some distain ever since we walked in the place accompanied by brother Navarone, of visible Hispanic descent.

After a few rounds of beers, one of the Blue Jackets approached our table and said something in Spanish to Brother Freddie. Roughly translated, either he asked, "how's the weather in San Diego" or "what the fuck are you doing with the Gringo dickheads?"

Whatever Oxnard Freddie said back to him was definitely lost in translation. The next thing I remembered was a large wooden chair rising from the smoke-filled room and splintering over his head. All hell broke loose. Chairs and table flew across the beer-soaked floor, blood gushed from an open wound in Freddie's head, the music died and the lights went black. We all hit the deck (customary in bar fights). Bodies, chairs and people flew in all directions. Large glass beer mugs whizzed past our heads, exploding on the glass mirror and sending shards of glass flying everywhere. Some of us tried to fight back as the wave of Blue Jackets descended upon us, but most huddled in fear on the beer and blood soaked floor. Unconscious and bleeding profusely, we pulled Freddie out from under the table and crawled across the floor, trying unsuccessfully to avoid being cut, kicked and stomped. As we reached the exit, we pulled our wounded friend out the door and escaped without paying for the beers.

When we stopped running, we were able to find a local Green Cross station conveniently located on the *Avenida de la Revolucion*. Attendants were able to clean and bandage Freddie's head wounds. Since we had all scattered in several different directions trying to avoid the Blue Jackets, it took what seemed to be hours to regroup at the cars. Needless to say, we escaped in one of the fastest border crossings ever known to U.S. citizens and Mexican border guards.

Kansas City-Blue Key-Aspen

One of the later road trips had its origin in the Chapter Room of the Red House when Brother Morgan entered a seemingly empty room one Sunday during Christmas break and announced "Anybody up for a road trip?" A still groggy eyed Brother McGinnis emerged from hiding and responded "Where to?"

We left the next morning in Brother Morgan's 1959 Chevrolet (aka the Morgmobile). After 2 days straight driving some 2400 miles and subsisting only on crackers and sardines, we arrived in Kansas City, where we knew not a soul, but did know the National Blue Key Leadership fraternity was holding its national convention. We purchased cheap tickets to the Big Eight Basketball Tournament (e.g. Hank Iba days at Oklahoma State, Kansas and other college teams of standing at the time). In the nosebleed seats, we just happened to encounter good friend and

UCSB running back Bob Dugman who had earlier informed us that he was nominated as the official Santa Barbara delegate to Blue Key convention.

As Blue Keyers ourselves, (albeit only for the yearbook photos) we quickly attached ourselves to conference events, which commenced that evening at *The Golden Ox,* a favorite Kansas City steakhouse in the middle of the odoriferous stockyards in the Foggy Bottom section of K.C. As the national group of Blue Key delegates seated themselves for Kansas City strip steaks, brother McGinnis rose for the toast and made (or made up) an impassioned speech about two dedicated Blue Key members who, although not formally invited, drove over 2000 miles from Santa Barbara to join their brothers in celebration of all things Blue Key. With brother Morgan tugging on his shirt and pleading for Brother McGinnis to cease the oratory for fear that our real intention would be discovered, he continued on for what seemed to be forever, until several of delegates at nearby tables came to tears (from emotion or pity we do not know). Several of the delegates proceeded to congratulate us for the sacrifices we had made to join the group.

The silliness went on until it was time to leave for the convention Hotel Muelbach (brothers Morgan and McGinnis had no reservations). Entry to Bob Dugman's room and a brief flirtation with a hotel maid led us to the window that allowed us to enter the vacant room next door for a peaceful night's rest. This involved an acrobatic maneuver exiting Dugman's window and climbing along an icy ledge to the next room, commonly referred to in criminal law as breaking and entering. At least we had a decent night's sleep after the three-day cross-country sojourn.

The next morning, after a courtesy breakfast from our Blue Key comrades and after searching for the Morgmobile, which we believed had been stolen, it was on to a 1000-mile drive Vail, Colorado for New Year's Eve (again crashing local parties and 'borrowing' a set of chains to drive up the mountain on ice slick roads). We purchased a bottle of vodka and a jug of Kalua to swig Black Russians on the way to Aspen. That was a big mistake. We successfully crashed a New Year's Eve Party in a club in Aspen but failed to anticipate the effects of the higher altitude on our alcohol-soaked brains. Partying was unfortunately cut short after "waking up" face down in snow, rolled, wallet missing and receiving a stern warning from local law enforcement types to leave immediately, or spend time in the local jail, borrowed chains and all.

Driving down the mountain and asking ourselves "what else could go wrong," we immediately skidded off the icy road into a ravine. Some dude in pick-up truck pull us out and we noticed with horror the condition of the bald rear tires. After a brief stop in Salt Lake City to collect wire transferred funds from parents to replace bald tires we returned to Santa Barbara with lasting memories, two tins of sardines and one box of Premier saltine crackers remaining in the trunk of the Morgmobile.

Pre-Programmed for Failure

Before the Internet became a universal confessional platform, our private thoughts and imaginations belonged to us and were not for sale. Personal data was available, but it was costly and time-consuming to collect and organize.

Today's undergraduate "screenagers" arrive on campuses with minds and suitcases stuffed with advanced pre-programmed entertainment and electronics, including computers, mobile phones, digital cameras, and media players pre-loaded with movies, television programs, and music. It is not surprising that they are quickly bored with lectures from live academics, professors who have merely spent their entire lives studying particular specialized fields. BOR-ING. Professors just do not move or talk fast enough for the alcohol fueled, Google-obsessed, IOScontrolled ADHD generation.

The challenge for most millennials today is to negotiate the digital world in a way that not only enhances their health, safety, and security, but also cultivates the use of social media in a time of unparalleled growth. This is even more significant today when 62 million of our fellow Americans—mostly poor and minorities—excluded from the digital revolution without direct access to the Internet.[1] The task before us calls for creativity to harness the contributions offered by new technologies and the discipline to regulate its threats.

Along with the application of new technologies, participants must recognize the virtually impossibility of protecting precious civil liberties in the Internet Age. Adlai Stevenson and Dwight Eisenhower warned us 60 years ago about the intrusion of business and government bureaucracy in our private lives. Many Americans did not listen then and do not listen now. They are either reluctant or unable to protect themselves from technological assaults on their individual privacy. Institutions can no longer ensure accurate records or that individuals or institutions are protected from corporate crime, government spying, hackers, fraud, or identity thieves.

Privacy and security are particularly sensitive in view of the enhanced electronic information gathering and espionage capabilities that now permit corporations and spy agencies to probe our innermost private conversations and records. This reality is prompting many to ask: Can we trust Google any more than we distrust government? [2]

Ignoring privacy risks, billions now communicate openly with others on unsecure electronic networks in easily traceable binary code, sharing intimate details of their private lives, exchanging compromising photographs, arranging "it's only lunches" with virtual strangers. Easy access to social networking sites provides ripe opportunities for cyber-criminals and guerilla marketers to gain personal information from personal website searches for bargains, companionship, social acceptance…and more. Users are vulnerable to malicious codes capable of accessing bank accounts, credit cards and retrieving private information, much of it voluntarily submitted. Such invasive technology presents new opportunities for invasions of privacy and new challenges for protecting individual Constitutional freedoms. Advanced technology and new multimedia outlets provide unlimited space for the collection of data, transmission of information and management of networks. While enjoying the benefits of advanced technology, those with access should realize the potential damage to family values and privacy rights. Most users don't.

Navigating the treacherous new digital landscape is probably not the thorniest challenge facing young Americans today, given the weak job market, complexity of the relationships and trade-offs inherent in every choice made—but the stakes are too high to simply ignore. Furthermore, obsession with technology may be hindering the ability of recent graduates and new hires to maintain a strong, qualified presence on the job. A recent study reported that 83% of distracted millennials born after 1980, and under aged 35, excessively used social media at work and that 82% texted at inappropriate times during the day. According to a recruiter for an international consulting firm:

> *"The biggest problem with most of our new hires is that they think everything can be done electronically. They are always on their computers or smartphones e-mailing or texting clients and colleagues. I constantly remind them that our business is based on personal relationships. I literally have to tell them to stop texting and go talk to people. That concept seems to be largely foreign to them."*

Corrosive consequences of new communication technologies are further evident with hours spent texting online, listening to pre-programmed playlists, and watching vulgar television reruns: activities that interfere with human contact, conversing with a friend, exploring a classic book or learning the origins of a dance, stage play or song. Access to digital technologies can be detrimental in other ways as well, including compromised personal privacy, loss of motivation, and voyeurism caused by always comparing yourself with other online 'friends.' God forbid that anyone would 'unfriend' you!

Googling for Fun and Profit

Personal privacy from the bedroom to the ballot box has always been necessary for the maintenance of democratic life. We tread on the most sensitive ground when attempting to weigh the issues of individual freedom and privacy against the societal need for laws to be fairly enforced and public services effectively rendered. Tradeoffs are inevitable and can only be objectively measured in the halls of government and the chambers of the courts. To rebuild lost public trust, government must pay closer attention to protecting individuals' privacy against the negative threat of Big Brother. *"Government is a contrivance of human wisdom to provide for human wants,"* wrote Edmund Burke two-hundred and fifty years ago. *"Men have a right that these wants should be provided for by this wisdom."*

When it was first created, Google was a noun describing a high-tech search engine: the term has now morphed into the neologism 'to google,' an active verb indicating the search for information on the Internet, endless web surfing and desperate social networking. Google and other search engines revolutionize the way people interact. Googling enables anyone with minimum access and technical ability to explore the web and connect with others: private conversations permanently embedded in Big Data files. The resulting "user-generated content" is uploaded to a "cloud" somewhere in the blogosphere, permitting individuals to interact through websites in a collaborative manner. It also provides hackers unlimited access to the same information. Computers, tablets, mobile phones and high-speed Internet connections make retrieval and crossreferencing of information not only possible, but quick and cheap. All those zettabytes of information are stored and accessible on the cloud (for a price) to marketeers and spies.

Lamenting the decision to attend an expensive private college, one of McGinniss' students observed: "Why do I need a college education, I have Google." She may be right. After listening to a Silicon Valley icon, founder of one of the tech-miracle companies in the 1990s, she finally said what others were reluctant to admit:

> *"What I found to be interesting in his lecture was when he got into the issue of Facebook, Google, Apple, and Microsoft all competing to be the top company. These companies are all competing with each other and this is largely unnecessary. Each company specializes in a different area and if they were to remain focused on that area they could all prosper. However, this is not the goal of any of these companies; they all want to dominate at every level. This can be seen the way Facebook is trying to develop a phone, Apple issues software (which is primarily Microsoft's domain), among many other examples. The reason these four powerhouse companies are doing this is because **they are competing for our imagination** (emphasis added). Each company wants to be the primary operating system of our lives. In other words, they want to dominate every technological area possible and shut out all their competitors, which seems reasonable in a capitalist society like the United States.*

Rapid advances in search engine technology, mobile apps and non-secure communication systems have led to new forms of interactive social media and re-kindled old forms of *anomie*, a sense of detachment from greater society: even the vigilant can never escape the all-seeing eyes of the data miners and surveillance cameras. Many of us will become even more reliant on social media and disconnect ourselves further from the face-to-face human interactions that the Internet has stolen from many of us. Unsuspecting people cooperate by volunteering personal information and posting compromising and easily retrievable pictures on *Instagram* and *Facebook* that could only have been extracted at a high price less than a decade ago.

Social media networks do serve to bolster and maintain safety zones among existing friends and family circles, regardless of physical location. Social networking also allows participants to meet others online in a pseudo-defined "safe spaces" and form *faux* communities with those who possess similar interests, or at least think they do.

Ignoring Risks/Travel Study Abroad

Not many millennials can resist checking their *Facebook* account when it is merely a click and a few seconds away. New media makes cultural products instantly available, and in huge quantity. Young people love music and tend to travel with playlists reaching into the thousands. Easy and inexpensive access to mobile phone service with text messaging is now commonplace in the poorest parts of the world. In fact, there are more cell phones in use worldwide than toilets. Travelers generally do not see this as a positive development for health and safety reasons, but it does permit closer communication from foreign destinations. As with Internet and entertainment access, new communication tools come at a cost not only to cross-cultural immersion but also, and more importantly, to the personal growth at the heart of travel.

CHAPTER 10: LOSING THE TWO-FRONT WAR

The world we thought we had closed-out, closed-in again at the end of the decade. By the early 1970s, most of the early Isla Vistans had left for careers, military service, B-school, grad school, Peace Corps, or law school. The ever-present specter of the draft made such choices about the future more difficult. Fearing the worst, yet unable to stay in school and unwilling to get married, some simply dropped out. Many struggled with conscientious objections to the direction of their careers and country: others took advantage of the insatiable demand for drugs and became enablers. Amid the chaos, one thing was certain: the festive milieu of our once isolated post-adolescent sexual playground was gone and a dark mood had descended over the campus and the rest of the nation.

Almost unbelievably, UCSB—now affectionately known as the University of Casual Sex and Booze—became nationally known as a hotbed for violent anti-Vietnam War activity, a reputation that would span several decades. With the exception of UC Berkeley, Columbia and Kent State, no other campus received as much unwanted attention from the national media for its anti-war activities.

Revolutionary acts at UCSB during the later years of the decade included bombing the school's faculty club resulting in the death of a custodian, burning the ROTC building (a federal crime), and torching the Isla Vista branch of Bank of America. These violent incidents were mere preludes to the unwelcome resurrection of Nixon himself and a sharp right turn in our national politics. Things were about to get much worse.

Reagan's response to the 'student inspired violence' was swift and brutal, imposing a dawn to dusk curfew and ordering the National Guard to enforce it with deadly force during the school year. Culminating the violent outbursts was the shooting death of an innocent UCSB junior and student protester. He died from a ricochet bullet fired by a police officer riding in the bed of a truck while on patrol in Isla Vista. Santa Barbara County officials conducted a whitewash investigation, which found that the officer had fired 'by mistake' and the homicide was ruled an accident. This incident would have profound and tragic consequences for the family of one of our close friends, a Red House brother whose life be changed by events that took place that night on Isla Vista.

During those years, a number of anti-war speakers visited UCSB on national speaking tours. Undoubtedly, J. Edgar's men were in the crowds listening to Jesse Jackson, William Kunstler, Ralph Abernathy, Tom Hayden, Abbie Hoffman, Eldridge Cleaver, Democratic presidential candidates Eugene McCarthy and George McGovern, while keeping a close eye on the activities of student protesters. The stage was set for violent political confrontations over the war. Nixon would take full advantage of the climate of confusion, fear and paranoia.

Johnson's Wars on Communism and Poverty

Franklin Delano Roosevelt's New Deal coalition discovered the hidden power of radio and early television to rally support from reluctant Americans to fight savage two-front wars in Asia and Europe. By the mid-Sixties, LBJ's vision for the future, the so-called Great Society, was making some progress toward equalizing economic opportunities and alleviating state-sponsored racial disparities: at least that is what political liberals and recipients of government benefits and believed. Federal programs were beginning to assist those living in the worst conditions. Federal laws promised educational opportunities and voting rights protections for minorities. Justice Department officials and U.S. Marshalls protected <u>Freedom Riders</u> from the violent actions of the KKK in the Deep South. Right-wingers continued to oppose to any type of federal government interference, but most citizens had not yet become jaded about public assistance programs to help those endangered by local racism. Unemployment was below 5% and society's downtrodden believed that recently passed civil rights legislation might help ameliorate conditions for low income Whites, Blacks and Hispanics.

Intrusive federal government presence did not sit well with White majorities, especially those from Southern states with long histories of lynching, slavery, and political tokenism. Tensions were high and tolerance for the federal intervention was limited on both sides of the color spectrum: White prejudice on one hand, and delayed realization of hopes of Blacks and other minorities on the other. Nixon and his right-wing cronies recognized the potential conflict and seized the opportunity.

Conservatives were adamant, as Tea Partiers today, about stopping federal government 'handouts' such as Food Stamps, Medicaid and anything remotely resembling or labelled social welfare. Economic minorities of all shades—Blacks, Hispanics, gays and poor women—were convenient targets for conservatives because they could not defend themselves against moneyed interests. Nixonites played on White fears of an uprising by hordes of rebellious militant Black Communists by threatening to use violent force against our own citizens to restore 'law and order.' Why should we upright white folks pay for 'them' lazy you-know-what's to lie around and do nothing except plot against us, especially if they are armed? Attitudes were changing faster than most citizens could absorb and process information.

Making things worse, Johnson sent the first contingent of U.S. ground troops into ground combat in Vietnam on March 1965. This was a crucial turning point for American involvement in the war. Escalation continued and opposition grew exponentially. At the beginning of the year, only 25,000 American troops were in Vietnam; by early 1966, there were 185,000. Draft calls to local boards went up and greater numbers of 18-year olds, still ineligible to vote, were inducted. Most were poor black and brown minorities unable to receive deferments for attending college. LBJ was trying to fight a two-front war, one against poverty at home and the other to protect other countries from "falling like dominos" to communist aggression in Southeast Asia. It was becoming increasingly apparent that federal resources and national will were insufficient to win either of these conflicts.

Federal protection was also necessary because of the violent suppression of lawful demonstrations by local police and Klansmen. Federal troops ordered to Alabama and other Southern states to protect civil right demonstrators and freedom riders who were intimidated, and sometimes hunted down and killed by white supremacists. For the first time since the Civil War, federal and state troops might fire upon each other. This did not happen, but the worst of civil unrest would explode in the streets soon after.

Black leaders who spoke publically against national authorities put their own lives at risk. Malcolm X, leader of the Nation of Islam, high on J. Edgar Hoover's list of subversive organizations, was assassinated on February 21, 1965. Republican leaders were openly connecting communist agitators with Black revolutionaries and civil rights demonstrations with the anti-war movement. Events intervened and violence erupted in hundreds of American cities. Police provoked most of the disturbances resulting in death or injury to Black demonstrators.

Major riots had broken out in large cities during labor disturbances of the 1930s and in Harlem during the late 1940s, but the civil disorders of the mid-to late 1960's surpassed anything previously experienced. The five-day Watts riot in Los Angeles during August 1965 resulted in 34 deaths and over a thousand injured; race riots in Detroit lead to 40 deaths in 1967. Following Martin Luther King's assassination in 1968, riots broke out in over 120 cities including Newark, Chicago, Detroit, and Washington. Hundreds more were killed and thousands injured. These violent outbursts were sporadic and continued in Boston during the 1980s and New York in the 1990s. They occurred following tragic events and police provocation and spread quickly at predictable intervals.

The South Central Los Angeles Watts Riots were the first major civil disturbances in a predominately-black South Central neighborhood of Southern California. Violence erupted when the police detained a 21-year-old African-American man on suspicion of DWI, driving while intoxicated. Police officers believed the black male was under the influence and radioed for his car to be impounded. Backup officers arrived and attempted to arrest the suspect using physical force. Ominous crowds began to gather in protest. Additional police arrived on the scene to break up crowds, but demonstrators hurled bottles, rocks and concrete.

After a night of increasing street violence, police and local black community leaders held meetings to urge calm, but opposing groups began shouting at each other and the meeting failed. Later that day, Los Angeles Police Chief William H. Parker, not known for his sensitivity with or understanding of minority culture, assessed the growing threat and called for deployment of the California National Guard. Rioting intensified and, by the end of the week, Gov. Reagan declared martial law and enforced a dust to dawn curfew in a vast region of South Central Los Angeles. In addition to the guardsman, thousands of Los Angeles Police officers and LA County Sheriff's Deputies flooded the area to quell the rioting. This would become a common pattern in future encounters and further exacerbate already strained race relations in urban ghettos throughout the nation. Thousands participated in the riots over the course of five days. While many other residents of the community were sympathetic to the cause, they did not actively participate.

Mainstream White America viewed those participating in demonstrations as thugs destroying and looting their own neighborhoods. Gun sales in suburban white neighborhoods exploded. Others viewed rioters as taking part in a justified uprising against an oppressive system. Black civil rights activist Bayard Rustin stated in a 1966 essay that: *"the whole point of the outbreak in Watts was that it marked the first major rebellion of Negroes against their own masochism and was carried on with the express purpose of asserting that they would no longer quietly submit to the deprivation of slum life."*

When police vice squad officers raided an after-hours drinking club or "blind pig" located in a predominantly black neighborhood of Northwest Detroit in July 1967, they expected to round up a few patrons, but instead found 80 people holding a party for two returning Vietnam veterans. Officers attempted to arrest everyone on the scene and, while waiting for buses to transport the arrestees, an ominous crowd gathered around the establishment in protest. The situation soon erupted as fires and looting spread to Detroit's East Side, engulfing 100 square blocks. Within 48 hours, the governor mobilized the National Guard, followed by the 82nd Airborne Division on the riot's fourth day. As a result of the riots, 2,000 buildings were destroyed, 43 people lay dead, 1,200 injured and over 7,200 arrested.

The Newark, New Jersey riot also began with the arrest and beating of a taxi driver, who allegedly drove around a double-parked police car. The riot spread from black neighborhoods to downtown Newark. After six days of rioting in July 1967, 23 people lay dead, 725 people were injured and close to 1,500 people arrested. These events among others confirmed the grim reality that military force would be necessary for the foreseeable future to maintain law and order in neglected inner city ghettos.

****

David Eggert faced a difficult dilemma after graduation. Although his father had been killed in an Air Force bombing mission during the Korean War, he was still draftable. He had a younger brother, who was also of draft age, so he could not claim an exemption under the "Sole Surviving Son" rule because of his father's death while on active duty. Instead of waiting for his number to come up in the local draft lottery, he decided to join the Peace Corps, providing a draft deferment so long as he stayed with the program. Naturally, his training for Peace Corps service in Nigeria took place in Watts, the predominately-Black neighborhood in South Central Los Angeles where deadly riots had occurred a few months earlier.

Years before, Mark McGinnis' brother had become a police officer in suburban community in Southern California. After talking with Eggert, they decided to drive over for a visit. This was about a month after the Watts riots, and his brother reluctantly agreed to go. As they were leaving, he casually grabbed his holstered service revolver and ammo belt.

"Are you seriously going to bring your gun?" ask McGinnis.

"I'll go to Watts, but I ain't goin' down there without my piece," he said, and proceeded to slip the gun under the front seat.

Millions of Americans shared this fear and began to arm themselves in the event that police would be unable to protect them during future race riots or individual acts of violence.

Just a few years earlier, Mario Savio, then leader of the 'Free Speech Movement' at Berkeley, had failed to stir students to political action. By mid-decade, the climate had changed radically. Endless beach parties and casual attitudes about personal relationships gave way to a deep sense of resentment toward authority. The reality of living in a police state was setting in, even for middle class white males.

1968: LBJ, Chicago and the Tet Offensive

Events moved quickly during that bizarre election year, much quicker than anyone, even the candidates, had anticipated. Anti-war sentiment was widespread and disruptive war protests were becoming more frequent on college campuses and in large cities throughout the world. Street demonstrations were occurring for three years, each time gaining in size and strength: an estimated 35,000 marched in protest on Washington, D.C. in November 1965; over 100,000 marched on the Pentagon to protest the War on October 22, 1967. Armed members of the 82nd Airborne ringed the building, as if unarmed hippies were a real threat to national security. The demonstration remained peaceful until after sunset when the TV crews disappeared.

When the cameras shut down and darkness descended, baton-wielding thugs used tear-gas to disperse demonstrators. People ran, trampling others, in a desperate attempt to escape the goon squads. This was a centralized and strategically directed operation and many of those who were assaulting the demonstrators had small earphones and spoke to commanders via Dick Tracy wrist radios. The repression took place in the shadow of the U.S. Capitol and within a few blocks of the Supreme Court: no Constitutional guarantees of freedom of assembly and speech when demonstrators challenge prevailing authority.

Following years of peaceful marches and Pentagon demonstrations, organizers began planning for even larger rallies at the Democratic National Convention in Chicago the following summer. Everyone expected Johnson would be re-nominated for a second term. Anti-war demonstrations and violent backlashes continued on other college campuses throughout the nation. In February 1968 three black students were killed and 30 wounded by police while demonstrating on the campus of a State College in Orangeburg, South Carolina. Local authorities and school administrators blamed the trouble on 'outside agitators.'

In early March 1968, Sen. Eugene "Clean Gene" McCarthy (D-Minn.) challenged the Johnson juggernaut and won a surprising moral victory in the New Hampshire primary, receiving 42% of the Democratic primary vote. Resistance groups were elated, believing that McCarthy, the antiwar candidate, could finally force Johnson to withdraw from Vietnam. Four days later, sensing blood in the political waters, Sen. Robert F. Kennedy (D-N.Y.) entered the race for the Democratic nomination. By late March, Johnson's critics were in full rebellion, angry over the seizure of the U.S. spy ship *Pueblo* by the North Koreans in January, and shocked by the *Tet offensive* in Vietnam in late January and early February.

By early summer, it was obvious that North Vietnamese regulars backed by the Chinese had joined the fight to drive foreign invaders from South Vietnam and reunite the country. They succeeded in creating the illusion that guerilla resistance was triumphing over superior U.S. firepower. Savage surprise attacks on the cities of South Vietnam destroyed the morale and fighting capability of the South Vietnamese Army, forced the U.S. to withdraw from Vietnam, and toppled the Saigon regime. The United States was divided into the 'war hawks' who wanted to 'finish the job' at any cost and 'peace doves' who saw only futility in continuing to sink resources and American blood into the quagmire.

Proponents who wanted to escalate the conflict (possibly even using nuclear weapons) conveniently ignored the reality that the war had turned decisively against American forces after *Tet* and once again screamed that American was about the "lose" another country to the communist menace. Or maybe opposition was just a cleaver distraction designed to free the Republicans, Nixon and Company to negotiate a separate peace with the Chinese and North Vietnamese on their terms?

Always ready to pounce, Nixon would charge that under the Democrats, America had become a lawless society and that we were losing the war because of political interference with field command decisions. The Johnson administration had failed to suppress civil disorder and Democrats must be held accountable for the rise in crime and violence, including urban riots, on the streets of America. Nixon was the 'law and order' candidate who was backed by the NRA and other radical right-wing groups intent on suppressing dangerous hippie anti-war demonstrators and unleashing military commanders to "finish the job" in Vietnam.

At the end of March in that infamous year, Johnson attempted to calm the country and bring peace to himself by announcing that he "would not seek nor accept his party's nomination for a second term." The rejoicing lasted only a few days. Reality set in and the mortally wounded Democratic campaign continued with Vice President Hubert Humphrey of Minnesota the "Happy Warrior" as the reluctant choice of the Johnson-wing of the party.

Repression at the Washington demonstrations would pale in comparison to the crackdowns on protestors at the Democratic National Convention in Chicago and, two weeks later, outside the Republican Convention in Miami Beach. The violence in Chicago culminated in made-for-television pitched battles between police and demonstrators. Thousands of anti-war protesters who were determined to force the party to reject Johnson's Vietnam War 'body-count" strategy clashed with Mayor Richard Daley's police. Inside the convention hall, Mayor Richard J. Daley fumed at his party's disarray. His appearances on television defending what former Illinois Governor Otto Kerner's National Advisory Commission on Civil Disorder later called "a police riot" presenting Democratic Party leaders to the nation as violent thugs unable to control their own convention and intent on suppressing legitimate protesters. After the conflict, all Daley could say in response to the criticism was "At least no one was killed."

Humphrey's fate was sealed by the heavy media coverage of violent police suppression of the demonstrators in this Democratic Party controlled city. Key organizers of the protests (known as the Chicago Seven) were indicted for conspiracy and incitement to riot. A few years earlier, federal laws were changed under the Omnibus Crime Control and Safe Streets Act of 1968, making it easier to arrest for conspiracy that actually committing a crime. Years later, the Supreme Court overturned the Chicago Seven convictions and this odious law.

The Chicago demonstrations did not draw as many participants as earlier protests—about 10,000 at most—because it was widely anticipated that Mayor Daley would deploy his police to prevent marches to the site of the convention. He did just that to show that Democrats could maintain law and order.[1]

Nearly forgotten because of the melee in Chicago, were two days of bloody rioting at Republican Convention in Miami Beach earlier that summer. Police cracked down harshly, killing three Black men and arresting hundreds of others. Nixon did not hesitate to use force against the 'rioters.' The Florida National Guard reacted quickly and, although demonstrators charged that that police had brutally suppressed the black community, the violence was contained.

To many in a stunned nation, the stark contrast between the two conventions reinforced Nixon's message that the Republicans' were better prepared to maintain law and order and that a vote for the Democrats would lead to further chaos, disintegration and street rioting.

One of the highest-ranking members of Johnson's administration remembers the weeks before and following LBJ's resignation "as a strange, almost psychedelic and schizophrenic time." The air was full of revolutionary fervor and monumental events occurred in just a few short months: American soldiers massacred 450-500 innocent civilian women and children at _My Lai_ hamlet in _Song My_ village in Vietnam; police crackdowns on demonstrators at the Democratic and Republican Conventions; epic riots in Paris and London. In New York City, writer Valerie Solonas gunned down Andy Warhol; in Baghdad, Iraq a coup d'état propelled a young, unknown man named Saddam Hussein into power.

On April 4th, 1968, as if to fulfill the final act of a bloody spring prophesy, Martin Luther King Jr. was assassinated in Memphis, Tennessee. His murder by a white supremacist set off a violent spasm of further rioting in over 100 cities that cost the lives of 34 people. Then, on June 5th, after impressive victories in the California, Indiana and South Dakota primaries, Robert F. Kennedy was struck down by a bullet from Sirhan Sirhan's .22 caliber pistol. Sirhan's motives remain a mystery to this day. The last hope of many Americans vanished. Nixon was elated.

****

By the end of 1968, around 15,000 U.S. service members had been killed in action—it was the worst year of carnage in Vietnam and it was far from over. The endless war, racism, and social injustices filled people with rage; millions demonstrated in protest across the world. We had lost faith in our leaders, hated Johnson because he would not run for a second term, and were distraught that charismatic champions King and Kennedy were gone. The Vietnam War broke a president, divided the nation, fragmented the Democrats, split generations and left U.S. global prestige at its lowest point since the end of World War II.

We did not know it then, but a fundamental shift was taking place in the minds of elite militarists about how to re-assert their power over American politics.

Nixon...Again?

In 1971, Lewis Powell, a prominent Nixon ally and Republican corporate lawyer wrote a memo to his friend Eugene Sydnor, Jr Director of the U.S. Chamber of Commerce. The infamous "Powell Power Memo" did not surface until after Nixon had been re-elected president in 1972 but it clearly inspired the creation of Republican "Think Tanks" such at the Heritage Foundation, the Manhattan Institute, the Cato Institute, Citizens for a Sound Economy, Accuracy in Academe, and other powerful right-wing lobbying organizations still active today.

Most notable about these institutions was their focus on education, shifting values, and movement building—a focus shared by many others, though often with sharply contrasting goals. Their long-term focus on restoring the "business of government" began paying off handsomely in the 1980s, in coordination with the Reagan Administration's pro-business and anti-regulatory philosophy. Although Powell's memo was not the sole influence, commercial and corporate activists took his advice to heart and began building a powerful network of institutions designed to shift public attitudes and beliefs.

For his efforts, Nixon rewarded the reliable conservative Powell with a seat on the U.S. Supreme Court in January 1972. The evidence as to whether or not Powell's political views influenced his judicial decisions is mixed. Powell did embrace expansion of corporate privilege and wrote the majority opinion in a 1978 decision that effectively invented a First Amendment "right" for corporations to be treated as persons and granted *card blanche* to influence political issues.[2] On social issues, Powell, like Nixon, was somewhat moderate. Right-leaning Republicans would nominate neither man to high office today.

Since then, the Supreme Court has been in lock-step with conservative presidents Reagan, Bush1, and Bush2 whose appointments to the high court (Kennedy, Alito, and Roberts) have bolstered a right-wing majority—at least until Justice Scalia's death in 2016—and given favorable treatment to corporations. (Scalia's premature death again set up a monumental conflict with greater implications for future.)

Nixon learned from his mistakes in 1960. While staging his political comeback in the primaries at the 1968 Republican Convention, he carefully scripted campaign events to the slightest detail, handpicking his audiences with the help of 28-year-old media strategist, alleged sexual harasser, and recently deposed Fox News head Roger Ailes. He trounced his chief rivals and primary opponents, Reagan, Rockefeller and Michigan Governor George Romney (yes, the father). Later, Nixon would become the first president to hire a full-time communications director. He ordered his economic advisers to work closely with public relations guru William Safire to clear all campaign communications. His mantra: deliver the message the voters wanted to hear first, then develop policy. (With Ailes as one of his key advisors, Trump obviously took more than a page from Tricky Dick's playbook.) Nixon's mastery of the electronic media would only have taken him so far if he had not also possessed another, less-noticed skill—and uncanny ability to read the darker moods of American voters, perhaps a reflection of his own sullen temperament.

By the end of the 1968 campaign, LBJ had solid evidence that Nixon had sabotaged the Vietnam War peace talks or, as he put it, he was guilty of treason and had "blood on his hands." Johnson planned a dramatic re-entry into the 1968 Democratic Convention to re-join the presidential race. Recently declassified tapes of President Lyndon Johnson's telephone calls at the time provide this evidence. He had recordings confirming that Nixon had interfered with the Vietnam peace talks...but said and did nothing. Perhaps his own personal guilt overwhelmed his political instincts, knowing that he, too, had the blood of young American soldiers on his hands.

Too many years of civil disorder, rioting and jungle warfare had eroded voters' confidence in Democratic leadership. The American war machine was killing Viet Cong, Godless North Vietnamese communists, innocent civilians and young American men, draining resources and frustrating those anxious for victory. After 15 years of war, we were still uncertain about the outcome of a conflict that had taken so much from so many families. With 500,000 U.S. troops now fighting in Vietnam, how could we lose?[3] Conscripted soldiers could only take so much and command pressure to increase the 'body count' inevitably led to deaths of innocent civilians. Villagers were terrorized by combat fatigued GIs and informed the Viet Cong on the whereabouts of American units. Without support from the people they thought they were fighting for, Americans were sitting ducks and easy prey for the insurgents. Grinding and humiliating defeats in battle after battle appeared live on national television. Americans were in disbelief because we had never before lost a war.

****

Following the campaign chaos of 1968, the people of the United States voted. In one of the closest elections in American history, 43.4% of the popular vote went to Republican Richard M.

Nixon; 42.7% to Democrat Hubert H. Humphrey; and 13.5% to the American Independent Party's "segregation forever" candidate Gov. George Corley Wallace of Alabama. The strategy used by Republicans to split the Democratic vote worked better than even they expected. Lacking a Southern candidate on the ticket, many conservative white Democrats switched allegiances to Republicans. Nixon's 'southern strategy' to divide and conquer democrats had succeeded.

Four years later, segregationist George Wallace ran again and was shot at a campaign rally. Nixon went on win another term over the hapless Democratic candidate, South Dakota Senator George McGovern. Ballgame over. Nixon overcame his disgraceful defeat and Republicans Ford, Reagan and Bush the First held the White House for 16 of the next 20 years, interrupted only briefly by Jimmy Carter's term from 1977-1981.

The twin issues of crime and rampant civil disorder as well as the slow pace of so-called "Vietnamization" finally won the presidency for Richard M. Nixon. Amidst the disarray, a slim majority of voters in 1968 choose their candidate based on their fears and frustrations about the present rather than their hopes and expectations for the future.

Nixon expertly played to collective paranoia and succeeded where he had failed just eight years earlier: a stunning reversal of fortune even for the unpredictable and vulnerable American Electoral College System. Nixon's message remained the same, but the social climate, war fatigue, increasing crime rates and fear of communist-inspired Black Power insurrection changed the political landscape. Riding public discontent with the party in power, Tricky Dick falsely promised an end to the war. After the election, he did just the opposite, escalating the war by bombing Hanoi and invading neighboring Cambodia, where Viet Cong were hiding, in a desperate final effort to force North Vietnamese to withdraw. Demonstrations and protests escalated with the bombings. Protests at UCSB and on other college campuses were the focal points for the anti-war movement. Meanwhile, heavier costs would be paid for challenging the right wing "bomb them into submission" status quo.

Following the failed carpet-bombing of North Vietnam and the invasion of Cambodia, Nixon tried to take credit for ending the Vietnam War. However, it was the massive protests and a global popular uprising that forced an end the conflict. After Nixon had lost credibility and resigned the presidency, it was only a matter of months before the U.S. withdrew its troops and abandoned Saigon.

On August 15, 1969, 400,000 people attended the 3-day Woodstock Music Festival in Bethel, New York to hear Jimi Hendrix, Janis Joplin, The Band, Joan Baez and other musicians who had become the conscience of our generation. In November, 250,000 people marched in the largest anti-war demonstration in the history of Washington D.C. Another 200,000 people gathered in Golden Gate Park, San Francisco to protest Nixon's escalation of the war. No one was surprised that all three of our political leaders had been lying to us during the entire decade. It took a Pentagon 'leaker' to reveal the truth.

The Pentagon Papers

Daniel Ellsberg worked for the Rand Corporation on a top-secret project documenting U.S. involvement in the Vietnam War. As the premier whistle-blower of his generation, he singlehandedly tore apart the thinly veiled rationales for the conflict and the Cambodian incursion by leaking secret documents to the press. During the aftermath in 1971, Ellsberg was labeled by the paranoid Neo-cons of the Nixon administration as the 'most dangerous man in America.' By then, even the perpetuators doubted the rationale for the so-called containment strategy requiring heavy American presence in Southeast Asia.

The Vietnam Study Task Force was founded in 1967 to write a definitive history of the Vietnam War. Analysts had access to top-secret files from the Pentagon to create the final product, keeping the study secret from political leaders in Washington and the public. Daniel Ellsberg knew the analysts involved in conducting the study and had access to the files. He took a huge personal risk in leaking the papers to the press: putting his future income at risk and potentially affecting not only himself but also his two children and his ex-wife. He lost status and access that accompanied a respected former State Department analyst who had spent two years in Vietnam and advised Former Defense Secretary Robert McNamara and Henry Kissinger.

In his memoirs, Ellsberg revealed that he believed that he would be incarcerated for the rest of his life for leaking the Papers. He was eventually indicted and tried as a spy but the case was dismissed because the Nixon gang had suppressed evidence, burglarized the office of Ellsberg's psychiatrist, illegally wiretapped his private conversations, and held secret discussions with the judge trying case about an appointment as FBI Director. Bribery was one of the least of Nixon's offences.

The Pentagon Papers had a major impact on the public's opinion of the war and sent shockwaves through the nation's collective psyche. Anti-war protests and teach-ins were underway for years before the leak, but the publication of the truth about the war stripped away the last vestiges of legitimacy and brought an end of the war. The leaks had a profound effect on Americans' view of government as well, influencing our willingness to take on faith the honesty and competence of our leaders. The Papers has a lasting effect on the history of the United States because they were a permanent, high-profile reminder that lies, mistakes, and plausible deniability may well lurk behind a government admonishment to 'trust the President' because only he knows the facts. Release of the documents also fostered skepticism among citizens toward government claims that some information must be kept secret in the name of the national security.

Ellsberg attempted to disclose the study's contents to President Nixon's National Security Advisor, Henry Kissinger, among other federal government officials, but was repeatedly turned away until he approached the *New York Times* in 1968. Kissinger would have nothing to do with the leaks, although the information was useful to him as he distanced himself from Nixon. He was too busy writing his memoirs and planning the so-called China initiative with Nixon to open diplomatic relations with our sworn Godless Communist enemy. Despite their conformity, loyalty and obedience, baby boomers were sold out.

History repeats itself with recent revelations by whistleblower Edward Snowden about National Security Agency domestic surveillance programs. These leaks may only be the harbinger of extended future military-intelligence-complex efforts to gather information about Americans under the guise of anti-terrorism. Post-9/11/01 legal authority in statutes such as the USAPATRIOT Act mandate greater compliance in the name of preserving homeland security and new technologies facilitate the legal assault on privacy without justifying the reasons for corporate or government intrusion.

Laws and regulations governing cyber-surveillance failed to keep pace with society's adoption of new data collection devices, social networking and other cloud storage technologies. In addition to embracing new social media applications, big databases overflow with reservoirs of information available to law enforcement and intelligence communities. The CIA recognized the value of free information voluntarily submitted to social media sites—the spy agency was one of the first co-investors in *Facebook*. The extent and 'precious diversity' of our personal information now stored by public and private organizations—Social Security data, credit ratings and transactions, driver's license information, medical records, military and state department communiqués, income figures, *Facebook* 'likes' and so on—far exceeds laws and regulations designed to protect individuals' from invasions of privacy.

Far more compromising information is uploaded voluntarily on *Facebook, YouTube,* and *Instagram* than would ever be collected by official government census reports or tax forms. New sources of data are monitored and cross-referenced by digital sensors almost everywhere: biometrics, blog postings, e-file tax records, climate sensors, video images, voting patterns, digital pictures, transaction records of online purchases, cell phones and GPS signals—to name a few. Today, prospective employers routinely check job applicants' social networking pages for any compromising information. If they knew, Adlai and Ike would be rolling over in their graves.

New York City has become a Virtual Police State, transforming its traditional reactive police response systems to proactive systems enabling officials to integrate databases, discover and respond to problems before they happen. Remember Tom Cruise in the film *Minority Report* and Gene Hackman and Will Smith in *Enemy of the State*? Science fiction is becoming scientific fact. There has been less attention paid to data protection than to data collection in the brave new world of Big Data.

These activities represent a new type of underground activism reminiscent of the *Pentagon Papers* leak, but without the patriotic intentions to end an unjust war. Ellsberg gave secrets to newspaper editors, so that journalists could edit and distribute information in their own manner. Wiki-leakers such as Bradley (Chelsea) Manning and Edward Snowden used new technology to dump all the classified material, which is then posted as .pdf documents and videos in its entirety. Distrust between citizen and government had already reached historic highs, even before the Trump election in 2016.

Just imagine what would have happened if Nixon had possessed such technology? Watergate would have been a minor skirmish in his total war against political enemies, real or imagined. The Internet rumor mill hums with accusations that the Trump administration was aware of Russian hackers and had access to private data about political enemies.

Remember that 'secret plan' to end the Vietnam War, which Nixon concocted but failed to share with the American public? Big surprise. He was actually planning a clandestine diplomatic initiative to Red China after seeking the advice of former Goldwater aide Henry Kissinger. They conspired to make a deal with Communist Dictator Mao Zedong to establish diplomatic relations with Red China and promote their membership in the UN. It would then only be a matter of time before China became a member of the World Trade Organization (WTO) and access lucrative world markets, including Europe and the United States. In return, Red China would back off its support (at least publically) for North Vietnam, which had already established a land bridge to resupply its troops in South Vietnam, effectively ending any possibility that the U.S. could ever 'win' the war. Sadly, for the thousands of draftees sent to Vietnam after 1968, Nixon kept this information to himself. Doubtless, Tricky D and Henry the K shared details of this treasonous plot and exchanged first drafts of their memoirs.

The Nixon Justice Department charged Ellsberg with espionage for his actions as the source of the leak, but all charges were dismissed in 1973 because Nixon administration officials had initiated a smear campaign against him. They did not learn much from the Watergate break-in. Among other actions, they hired operatives to burglarize Ellsberg's psychiatrist's office, copy his private medical records, and then used them to publically crucify him. Ellsberg continued his distinguished career as a political analyst and anti-war activist. A 2009 documentary, T*he Most Dangerous Man in America: Daniel Ellsberg and the Pentagon Papers* earned a Peabody Award and the film was nominated for an Academy Award. The full text of the secret study of the Vietnam War was released 40 years later, in June of 2011.

Within a year of their attempt to discredit Ellsberg, Nixon's entire senior staff was indicted for the Watergate break-ins and he resigned in disgrace. By then, he had turned to alcohol for solace. As the Watergate investigation closed in and with his impeachment imminent, Henry Kissinger observed him fully inebriated in his underwear on his knees talking to the portraits of ex-presidents in the East Wing of the White House. The conversation probably went something like this:

"Well, George, we really fucked things up, didn't we?" Nixon moaned kneeling before a portrait of Washington dressed resplendently in military uniform on his white Stallion, Lord Nelson.

"What do you mean 'we,' you horse's ass! You are the one that ripped a new one in the New Kingdom that I created," answered Washington angrily.

"I wanted to be addressed as I should be as King George. We beat whose limey Red Coat bastards and all you did was surrender to the Reds."

"Oh, come on GW, I tried my best, but those fuckin' Democrats, Kennedy and those Eastern faggots had it in for me from the beginning," Nixon pitifully replied.

"Excuses, excuses, you wimp. I should horsewhip you, like I do when Martha and the slaves fuck up."

"I am sorry, George, I know…you know I meant well…it was those fuckin' Cubans who let us down. I should never have trusted those bastards. They never come through in the end. They shot Kennedy, don't ya know."

"Yeah, that Jefferson is a wild motherfucker, always into the Black stuff…I mean once in a while is ok, but privacy, please…keep it in the house."

"You are absolutely right, George, Pat dried up decades ago and I had plenty of chances… that blonde divorcee in Key Biscayne, she was comin' on to me at Bebe's Christmas party, but I had inner strength, you see…that's how I beat those sons-of-bitches…inner strength.

"Right, Dick, you drunken sod, your strengths smell like bourbon whiskey, cheap at that."

"Actually it's pretty good stuff," mumbled Nixon, looking down at a bottle of Wild Turkey tucked between his knees.

"Get the hell out of my house, you dick, you disgraceful excuse for an Englishman."

"Actually, our family was German, look solid Nordic stock…."

"Shut the fuck up, I'm outta here. Giddeup Nelson."

This was not Nixon's lowest point. After the infamous Watergate resignation, he remained in a deep depression, often threatening suicide. During one particular episode in front of his Casa Pacifica home in San Clemente, he plunged into the heavy surf in Pacific Ocean fully clothed in a drunken stupor. He tried to swim to China where he assumed he would be worshipped. The Secret Service agents who reluctantly rescued him from the surf said that he was mumbling something like:

'Mao loves me…he listens to me… they respected him. I didn't lose that fucking war, it was Westmoreland and those pussy generals who wouldn't fight. Why do those reporters hate me?"

He whined as agents dragged him back to the house, his Gucci tie-down shoes making deep furrows in the brown sugar sand.

Nixon died on April 22, 1994, deeply engaged in an imaginary debate with Lincoln's disgraced successor, Andrew Johnson, over the Constitutional merits of impeachment.

CHAPTER 11: Bank of America, Isla Vista Branch

With tensions mounting on campuses worldwide alongside national political unrest and opposition to the Vietnam War, the 1969-1971 school years were the worst in UCSB's history—at least until the senseless massacres of students by deranged social misfits in 2001 and 2014. For eligible males, Nixon's escalation of the war increased the risk of becoming cannon fodder for a protracted war with no purpose other than enhancing Tricky Dick's image as a diplomat and peacemaker. The draft brought home the reality of combat for those who lacked the voting franchise and were unable to question the war's justification. Friends and older brothers who had served in Vietnam would relay uncensored horror stories which starkly conflicted with official media accounts of the "heroic struggle for democracy" taking place in Southeast Asia. Not all males were equally vulnerable: scions of wealthy families could always receive deferments from a college while lower income black and brown teenagers were inducted.

As patriotism waned and opposition increased, it became obvious that America armed forces were sinking further and further into a bloody quagmire. Symbols of big business, capitalism, Nixon and the Vietnam War—with their ties to the military-industrial-complex—were inviting targets for anti-war protesters.

****

The Bank Burning and its Aftermath[1]

On Feb. 25, 1970, second-year UCSB student Matt Welch looked out his window and saw flames shooting into the night sky on the normally peaceful center of Isla Vista a few blocks away. Puzzled about what was going on, he picked up his camera and joined the crowds rushing towards the flames. What he saw and photographed that night would haunt him for the rest of his life.

"I woke up in the middle of the night and saw the sky glowing red. I walked over to Del Playa and there was pretty much dead silence as the fire burned. It was a weird sensation like watching a war movie, only the smoke and cracking fire was real," Welch remembers.

After a year of tension, unrest and anger on campus, rioting students looted and set fire to the local Bank of America branch on Isla Vista. To some, this was seen as the last desperate attempt

159

to reverse course in Vietnam; to others, including most of the so-called 'silent majority," it was an unjustifiable act of civil rebellion and wanton destruction of private property.

Welch remembers that:

"It was a freaky scene that night. People were in lots of different moods, celebrating, shocked, and stunned by what was going on. Neither the police nor fire department ever came. They just sat there and let it burn,"

Earlier that afternoon, William Kunstler, the lead defense attorney for the Chicago Seven defendants in the Chicago conspiracy trial at the Democratic Convention, spoke to a packed stadium on campus. Authorities anticipated an inflammatory reaction and showed up in full riot gear to control the crowd. After the speech, groups of students peacefully walked back from campus toward Isla Vista. Police descended upon the crowd, beat up a 22-year-old student and arrested him for carrying a bottle of alcohol that was misidentified as a Molotov cocktail. The same tactics that had been used Blacks in Chicago, Detroit, Newark and Watts were now being used against protesting middle-class white college students.

According to Rick Whitely, a second-year student living on Del Playa Drive near the bank, police actions fueled repressed student anger.

"When the cops beat up this guy, the news spread like wildfire and set everything off. Tensions were high all week, with radicals waiting for something to get fired up about after Kuntsler's speech," Wiley said.

"It was like they threw a match into a gasoline can, everything just exploded."

The fire still smoldered on Feb. 26th when Reagan declared a state of emergency for IV. Dump trucks full of cops patrolled the streets at curfew every day; tear gas canisters were lobbed at any gathering of more than a few students; and gawkers recklessly came out just to see what would happen if they violated the curfew. Some wore gasmasks. Other taunted the police with rock and bottles. It took days for the bank vault to cool enough for a wrecking ball to break it open. Most of the cash burnt beyond recognition and Isla Vista became occupied territory.

Santa Barbara County Sheriff's helicopters whirled overhead announcing over bullhorns that anyone caught outside was in violation and subject to arrest. Many of the students targeted their rage at cops patrolling the streets of Isla Vista. Local police were outnumbered and Reagan ordered LAPD and LA County SWAT teams to assist.

The imported LA cops were reserves unfamiliar with the I.V. vibe and overreacted to student's protests. LA cops were particularly brutal, breaking into students' apartments and beating them for no apparent reason. People were glad when the National Guard showed up some days later to stop the random Gestapo-style violence.

"That little bank was the biggest capitalist thing around," remembers Tina Wilson, a fourthyear student and then editor-in-chief of *El Nacho*, the student newspaper.

"It symbolized opposition to corporations that profited from war and were oppressing people all over world, in whose interest the government was acting," she said.

Others believed that the bank was set on fine purely out of anger and frustration with the treatment of students and the overwhelming police presence in I.V.

"The bank was in cahoots with defense contractors providing armaments to kill innocent Cambodians and Vietnamese. At least that was the rationale given, but there was more to it than that simple explanation. Repressed anger toward police that had developed over time. People were just pissed off about everything. They were really pissed off."

"When I started school in fall of 1968, only a handful of people were demonstrating, just a quiet peaceful little vigil with signs and candles in front of the library. Nobody really gave a shit about the peace movement or the war," Welch remembers.

"Two years later it had become a widespread movement with probably most students against the war. By that time, everyone knew someone who have been drafted or hassled by the cops. It changed the whole vibe on I.V., became much more personal, more real."

Behavior was becoming totally surreal. One woman wandered around all night calling out obscenities, taunting the cops and guards, teasing them, apparently never getting caught. Rick Wiley found a spent shotgun shell on his front door step one morning. Afterwards, he slept in the bathtub and kept away from the windows.

The super-charged political atmosphere of the late Sixties was evident well beyond the confines of Isla Vista, too.

"It's hard to imagine now, but the whole country was just boiling over with rage, with the Chicago Seven trial in Chicago, the war, people getting drafted … the whole country was pretty much out of control," Whiteley remembers.

"Tensions were high in I.V. toward anything and anyone remotely connected with the status quo, Nixon-Reagan style, and the most immediate and visible targets turned out to be cops and narcs," Matt Welch said.

Beyond these broader societal trends, the growing drug culture and hippie lifestyle of the time widened the generation gap between adults, students and police, who patrolled Isla Vista and campus in full riot gear and used tear gas regularly to disperse crowds.

"Police saw students as enemies of the state who were at odds with civil authority. Anyone driving a Volkswagen van painted with flowers or had long hippie hair was going to be harassed by police, stopped in traffic, and pulled over. That's just the way things were," remembers Wiley.

"Isla Vista had changed for the worst," Welch said.

In the weeks after the curfew was instituted in Isla Vista, nearly 300 people were arrested and taken to the county jail.

"Everybody sensed huge confrontation the night after the bank burning. I went out on street again to take photographs in the early evening. When I was on Ocean Drive taking pictures of police at the San Rafael parking lot...they arrested me and took me to their staging area. We were then bussed out to fire station down on Storke Road and eventually over to the new county jail, which hadn't even opened yet," Welch explained.

Culminating the violent outbursts was the shooting death of Kevin Morgan, a 20-year-old student activist, protester and UCSB Junior. Like thousands of others, Morgan was drawn to the scene by the flames, smoke and confusion. Police arrived in armored trucks, dressed in riot gear and armed with rifles and tear gas. Morgan and several others were trying to put out the fire with neighborhood garden hoses. Amid the confusion, shots rang out and Kevin was fatally wounded.

His older brother Rick had since moved from I.V. to law school at Boalt Hall in Berkeley and remembers how he first learned of his brother's death.

"I had been studying late for a moot court hearing the next day. The phone rang and it was my mother, sobbing uncontrollable. This was unlike her, always in control, always directing. At first, I couldn't understand what she was saying...something about Kevin. Perhaps he was in an accident? No, she blurted in her usual protective way that something worse had happened and that I needed to get down to Santa Barbara right away."

"I was confused. I knew of the student unrest at UCSB, but thought it was just like the protests happening every day on Telegraph Avenue in Berkeley."

"What do you mean?" I asked hesitatingly…as it finally hit me that perhaps…no, not him!"

The cacophony of events during the next several weeks overwhelmed all his senses. The more he learned, the worse it became. Although the police first claimed the bullet originated from a sniper in the crowd, a ballistics test determined that it came from a police officer's rifle. Kevin was an innocent by-stander, among a larger group of students helping to put out the fire with garden hoses near the burning bank.

Months later, after a perfunctory hearing, the incident was deemed an accident, and the officer exonerated.

"My brother had done nothing to provoke the police and was only trying to help put out the fire," Morgan later told newspaper reporters.

His life took a difference turn after he left Isla Vista for law school. His distrust heightened after he learned about the police shooting on Isla Vista that took his brother's life. Until that tragedy, Rick had never thought too much about law enforcement. But the actions of the police that night convinced him that he could do more to prevent such unnecessary 'mistakes' from happening in the future by becoming a federal officer. He did just that and served for 32 years with distinction as a federal prosecutor in the U.S. Justice Department.

That night, he dreamed that his Mother was playing a piano alone in an apartment. His Dad came in later (or he imagined that he did), lost clothes, hunting around the strange building in torn T-shirt, his penis dangling from his pants. He had been kidnapped and had to steal from someone's clothes bag, worried that old ladies were watching him and would turn him in…back to Mother's apartment. She was playing piano beautifully. My sister Valarie was living there, we embraced, but she was leaving to go back east to visit her kid? The floor was dirty with cigarettes, mother said we spilled something, and I got broom and tried to clean up the mess.

Rick's brother would not be the last casualty in the domestic protests against the war. Less than a month after Kevin Morgan's death, President Richard Nixon publicly acknowledged that he had widened the war in Southeast Asia to include Cambodia. Immediately, students at UCSB and others across America rose in opposition to this escalation of the war. On Monday, May 4, 1970, Ohio National Guardsman fired live ammunition into a crowd of unarmed students at Kent

State University in Kent, Ohio. The guardsmen fired 67 rounds over a period of 13 seconds, killing four students and wounding nine others, one of whom suffered permanent paralysis. Some of the victims were protesting Nixon's Cambodian incursion and others were shot dead walking to class nearby or observing the protest from a distance. An international response followed the escalation and the shootings: four million students refused to attend class and hundreds of universities, colleges, and secondary schools closed throughout the United States. The events further negatively affected public opinion about Nixon and the course of the war.

****

In the weeks following the fire, Bank of America declared prematurely that it would not withdraw from Isla Vista and set up a portable trailer as a makeshift bank. Despite 24-hour security protection, it quickly became a target for distain, graffiti and numerous street demonstrations. On April 18th, a rally was scheduled against the temporary bank. Associated Students President Bill Thompson went on the radio to speak against further violence, urging students to protect the bank from vandalism. On June 3rd, 17 persons, mostly community and student leaders, were indicted for the bank burning, after being identified from photographs supposedly taken on the night of Feb. 25. The indictments were immediately met with controversy because several of the students had solid alibis.

On the same day, a Santa Barbara Grand Jury indicted "Isla Vista 17" on charges of burning the Bank of America. They faced a total of 609 1/2 years on 72 counts. Bail was set for one of the 17 defendants at $120,000, despite the fact that he had an airtight alibi: he was in the County jail the night the bank burned.

In retaliation, on June 4th the people of Isla Vista again attempted to burn the temporary bank, skirmishing with police in the streets. When the fighting ceased, 667 people had been arrested. Incomplete figures showed numerous instances of police brutality, including: 92 cases of unprovoked beatings, 43 cases of illegal entry, 26 cases of willful destruction of property, 6 cases of threats of death accompanied by the use of weapons, and 5 sexual offenses against women.

On Wednesday, June 10th, 1500 Isla Vistans peacefully assembled in Perfect Park to defy a 7:30pm curfew and to express their opposition to the brutal treatment of Isla Vista residents. Within 15 minutes, arrests began and soon gave way to beatings and the firing of teargas into the crowd.

"It was obvious that all of those indicted were all well-known campus activist radical leaders," said Vice Chancellor Samuel S. Goodman, a friend of the students.

"The idea that a particular group of well-known people were all together around that building was ridiculous. Especially since some of them were among those arrested the day before and were actually in jail when the bank burned," countered Welch.

At the time, Goodman publically estimated that:

"Perhaps 100 hard-core revolutionaries lived in Isla Vista and another 400 to 500 leftists sided with them…perhaps another 4,000 to 5,000 moderates who can swing either way, and swung left during the riots."

This could have been a white wash to protect students from further persecution by Reagan or an attempt to isolate the university from the political repercussions of failing to control the collapse of 'law and order' in Isla Vista. The rallies, tear gas attacks and arrests continued throughout the course of the year, and fundamentally changed the environment of the community.

"The riots nearly destroyed Isla Vista. Before the crack-down it was cute little place, nice cinemas, new bookstores, more like a Laguna Beach or Santa Cruz or Westwood, and after… it was …burned out. They completely killed the village," Matt Welch said.

Showing its true colors, Bank of America abandoned the Isla Vista branch in 1981, opting instead to open an unmanned ATM on Embarcadero Del Norte.

Today, a residence hall is in place where the bank once existed. A small and barely noticeable plaque in front of the dormitory commemorates Kevin Morgan's needless death. Recent murders of students took place within a few yards of this now forgotten memorial.

Arrests were followed by several years of federal prosecutions. UCSB administrators and SB officials yearned for the "good old days" when the worse offences were intoxicated cheerleaders, panty raids and gotcha parties. As bad as we were, they (remember them) preferred our drunken frat parties to the violent actions of mass murderers, radicals and doomsday anarchist cults.

Das Institute: Soft-Hearted Anarchists

Controversy haunted Isla Vista well after the bank was torched and some of the old beach houses and fraternity residences were torn down and replaced by sterile apartment buildings. The presence of revolutionaries, an influx of hard drugs, and sporadic student anti-war demonstrations led to lower enrollments as well as a general slump in the fraternity system that led to bankruptcy for many houses, including ours.

165

The defunct house was soon occupied by a radical anarchist cult. Members not only possessed many guns, but were also rumored to perform ritual animal sacrifices in order to forestall alien invasions. (Many locals believed that they were affiliated with the Church of Scientology, but this was never confirmed.)

Sometime in the night of July 4, 1970, three men camping on the beach near the UCSB Campus Point were attacked by someone with an axe or a machete. Two of the victims died at the scene. The third victim somehow survived the attack and told authorities at least one of his attackers had long hair and a beard. No money or jewelry was taken so money was not a motive. The violence continued as five other murders on nearby beaches occurred between February, 1970 and June, 1972, three in Santa Barbara, and two in Isla Vista. D.I. members were suspected, but their involvement could never be proven. Isla Vista was frozen with terror.

According to one of the D.I. leaders, a local ex-Red House brother who was involved with a woman living at D.I., several of its members were armed drug dealers. He feared for his life because he had published as expose about the biggest heroin dealer in Santa Barbara County, an FBI informant who was released by the by the feds every time he ratted out other dealers.

"He (the dealer/informant) started stalking me and almost shot me twice (once in public at a restaurant). Lots of fun looking down the barrel of a .45 automatic pointed at your face at pointblank range..." (name withheld)

According another one of its ex-members, D.I. was made up of two groups, radical revolutionaries who expected Nixon or Reagan to declare martial law and cordon off IV at any moment, and the other typical left-leaning Isla Vistans. He recalled that:

"I became friends with some of the more radical element, which included 'Willie' (a selfdescribed anarchist). We loaded our own bullets and had lots of guns, and often went target shooting in the San Marcos Pass area."

"At one point, Willie offered to "take care" of the FBI informant for me. However, when push came to shove (literally) he chickened-out and proposed to hit the guy and knock him to the ground. Willie was a softhearted anarchist and said he just did not have it in him to kill someone so deliberately. Eventually the crisis passed and, if I remember correctly, friends of Willie and the others went bowling together on many occasions at midnight. I lost track of him when I moved away in November 1972."

One more story involving 'Willie' (not his real name) illustrates the tension that gripped IV. "On the night after an informant hit me in a restaurant while flaunting his gun, we heard rumors that he and his drug dealer friends were going to break into Das Institute and shoot everybody in retaliation for ratting them out to the FBI."

These guys had beaten up other residents before, so it seemed a plausible threat. Our ex-brother and his girlfriend had moved into a vacant room at the end of the hall, and "noncombatants" moved to the second floor while everyone else on the first floor armed themselves with weapons. Any movement outside would awaken jittery D.I. members who would reach for their guns. A shotgun leaned up next to the door. In the middle of the night, one of the women residents got up to go to the bathroom and tripped over a bicycle in the hallway. All hell broke loose when she became entangled in the bike.

"All I remember is suddenly lying on the floor with my finger nervously gripping the trigger the shotgun, head and arms out the doorway into the hall, aiming at the dark silhouette who was screaming 'Don't shoot! Don't shoot!' After what seemed forever, someone turned on the hall light exposing woman, stark naked, frozen with one hand up high and the other covering her genitals with guns, rifles and shotguns pointing at her from every doorway! If any one person had started shooting we all would have, and she would have been cut to pieces."

Needless to say, UCSB Administrators and Santa Barbara County officials were not amused by trigger-happy members of Das Institute. The House was eventually raided by the CIA, ATF, FBI, and the Santa Barbara County Health Department.

It took nearly a decade for UCSB to re-establish its academic reputation and almost another 10 years for students and parents to forget the events that took place on Isla Vista. As the rising costs of higher education made state-subsidized higher education as attractive option—especially for families struggling with economic recession and debt—the number of applicants ballooned.

The Angel of Death and the Tweaker

All the favorable publicity and rebuilding efforts ceased on February 23, 2001 when a druggedout misfit drove down Sabado Tarde Road at high speed and deliberately hit a crowd of students. He was David Attias, then 21, the scion of a wealthy Los Angeles family. He emerged from the car and triumphed "I am the angel of death!" as four people were dead or dying on the street. He was known to students as "Crazy Dave" or "The Tweaker." He was convicted of four counts of second-degree murder in 2002, but the same jury later found him to be insane. No doubt he was. Attias was sent to a state hospital for the criminally insane for 60 years. With an influential legal team arguing for him, a Santa Barbara judge later decided that he was no longer a threat to society, and ruled him eligible for release in 2012. His present whereabouts is unknown.

The site where burnt-out Bank of America once stood is now a University office building, across the street from where 6 students were gunned down on Friday, May 23, 2014—seven others were wounded, and suspected gunman Elliot Rodger, 22, died of a self-inflicted gunshot. Both Attias and Rodger were spoiled children of the Hollywood entertainment elite. Attias was the son of a Los Angeles-area entertainment director and Rodger was the son an assistant director on the violent Hollywood blockbuster film *Hunger Games*. Rodger's pre-recorded "hate manifesto" described his "troubled childhood" in Beverly Hills, family conflicts, frustration over not being able to find a girlfriend, hatred of sorority women, contempt for racial minorities and interracial couples, and plans for killing spree. Even the privileged few are resentful about being rejected from the coveted Isla Vista social scene.

As can be seen from an editorial opinion from the UCSB student newspaper following the April 2014 Deltopia riots, little has changed in Isla Vista.

Isla Vista is a volatile cocktail. Some of the explosions that pop in this melting pot are shameful rapes and "riots," stabbings and pollution — and unfortunately, these are the headline grabbers. When friends and relatives from around the globe are worrying about whether or not we survived Deltopia, a reputation builds. It's easy to interpret these events as evidence that Isla Vista is an economic drain on the county and a vapid cultural black hole, but this zoomed-out viewpoint that the media latches onto is not an accurate reflection of our square mile. There's so much going on that slides under the surface and gets swallowed by the noise. The energy here is always palpable, and when it's channeled in the right direction, a truly unique culture emerges. The obvious truth is that Isla Vista is far more complex and sophisticated than the papers, periodicals and primetime newsbreaks portray. The obvious truth is that something is wrong with Isla Vista. But the even more obvious truth, under our very noses, is that there is a vital and lively culture in Isla Vista that thrives and somehow puts all this madness in context. It's only a matter of finding it amidst the chaos. This neighborhood is too strange and vibrant to simply abandon to the rising tides of a party culture which, now more than ever, threatens to drown our voices. It's true that most of us are only here for a few years, but that shouldn't dampen or misdirect our enthusiasm. These are still four years in our very limited lives, and we are lucky enough to be in a place that offers as much room for creativity, freedom and experimentation as it does for drunken shenanigans. College is not just a throwaway time before "real life." We're all at critical points of transition, establishing habits and values that we'll carry far away from this corner of the coast.

SOURCE: Adrian Gronseth and Sean Nolan, *Isla Vista: Born from Fire*. Opinion page of the *Daily Nexus* or UCSB, May 1, 2014.

This perceptive but naïve opinion editorial was written by UCSB students just 3 weeks before Elliott Rodger's murderous Isla Vista rampage.

At some point, someone has to assume responsibility for the craven acts of violence that have repeatedly plagued Isla Vista. Too often, 'outsiders' have been blamed for the carnage that now stalk the once pristine campus-by-the-sea. Nothing could be further from the truth. The pattern of incidents followed by media frenzy, collective sorrow, blaming others, hand wringing, and the resulting patchwork deployment of a few more police patrols does not and will not work. School shootings have become so commonplace that they quickly recede from public memory within weeks only to re-emerge again at regular intervals with the next horrifying act of domestic terrorism. Where is the outrage? Where are the demonstrations against these atrocities?

People have become so callous and indifferent that they no longer feel the pain of others cut down in this volley of hateful gunfire. Feeble attempts to prevent the next round of slaughter have replaced national efforts to determine and address its underlying causes. Classroom teachers are now armed and police officers protect churches. This avoids dealing with a societal malaise so deep and so pervasive that it is nearly impossible to understand. Violence in schools may be predicable, but not preventable.

****

In late 2012, a California middle school student wrote a poignant poem about the horrific shootings a Sandy Hook Elementary in Newtown, Connecticut. When the poem was discovered by a teacher, the girl was summarily expelled from her charter school. Her poem spoke about the possible motivations that could have inspired Adam Lanza's murderous rampage, but apparently that freedom of expression was not allowed at the school; she was suspended and they threatened to permanently expel her. Her school, a charter school in San Francisco, California, saw the poem as a threat and said it violated their zero tolerance policy on violence. The British *Daily Mail* posted an extract from the poem:

> *They wanna hold me back*
> *I run but still they still attack My*
> *innocence, I won't get back I*
> *used to smile*
> *They took my kindness for weakness*
> *The silence the world will never get*
> *I understand the killing in Connecticut*
> *I know why he pulled the trigger*
> *The government is a shame*
> *Society never wants to take the blame*
> *Society puts these thoughts in our head*
> *Misery loves company*
> *If I can't be loved no one can*

Source: Article "California Student Suspended for Newtown Poem"

http://cbldf.org/2013/01/californiastudent-suspended-for-newtown-poem/

President Obama presided over services for 17 mass shootings and terror attacks during his presidency. Each time, the mass murders killed more victims, the latest at an LGBT club in Orlando on June 11, 2016 where 49 died and 53 wounded by an apparent ISIS-inspired hater.

CHAPTER 12: Bless Them Godless Russians and Chinese

Waiting for a flight to Beijing at San Francisco Airport forty years later, a much older (and perhaps wiser) Dr. Mark McGinnis struck up a conversation with a fellow traveler who, he learned, had worked as a construction manager in China for several years. This was Mark's first face-to-face encounter with the Evil Communist Empire, so he was curious about its totalitarian ideology and the oppressed people he had sworn to hate and, if necessary, kill on the battlefield so many decades ago. He wondered if the stereotypes he had heard were true?

- Did they really discard their disabled children on the streets?
- Were they massed on the border and ready to conquer other nations?
- Did they abort millions of their baby daughters?
- Do public officials execute those who practiced certain religions and sell their body parts?
- Do they eat cats and dogs?
- Did they let their babies squat in the dirt and on the street to defecate and urinate?"

During the conversation, the manager related a story illustrating we were deceived during the four decades after the end of the Vietnam War and how much we still didn't know about the Chinese culture, people, or how they achieved the economic miracle of double-digit growth for over thirty years.

The young son of one of the manager's Chinese colleagues was tired of playing with toys made in China so he asked the manager to bring his son a real toy "Made in America" on his next trip home. He gladly obliged, remembering his own joyful childhood filled with BB guns, board games, Gilbert erector sets, Hasbo toys, and a boy's dream gift—a smoke-belching steam engine pulling a Lionel train set.

Upon returning home, the man went from store to store searching for toys 'Made in America." After numerous futile trips, all he could find on the toys were labels "Made in China," "Made in Mexico," and "Made in Thailand." No American made toys could to be found anywhere. Despite the aggressive U.S. anti-communist stand for nearly 50 years following the Second World War, the simple reason our products no longer sell on global markets is that corporate elites have outsourced our industrial base to China and other emerging nations, irrespective of ideology. How we did this is better known than *why* did it was done and *who* benefitted from the massive reverse income redistribution accompanying economic globalization.

We can thank Nixon and his Republican cronies for the so-called "China Initiative" and congratulate Reagan and the Bushes for turning a blind eye to the consequences of outsourcing. Bill Clinton tried to reverse the tread, but he is best remembered for his promiscuity, job creation, NAFTA and balancing the federal budget by reducing spending for four straight years from 19982002. George Dub-ya quickly decimated the Clinton era federal budget surpluses with two unpaid for wars in the Middle East, tax cuts for the rich, and a prescription drug benefit that no one requested—all of which led to the worst recession since the 1930s. Just think of the sophomoric way Bush rationalized the wars: *"What better reason to invade a country than wanting to 'kick some ass' after the 9/11 attacks?"*[1]

Massive federal deficits, accumulated debt, and Congressional gridlock have neutered the fiscal capability of the federal government to accomplish more than sinking deeper in debt. The debt problem is compounded by the fact that "on-budget" federal revenues as a share of the total economy already reached its lowest level in 60 years! (13.1 percent of GDP in 2014 vs. 13.4 percent in 1950.) This is hardly "overspending." Yet conservative Republicans deficit hawks continue beat the tax cut drum and blame "big government spending" without bothering to acknowledge the harmful effects of the generous tax breaks and loopholes still enjoyed by the wealthiest Americans.[2] Greater citizen involvement at the state and local government level is actively discouraged; local elected officials do not want to make changes that might cost them their jobs. Meanwhile, politicians in Red States block most progressive policies because their enactment would undercut Republican Party Congressional strength.

As Americans cope with a dwindling share of a shrinking number of high-paying jobs, enormous increases in productivity have occurred elsewhere, especially in China. Despite Trump's false promises, even if jobs do return, this may only happen by converting higher-paid jobs to lower-paid ones to match our competitors—hardly a long-term strategy for economic recovery.[3]

Corporate elites have pursued globalization in such a disingenuous way that it has further shifted bargaining power away from American workers and concentrated even more wealth in the overflowing coffers of the owners of multi-national corporations.[4] High paying jobs are relocated to cheaper labor markets overseas because it is less expensive to 'outsource' them than to keep factories open in the United States. Trump's threat to slap a 20% border tax on goods manufactured outside the U.S. will only cause a trade war and increase to price of goods to American consumers. Global corporate elites must consider how much profit they are willing to relinquish for greater income distribution and employment opportunity for all. Individual Americans have seen little economic social progress domestically since the mid-1970s. The challenge ahead for corporate and political leaders is to muster the courage necessary to eradicate this debilitating disease and its malignant social symptoms. Meanwhile, certain groups, which exercised identity-based political muscle, have made substantial progress.

College-educated women in America not only receive equal treatment under law, but also excel in careers such as law, politics and medicine formerly accessible only to males. Women can now decide for themselves whether to serve as jurors, join the military or run for political office; they are doing so in record numbers. Twenty-one women now serve in the U.S. Senate and 81 in the House, an all-time high for the U.S. Congress. Janet Yellin was tapped by Obama to succeed Ben Bernanke as Chair of the U.S. Federal Reserve Bank, the first women to hold that powerful position since the FED was created a hundred years ago.

Challenges remain, as more and more of the 31 Red State governors and legislatures gut Obamacare, further restrict immigration, and repeal voting rights protections and civil liberties for women and minorities. Republican social conservatives and religious fundamentalists have shut down abortion clinics and denied LGBT rights in states such as Alabama, Mississippi, North Carolina and Texas. These tactics are thinly veiled and successful attempts to suppress Democratic Party voters, issues and values, including civil and voting rights for youth and minorities and reproductive rights for women.

Even as the so-called Great Recession lingers, and lingers, and lingers, many more Blacks and Hispanics have opportunities to compete for better-paying jobs. Unfortunately, too few goodpaying jobs are available and beleaguered angry working class white males object to anything that looks remotely like identity-based affirmative action.

The Obama administration stabilized the economy and achieved substantial social progress: unemployment rates declined, gay marriage is legal in every state, and Obamacare is the law of the land. The United States has not seen such economic growth since 1999; the unemployment rate has plunged below pre-crisis levels; oil prices have declined as Americas have grown less dependent upon the foreign oil and gas industry; the federal deficit has been cut in half; and 23 million more people insured under Obamacare. Ironically, the wealthy investment class, which typically aligns with Republicans, prospered under the Obama presidency: some CEOs are even criticizing Republican Tea Party intransigence and realigning with Democrats, if for no other reason than their own economic advancement. At this writing, the Dow-Jones industrial average, a leading indicator of economic recovery, is above 20,000—triple what it was when Barack Obama first took office in 2009. More measures would help working families achieve financial security, push higher minimum wage higher, and provide higher education opportunities for low and middle-income students. Unfortunately, none of this will happen during a Trump administration.

The mind fucking of the American Electorate continues unabated: 60 million Americans actually voted for Trump's elitist, racist and plutocratic appeals in the 2016. Hillary received almost 3 million more votes than Trump, but lost because of the vulnerabilities of our antiquated and dangerous Electoral College.

It took Republican counter-operatives less than two election cycles to master the technology and counteract the Democratic Party's voter registration advantage. Among the apparent consequences were suppressed Democratic turnouts and Republican sweeps in the 2014 and 2016 elections. The negative ad strategy was especially effective in silencing low-income persons, minorities, women and youth. In addition to the prolonged recession, one of the major reasons eligible voters failed to participate is that half of all Americans still do not have access to the Knowledge Revolution due to lack of resources necessary to connect with New Media.

Romney reminded us in 2012, with foot squarely in his mouth, that nearly one-half the population (47%) pays no federal income taxes: he labeled them slackers, too many so-called 'freeriders' including aging boomers who snag meager public benefits such as Medicare and Social Security. He neglected to mention that for a family of four to pay no federal income taxes they must earn less than $24,250 per year, barely above poverty wage. Most of those "digital dropouts" are among Romney's lower 47: the rest are among the millions of non-voters who eschew both political parties and candidates. In his haste to shore up right-wing support and blame the poor and aged for being poor and aged, he neglected to mention that the "lower 47" pay social security, payroll, state and local taxes: still, too many voters resent having to shoulder

174

the burden for those who receive 'stuff' (Romney's word) without paying their so-called "fair share."

In the four decades since the end of the wasteful and demoralizing Vietnam War, there have been two futile Gulf Wars, numerous stealth invasions, and a travesty unfolding in Iraq and Syria. Inequities and social injustices remain today as they did 50 years ago and economic conditions for most Americans have worsened. Despite volumes of lawsuits, Justice Department interventions and enforcement of federal regulations, there has been little progress toward equalizing opportunities. Wars in Iraq and Afghanistan are this generation's Vietnam—enormous subsidies to Bush and Cheney's allies in the military industrial complex resulting in humiliating losses of American lives and treasure. No one was surprised that so much Defense Department money found its way back to the pockets of Republican candidates as campaign contributions. Republicans newfound commitment to fiscal austerity, in the form of insisting on lower taxes for the wealthy while slashing educational, healthcare, social services and unemployment benefits for youth, elderly and the poor, is the height of hypocrisy. The bad news for the U.S. is that many of its economic and social institutions are failing.

Racist and xenophobic rhetoric still finds supporters and turns out voters in droves. Rather than focusing on a single unified social body, media-hyped hyper-linked campaign consultants scrutinize micro-segments of the voting population as disaggregated sets of niche markets with different interests and risk profiles. Rather than viewing the electorate as a unified holistic body capable of making decisions for the betterment of society, candidate media ads are custom-tailored to match fragmented voter preferences. Taking a lesson from Nixon's playbook, politicians customize their messages based less on principal than political expediency and voters form opinions from the information given to them by the media. The free exchange of information inevitably includes "alternative facts" (aka false information) and the most effective and organized actors inevitably succeed.

Discouraged from actively participating in political campaigns by pot-smoking Libertarians, militant right wing Republicans and debt-ridden parents, cynical youth have come to believe that the fix is in. Others take the bait and aspire to join Romney, Ryan and now Trump to become *uber*wealthy 1-percenters. While right-wing politicians deliberately ignore social issues, many naïve students attempt to become more politically active: LGBT, civil and voting rights issues predominate, and struggles for living wages, gay rights and marriage equality have become the civil rights causes of today. Political unity further fragments as an increasing number of Americans shun media sources providing several different points-of-view in favor of one-sided news sources that reflect their beliefs.

Despite some civil rights and equal opportunity progress domestically, the U.S. economic engine has stalled with structural unemployment doubling from an average 3-4% in the 1960s to 5-6% today.[5] Trump and other right-wingers insist that the actual number is much higher because many millions have given up. Prospects for a renaissance of the American labor are bleak: the United States is becoming a wholly owned subsidiary of the Big Red House—China, Inc.

China, Inc., Walmart and *Waiting for Superman*

During the Depression and WWII years, America stood solidly behind Democratic Party Leader President Franklin D. Roosevelt and Republican opposition leaders did not try to undercut his authority by making 'side deals' with warring factions. Leaders of the G.I. Generation were also magnanimous victors who helped demilitarize and restore the economies of former enemies with the Marshall Plan in Europe and the Allied Occupation of Japan. We so deeply believed in the righteousness of our cause that we invested billions of dollars to rebuild the shattered economies and political systems of our foes. This strategy appeared to work so long as we insisted that the vanquished convert to our democratic ideology. Under our strong hand, former enemies remade in our image as strong capitalist democratic economic competitors. We successfully instilled the virtues of democratic governance and free-enterprise capitalism in their hearts and minds.

After pseudo-détente with the Soviets in the late 1980s, we also thought we won the Cold War and "rescued" another 3 billion eager capitalist entrepreneurs from the yoke of communism. In retrospect, this judgment may have been naïve and overly optimistic. Most of these eager neocapitalists were from repressive nations, particularly Communist Red China, Russia and its former Soviet puppet-states in Central and Eastern Europe. Many of these nations (kind of) jumped on the capitalist free enterprise bandwagon, but on their own terms. They embraced the free enterprise elements of capitalist systems, but maintained their own authoritarian political systems. Unlike the vanquished Germans and Japanese, our former communist enemies adopted only those aspects of capitalism that best suited their economic interests, while rejecting most democratic political values, principles, and institutions.

We now depend on Chinese financiers for capital to bankroll our public and private infrastructure investment—on their terms. Chinese banks and financial institutions are creditors and bondholders for 10% of our massive $20 Trillion cumulative public debt. Chinese factories produce nearly all of our imported manufactured goods, toys and electronics. We are beholden to China for much of our foreign debt and nearly all of our consumer products.

Chinese economic growth and manufacturing prowess became the envy of the world thanks in large part to its repressive one-child per family birth control policies (at least when judged by Western moral values). That policy is now being phased-out due to a softer economy and shrinking workforce, but China is still the leading exporter of finished goods and has one of the fastest growing economies in the world. China overtook Japan as the second leading consumer of coal and petroleum several years ago and will overtake the United States to become the world's largest economy. Why?

Because the U.S. economy has created too few jobs, produced too many high school dropouts and far too many underemployed college graduates. The number of Americans with baccalaureate degrees increased 25% to 41 million between 2002 and 2012. Three times more Americans have bachelor's degrees now than two generations ago but the number of well-paying jobs has decreased. In 2010, 15% of taxi drivers and 25% of retail sales-clerks had bachelor's degrees. There are too many overeducated and underemployed job seekers: 13 million more job applicants with college degrees than jobs requiring such degrees. Reputable economists estimate that the United States lost 20 million jobs to China and other fast-developing nations during the past decade.

The so-called 'job producers,' aka greedy corporate Wall Street magnates, hoard over $2 Trillion in cash, massive caches of profits used to stonewall progressive change and extort the Obama administration for more corporate welfare. They sponsor right-wing causes, such as campaigns to defund Obamacare, reduce the size of government and further lower taxes for the wealthiest Americans. They cling to Reaganonics and supply-side economics and ignore the consequences for the rest of society. They supported political campaigns of Republican members of Congress committed to blocking any policy initiatives of the Obama administration. At the same time, they pass legislation favorable to the right-wing supporters and their opportunistic foreign donors.

The five descendants of the retail giant Walmart, who inherited their billions from the family patriarch Sam Walton, are among the primary buyers of Chinese merchandise. They grow richer and richer and pay less and less in taxes. Incredibly, their inherited family wealth of $152 billion alone exceeds the cumulative net worth of the bottom **42%** of *all* American families.[6] Thanks to the Walton's and their Communist Chinese allies, thousands of family-owned and operated neighborhood grocery, hardware and retail shops in America have permanently closed or gone bankrupt. Chinese middle-class families have prospered while the U.S. middle-class has nearly disappeared.[7] Structural inequalities and generous tax loopholes for the rich have increased as median family incomes dropped by almost 10 percent during the Great Recession. In some regions of the country, over 40% of youth and minorities are un- or underemployed. Donald Trump's hollow promises "to bring jobs back" only worsen prospects for economic recovery by raising hopes of dispirited workers.

The United States government sponsors a Trump University-like swindle called the EB-5 Investment Program for Foreign Investors. (To some, the EB stands for "easy bucks.") It allows foreign nationals can purchase U.S. visas for themselves and their families by investing in United States economic development projects. The high demand for capital creates a rich environment for foreign nationals to buy their way into the country. Democratic values again subservient to the highest bidder. Foreign investors have to make a $500,000 US investment and a commitment to create 10 jobs for friends and relatives. Investors, including citizens from such robust democracies as China, Nigeria, and Russia have collectively contributed tens of millions of dollars to finance private development projects in selected regions of the United States. Wealthy states such as Arizona, Florida, and New York are prime beneficiaries and, because much of the foreign money funds charter schools, American public schools are the biggest losers.

Despite only mild political backlash, Chinese investors have already contributed millions of dollars to fund businesses and charter schools in the U.S. Charter schools are a privately run public school defrauds that benefit from an influx of foreign funds during the current economic recession. Charters divert resources from public schools by "cherry picking" the best students with hollow promises of higher quality education and better paying jobs. Advocates say these publically funded private schools stimulate competition and offer a greater range of choices for families. Detractors see them for what they are: thinly veiled attempts to drain money from the already cash-starved public schools and break the power of teachers' unions.

Patently false and misleading 'opportunities" for self-improvement and admission to the middle class are depicted in the charter school propaganda film *Waiting for Superman* (The title comes from one student's fantasy dream of being rescued from poverty by Superman.). He ain't comin,' folks. Sad but true.

The "for-profit" model of charter schools uses education management organizations (EMOs) to skim off large portions of taxpayers' money even when the school is purportedly managed as a not-for-profit. At this writing, about 200 different EMOs operating in 28 states. Charter schools are deregulated and free from most state laws other than those governing health and public safety. In Louisiana, deregulation has become so extreme that no teacher certification is even required. In the American Southwest, the pervasive influence of the University of Phoenix, the original forprofit online institution, graduates many who enter the teaching profession. New teachers are evaluated by former UP graduates.

Throughout our history, confidence in the future has fallen or risen in response to changing economic and political circumstances. While negativity persists, confidence in economic recovery and growth are retarded: families hesitate to spend; businesses reluctant to invest; individuals lose confidence in the future. American life no longer has the energizing narrative that has given us meaning and purpose from the beginning of our national existence.

Wither the Obama Coalition

Like Nixon, Superman is dead, as moribund as our public schools. Many of our high school graduates don't even qualify for entrance to our own universities! Only one-third of high school graduates apply for college and must take the ACT or SAT entrance tests. They are often unprepared for the most rudimentary subjects. Remedial courses in community colleges full to the brim with students seeking to master basic math, reading, and writing skills that should have been acquired in high school. Recent studies by the SAT test-masters confirm the downward slide in scores and the lack of preparation for college-level courses.

Despite the continuing poor performance of our students, global competition for brainpower and human resources continues unabated. Growing numbers of Chinese students are better qualified to enter elite American universities than many U.S. high school graduates. According to the Institute of International Education, more than 250,000 Chinese students study in United States colleges and universities, fully 25 percent of total number of international students in the entire country. It is unlikely that they are studying democratic institutions. In a bizarre twist, some elite universities have placed 'quotas' on the number of international students that are admitted in order to accommodate less-qualified Americans. Imagine affirmative action necessary for American students to attend our own colleges and universities?

Even the Chinese feel the pressure from a weakened economy, Trump's election, disaffected workers and other Asian Tiger competitors. In the ultimate degradation of the boomer generation, America now trades with Semi-Communist Vietnam--a humiliating and disgraceful testament to the two million American men who served in Vietnam and the nearly 60,000 who were sacrificed on Kennedy, Johnson and Nixon's Alter of Capitalism.

Rather than living in an egalitarian society envisioned by Sixties reformers, boomers were deceived by their government, unaware of dozens of ill-conceived covert CIA-sponsored invasions of countries with disagreeable leaders, fooled by false promises of racial harmony, and forced to take sides in conflict that few understood. Too many suffered from two decades of *overt* warfare in a God-forsaken distant part of Southeast Asia allegedly fought to 'protect the rice crop' from the Godless Chinese Communists. Resources diverted from necessary domestic infrastructure to protect corporate interests globally.

Income Inequality and Political Stagnation

Americans have experienced nearly 10 years of weak economic growth (at this writing) accompanied by a steep drop in property values, disappearance of retirements funds, and a jobless economic recovery. Income inequality has further segregated economic elites from the rest of society. Economist Joseph Stieglitz identifies reasons why inequality holds back economic recovery and forces millions into poverty.

The immediate cause is increasing middle class debt that has historically supported consumer spending and primed the economy. Growth in the decade before the economic crisis was unsustainable—relying on the bottom 80 percent of the population consuming about 110 percent of their income. In the U.S., where the gap between rich and poor has grown at a faster rate than any other developed country, the top 1 percent captured 95 percent of post-recession growth (since 2009), while the remaining 90 percent of Americans held steady or became poorer.

Heavy debt was inevitable. The deterioration of the middle class since the 1970s, a phenomenon interrupted only briefly during Clinton-Gore years in the late 1990s, has made it nearly impossible for most Americans to invest in their future, educate their children, start, or improve businesses. The premeditated destruction of the middle-class, which began during the

Reagan years, has held back tax receipts, especially because the wealthiest top 1-percenters are so adroit at avoiding taxes and getting Washington to give them additional tax breaks.[8]

Income inequality is associated with more frequent and severe boom-and-bust cycles making the economy far more vulnerable to foreign influence. Although inequality alone was not the only cause the most recent economic crisis, it is no coincidence that the late 1920s — the last time inequality of income and wealth in the United States was so high—ended with the Great Crash and the First Great Depression.[9]

Our skyrocketing inequality—so contrary to the past meritocratic ideal of America as a place where anyone who works hard can succeed—guarantees that bright youth born of parents with limited means are far less likely to live up to their potential. Children in other rich countries like Canada, Denmark, France, Germany, Japan and Sweden have a better chance of exceeding their parents' expectations than do most American kids. More than one-fifth of our children live in poverty—the second worst of all the advanced economies, putting us behind countries like Bulgaria, Latvia and Greece.

After nearly four decades of political gridlock, stagnant wage growth and the greatest economic downturn since the Great Depression of the Thirties, almost nothing has changed.[10] Unemployment rates have further depressed job opportunities and wages. American middle-class family incomes have suffered most. As Washington Post columnist, Dana Milbank recently observed: "The gap in wealth and income between rich and poor is the worst since the Great Depression, and the gap between the rich and the middle class is at its highest since the government began keeping such statistics 30 years ago. After more than three decades of income growth for the wealthiest 10 percent and stagnation for everybody else, the top 3 percent now has more wealth than the bottom 90 percent."

The most important economic asset for most Americans is (or was) their home. As prices plummeted during the recession so did household wealth, especially since so many had borrowed so much to pay the inflated values of their homes in anticipation of continually escalating real estate prices. Large numbers had negative net worth as median household incomes fell from $56,000 in 1999 to $51,000 in 2012. Rapidly plunging house prices and a stock market crash were the immediate contributors. Some of that loss has been recovered with the stock market rebound, but many family fortunes are still well below pre-recession levels.[11] The wealth gap between Whites, Blacks and Hispanics has reached record levels. When the economy tanks, the poor lose everything and the rich loose only a percentage.

According to Joseph Stieglitz and other compassionate capitalists, we could have enabled homeowners who were "underwater" (owe more money on their homes than they are worth) to get a fresh start by writing off principal in exchange for giving banks a share of the gains—if and when home prices ever recover. Better yet, we could have recognized that when young people are jobless, their skills atrophy. We could have adopted policies which ensured that every young person was either in school, in a training program or on a job. We could have encouraged young adults to serve their nation or communities in exchange for loan forgiveness. Instead, we did nothing and let consumer debt, student debt and youth unemployment double during the Great Recession.

Not only are income inequality and wage stagnation at their highest levels in nearly a century, but an 'empathy gap' further separates the rich and the poor. The widening income gulf between the haves and have-less is troubling, but perhaps less so than the disdainful attitudes expressed by right-wing politicians and their followers. Those who have benefitted from the "Reagan Revolution" firmly believe that "the poor are poor because they are poor." Apart from the financial inequities, an entirely different gap exists due to the inability to see oneself in a less advantaged person's condition. The callous indifference of the richest Americans toward others affects economics in our society as well as globally. Reducing the economic gap may be impossible without also addressing the chasm in empathy between the have and the have-nots.

CHAPTER 13: The Political Assault on Freedom and Literacy

In a prophetic foreshadowing of our current educational crisis, the President's Commission on Higher Education in 1947 warned that:

> *"If the ladder of educational opportunity rises high at the doors of some youth and scarcely rises at all at the doors of others, while at the same time formal education is made a prerequisite to occupational and social advance, then education may become the means, not of eliminating race and class distinctions, but of deepening and solidifying them."*

Those words offer a strikingly prescient depiction of education in our times.

The American dream of universal education has deteriorated from enabling upward mobility to exacerbating economic decline and social stagnation. College-going now resembles a medieval caste system, further separating Americans who grew up in different social strata and widening economic divisions between them. The consequences are vast, including stark differences between graduates and non-graduates in employment rates, lifetime earnings, health, and civic engagement. Even lifespan is affected: non-college graduates can expect to live an average of 15 years *less* than college graduates do. Rather than questioning why this happened and how the regressive status quo could be changed, too many accept the current realities of separate but unequal economic segregation as a future inevitability.

The struggle for educational equality took center stage in American life during the later decades of the 20th century. The historic *Brown v. Board of Education* Supreme Court ruling in 1954 led to the expansion of public education during the Great Society years and dramatic increases in college accessibility from the mid-1960s to the mid-1980s. Equal educational opportunity legislation provided hope for the future in the minds of millions of low income Americans previously excluded from both private and state-supported higher education. With these rulings, the infinite human potential to develop science, technology, art and culture was unleashed—it least that is what many thought.

Today, public education lies in tatters, an openly class-based system. Corporate vultures and their political lackeys "cash in" on the growing for-profit education "marketplace"—treating education as a personal business opportunity rather than civil obligation. Sixty years after *Brown*, public school districts are starved of funding, segregated schools have become the norm again, and the inflated costs of higher education are an interminable nightmare for massively indebted low-income students and their families. Politicians divert attention by falsely blaming teachers for student failures while ignoring the effects of family income on education. This is a distraction from the intractable problems of American education—not test scores, teachers or curricula—but racebased re-segregation and the terrible growth of poverty.[1]

In the meantime, big businesses siphon off taxpayer dollars for education alongside the banks and hedge funds, which view American education as an "emerging market" worth an estimated $50 billion annually. In addition to direct funding of charter schools and for-profit colleges, the federal government provides generous tax breaks encouraging banks, financial institutions and individuals to invest in private school construction. One ballsy Chinese-American entrepreneur even "guarantees" admission to an Ivy League University for a mere $600,000. Such a deal, if you can afford it!

The Assault on Public Education

As a nation used to global leadership, we face a perilous future. Academic achievement levels in the U.S. continue to plummet. Our graduates now rank in the mid-20s to lower 30s on comparable math, science and reading tests with students from other countries, especially Chinese. Even oil and natural gas companies pony up big cash to air television commercials decrying the decline in U.S. math and science scores. Concurrently, scarce resources drain from inner city and rural schools cynically labeled "dropout factories." While politicians lament the decline in public school achievement, they enroll their own children in pricy private schools and force minorities to scramble for limited admission to charter schools. The rise of for-profit colleges, deep cuts in federal student aid, and the demise of state funds for public colleges and universities helped produce these circumstances.

Why has the United States drifted so far from its noble aspirations following WWII?

Cuts in public education and college tuition increases alone do not explain the depth of the crisis in education. We need also to consider what has become of government's support for students and institutions. In reality, few students who attend elite private nonprofit colleges and flagship public universities—which advertise high sticker prices—pay full fare. Even if they do, what they borrow amounted to a valuable investment…until now.

Hundreds of academic institutions teeter on the brink of financial disasters similar to those which preceded the housing market and mortgage meltdowns. Sudden academic deflation could have even more catastrophic effects than the meltdown decimating housing values a decade ago, one of the leading causes of the Great Recession. If we continue along this dysfunctional path, we will slide further away from the meritorious ideal of greater equality and widespread upward mobility that characterized education in the mid to late 20th century.

Loss of hope for the future has occurred primarily among people earning low to moderate incomes. Individuals in those groups are less likely to graduate from college than those in their parents' generation. This disturbing trend has developed during the same decades in which economic inequality has widened and a college degree has become more important than ever in determining Americans' lifetime employment opportunities and income. Moreover, that doesn't even take into account the kind of degree attained.[2]

Despite considerably lower price tags at the state-supported public colleges attended by eight out of ten American students, soaring tuition consumes substantially more of the average family's income than in the past, making enrollment, even at lower costs, unaffordable for many. As resources are stretched thin at public institutions, class sizes have swelled, more sections are taught online or by adjuncts or graduate students rather than in person by full-time professors. Budgetary constraints have forced colleges to offer less academic support for students. This has contributed to lower graduation rates, especially at large overcrowded state universities. Fiscal conservatives misuse numbers to justify budgetary reductions forcing parents into private alternatives. The wealthy have always had greater advantages in finding their way to college and in succeeding once they get there. Here again, we need to consider how social priorities have been neglected over the past 50 years.

Tuition rates have grown for reasons unrelated to government's role, and student aid has failed to keep pace. Higher education spending in the states has been effectively displaced by spending in such areas as corrections, law enforcement and health care. In part, the mandatory features of these programs compel states to provide those services, while aid for colleges is considered "discretionary" and therefore more vulnerable to budget cuts. Echoes of Ronald Reagan: higher education seen as 'luxury' public expense that can be provided by other for-profit and private universities. Stark correlations exist between increased prison spending and education cuts, with many of the states with highest incarceration rates making the deepest education cuts.[3] Lower tax receipts resulting from the Second Great Recession, and the rising value of the dollar vis-à-vis foreign currencies, have forced nearly all state and local governments to cutback services vital to qualified students, particularly those at the bottom and middle rungs of the economic ladder. Between 1990 and 2015, state governments decreased higher education funding even as operating costs increased. To close the gap, colleges raised tuition 113 percent in real terms between those years. As institutions became increasingly privatized, low-income students and their families shoulder the burden of inflated costs of public higher education. Some state university campuses have been designated "enterprise units," a political contrivance, which virtually cuts them off from state, appropriates and requires them to compete with private universities for funding. State community colleges and universities are particularly hard hit by budget cuts.[4]

Among the current issues facing education in America: under performing schools; imbalanced student teacher ratios; large disparities between urban and suburban neighborhood schools; and the politicization of public education. As the entire country worries about the U.S. lagging behind educationally and innovatively, states try to find answers, other than more money, to solve their educational woes. Many schools have received failing grades by their states and remained "F" schools over extensive periods. In response to failing schools, states have tried different reforms like extending the school day for those particular schools and/or removing the entire administrative leadership and replacing them with new administrators. States have also begun closing failing schools, leaving many students to be pushed to another school in their district, leading to higher levels of attendance in buildings with classrooms and teaching staffs that remain the same. This leads to disproportionate ratios of students in classrooms to the number of teachers on staff and further segregates public schools.[5] Which families are hurt the most?

While commonly assumed that when it comes to paying for college, the middle class is squeezed (because rich kids are supported by their parents and poor kids get financial aid) but, in fact, it is the poorest students who are under the financial pressure.[6] When you match students by income, race, and academic preparation, an entering student is more likely to receive a bachelor's degree if she starts at a four-year institution than at a community college. For-profit colleges often produce poor results as well. Mountains of reports, economists and education experts have documented the stratification in American college going; they have shown a commensurate rise in inequality in college attainment. *Students from rich families are nearly nine times more likely to complete a four-year BA degree than those from poor families.*[7]

In the United States now, as in the past, attending college is the only sure way to move up the economic ladder. The total price for tuition, books and living on campus at the average public university costs over $25,000 per year. At private colleges, the total can run a staggering $65,000 per year. Four years of college costs between $90,000 and $260,000. Think of the generational change this way: average tuition and fees for four years at a top-ranked public university cost the same in the Sixties as just *one semester* now costs at a comparable institution. That is the stark reality of inflated prices charged and paid for higher education, under the delusion that a college degree is the only sure vehicle for social mobility. For all but the most affluent families, borrowing more and falling further into debt becomes an economic deathtrap.

While public university budgets are slashed, lawmakers have permitted the for-profit education industry to capture a huge portion of federal student-aid funds, despite its poor record of serving students. For-profit colleges charge more than the public institutions, forcing nearly all students to borrow far higher amounts. Beginning in the late 1990s, lawmakers relaxed accounting restrictions on the sector, making it even easier for administrators to take advantage of federal largess. Congress did this despite these institutions lacking established forms of self-regulation and quality control that have long been in place at most public and nonprofit colleges. Despite the absence of such self-governance, advocates of more-extensive public oversight for the sector have faced an uphill battle. Efforts by the U.S. Department of Education to regulate for-profits produced a watered-down set of rules in 2011, most of which were discarded by a federal judge one year later.

Student debt exceeded credit-card debt for the first time in 2010 and continues to mount. The average graduate has about $30,000 in student loans, joining the tens of millions of other adults who collectively owe more than $1.8 trillion in student loans. That burden is largest in many Northeastern and Mid-Atlantic states, a few Southeastern states and in California. Some of those states—especially in the Northeast and Mid-Atlantic—have the highest share of adults with bachelor's degrees. Student debt can almost never be wiped out, even in bankruptcy. Little-known laws in 22 states on the books as far back as 1990 allow authorities to garnish wages and revoke driver's licenses if someone falls behind in student loan repayment. Advocates for repeal say that these restrictions have real consequences for people who cannot make a dent in their student debt. Parents who co-sign loans cannot have the debt discharged even if the child dies. The debt is still collectible even if the school, operated for-profit and owned by exploitative financiers, provided an inadequate education, enticed students and their families with misleading promises, or failed to prepare them for a decent, well-paying job. Dropout rates for some for-profits exceed 50% and that industry spends more money on marketing than it does on instruction. Why don't corporate big-shots flush with all that cash follow the socially responsible actions of Buffet, Gates and Zuckerberg and offer to pay off those loans in exchange for American students' focusing on careers necessary to restore American manufacturing?

On the opposite end of the scale, retirement accounts for many war baby boomers have all but disappeared as their numbers grow and the jobless recovery deepens. More Americans are now over 65 than at any other time in our history: 76 million aging boomers, a 7.1 percent increase over 2010, when the nation's total population rose by only by 1.7 percent. This creates yet another crisis of confidence for elder boomers—especially for the prematurely unemployed—that affects economic security, hope for the future, and personal well-being.

Bureaucratic Homeopathic Pluralism

Unlike their parents or grandparents' generations, boomers look for alternatives to impersonal, high-cost and high-tech industrial medical care. Most accept alternative treatments and use less costly holistic medicine as a matter economic survival. Fiscal responsibility mandates major changes in healthcare delivery systems. The two largest federal programs, Medicaid, government-funded healthcare for the poor, and Medicare, the healthcare system for boomers, grow at such unsustainable rates that they, like all other federal so-called "entitlements", are targeted for deep cuts and additional restrictions in the future.

As the 21st century recession and jobless recovery lingers, the costs of basic necessities such as food and healthcare continue to rise, albeit more slowly. Despite the increased access to healthcare brought about by Obamacare, medical-industrial-complex now consumes 18% of total U.S. GDP or wealth. No other advanced industrialized country in the world even comes close to spending that amount, much of it wasted on gold-plated procedures and unnecessary testing. During the 1960s, in sharp contrast, just 5% of our now dormant GDP was consumed by healthcare.

Soon, $1 out of every $5 of our debt-ridden national economy will be devoured by emergency room care, drugs, hospitals, insurance premiums, and physician's salaries. Despite the fact that nearly half of all healthcare revenues come from government, the medical establishment fights tooth-and-nail to oppose any form of reasonable market-based cost controls to bring down the rate of increase in costs. As costs have ballooned, satisfaction with access and quality has declined. Worse, younger Americans live in poorer health and will die earlier than their counterparts in other developed countries, with far higher rates of death from diabetes, firearms, car accidents, obesity and drug addiction.[8] For unarmed elderly not-as-great boomers, there is a thin positive aspect in an otherwise dismal forecast.

Medical marijuana use is now legal in 28 states and the District of Columbia. Seven states and DC allow recreational use of marijuana without a prescription, soon to be followed by dozens of others. Colorado legalized and licenses marijuana stores for recreational use since 2012. Governments desperate for cash are imposing 15-25% 'sin taxes' on the purchases of the dreaded Gateway Drug. Damn the federal government and full-speed ahead! Colorado has earned so much money from its marijuana tax that the state must rebate money to taxpayers. President Obama, who was a former member of a <u>choom gang</u> himself, had no interest in using the FBI or any other federal agency to pinch potheads. Purchasing dope from the local Cannabis Store is certainly less adventurous than clandestine road trips to Mexico, but it makes good economic sense when compared to the high cost of enforcing outmoded drug laws. Bob Marley's descendants are betting that his image will sell "premium" marijuana to the masses.

Marley Inc. has created *Marley Natural*, a global cannabis brand that will offer "heirloom Jamaican cannabis strains inspired by those Bob Marley enjoyed." *Marley Natural* will also produce and market cannabis and hemp topicals such as sun-repair creams and lotions containing Jamaican botanicals. The herb has gone mainstream and created demands for other weed-laced products. One California firm is marketing a marijuana tampon to ease the pain on menstrual cramps. Maybe those Sixties rumors about tobacco companies patenting names like Acapulco Gold, Maui Wowi and Panama Red really are true?

Following the lead of Holland, Portugal, Switzerland and other European countries, most Americans have finally accepted marijuana as a leisure recreational substance, not unlike beer or wine, licensing, selling and taxing cannabis in state-regulated outlets. Local political opposition to its controlled consumption withers as political coffers begin to fill with sin tax money. Cannabis oils treat serious childhood afflictions such as ADHD, autism, and epilepsy.

This sea change in attitudes and its implications for government spending—one of the leading drivers of public debt and deficits—are apparent. Scientific research is confirming the positive medical effects of marijuana, including its potential for treating a wide range of diseases, from sleep disorders, to Alzheimer's to glaucoma.[9] Plentiful availability and widespread use of the forgetful drug may also treat diseases such as cancer, heebie-jeebies, PTSB and, concurrently, reduce dependence on expensive high-tech industrialized medicine, opioids and big pharma.

Ironically, open access may ease the pain baby boomers have inflicted upon themselves with their high-risk lifestyles.

Boomer's reckless behavior can be partially explained by loss of faith in just about everything: corporations, leaders, politics, Roy Rogers, organized religion, economists and the media. The fires of cynicism have been fanned by simplistic right-wing Reaganesque propaganda hammering away at 'liberal' Robin Hood social policies that have allegedly taken resources from the rich and given to the poor. Whom do they think they are kidding?

Ever since the Reagan-Bush snow job, the richest elites have stuffed their bank accounts with more loot. The top 1% took home 95% of income growth from 2002 to 2012; lower and middle-class households, those most likely to spend their incomes rather than save them, earn lower minimum wages today, when adjusted for inflation, than they did in 1967! That means no increase in purchasing power for two generations! No wonder there is boom in marijuana sales, legal and illegal.[10]

American Plutocracy

Boomers be the last American generation to experience liberal democracy and the first to experience authoritarian plutocracy. Since John F. Kennedy's assassination, citizen interlopers have been eliminated from politics by security measures and repressive methods initiated by Nixon and later expanded by Reagan. Nixon's phalanx of corrupt advisers (Haldeman, Erilichmann, and Kissinger) later known as the "Berlin Wall," isolated him and stonewalled the Congressional investigation years later during the Watergate investigation. Direct citizen-topolitician contact without media interference, talking heads, threats, or security concerns vanished, along with citizens' access to unfiltered face-to-face contacts with prospective political candidates. The same institutions and interests benefitting most from apathy, cynicism, and low electoral participation have actively discouraged civic participation.

The gargantuan and unintelligible federal tax code permits purchase of media ads by "unaffiliated" individuals or groups who purchase air time in behalf of their Congressional, presidential, or state and local candidates, without having to disclose the amounts spent or the names of contributors. The Supreme Court has obligingly endorsed this oligarchical charade in *Citizen's United vs. Federal Election Commission (FEC)*, *McCutcheon v. FEC*, and *Speechnow.org v. FEC*. Interest group lobbies representing big corporations and foreign investors engulf political parties and dominate congressional committees, forming an impenetrable Iron Triangle of reciprocal influence peddling.

Since Nixon, the American voter has been excluded from having any real impact on public policy making. Their opinions and votes, to paraphrase Sigmund Freud, have been relegated to the status of "sheep debating dinner menus with hungry wolves." The wolves were gathering for the kill long before big money dominated national politics. In his farewell speech, over five decades ago, President Dwight D. Eisenhower showed his true moderate convictions and warned,

> *"In the councils of government, we must guard against the acquisition of unwarranted influence, whether sought or unsought, by the military-industrial complex. The potential for the disastrous rise of misplaced power exists and will persist. We must never let the weight of this combination endanger our liberties or democratic processes. We should take nothing for granted."*

Today, most cynical and skeptical citizens take just about everything political for granted. We can add the national security-industrial, media-industrial and medical-industrial complexes to Ike's growing list of interests dominating electoral politics. The two major political parties are wholly owned subsidiaries of big money interests, media conglomerates, large corporations and American family dynasties.

The dark art of political persuasion via the mass media has been perfected ever since the Sixties. Today, access to the White House, state houses and courthouses is less a bottom-up democratic process than a top-down money-addicted, sanitized and privately funded mediaindustrial circus. The Internet has transformed modern political interactions from aural and visual to online and interactive. The power of new social media to guide marketing and public opinion was painfully demonstrated in recent campaigns. This emerging and unstoppable trend is having neither a positive nor unifying effect on civic dialogue, political participation or voter turnouts. Quite the opposite, the cacophony of deceptive and negative ads is squashing meaningful dialogue, suppressing issue discussion and discouraging electoral participation. Collective anger and emotion prevail over information and rational discourse.

Since the 1994 elections, constructive bipartisanship has all but vanished from the political arena. Both chambers of Congress are more polarized today than at any time since the post-Civil War Reconstruction era. Both parties have become more internally homogeneous and unified, and moderate Republicans have all but vanished. This uber-partisan environment not only hinders public officials from enacting bold new landmark laws, but also prevents them from performing even basic tasks such as budgeting. When factions within Congress have managed to unite in the past two decades, the interests they respond to most reliably have been those with the deepest pockets.

Money lubricates political machinery stuck in gridlock—endowing our political system with features of a plutocracy, with a wealthy class effectively controlling government. We need to reject the advantage that powerful corporate interests have over our futures—at least when we vote.[11]

K-Street lobbyists are hired guns for Wall Street billionaires with only one mission—winning elections. Experts and "talking head" media specialists are drawn from centers of power and relied upon to interpret reality and explain policy. They, in turn, depend on press releases written by corporations for their scripted responses. Hard news media vacuums are filled with celebrity gossip, cooking shows, lifestyle stories, reality shows, sports and trivia. Corporations own the press outright, hire journalists as messengers for the elites, and promote themselves as celebrities. Journalistic super-stars earn millions of dollars for their networks and closely align with the interests of political parties.

During two terms in office, President Obama waged full-scale domestic warfare against selfish Congressional Republicans equally adamant against any changes in tax codes favoring the ultrawealthy since the so-called 'Reagan Revolution' in the 1980s. How many times can we be fooled?

The ultra-rich benefit from huge wealth transfers from a dwindling middle-class—too many victims do not realize that they being ripped off. The American plutocracy not only survives but flourishes after the 2016 Presidential Election.

From Seclusion to Delusion

As the old saying goes, "if you remember the '60s, you probably weren't there." No matter, Madison Avenue takes you back with a slew of ad campaigns celebrating the sights and sounds of the decade…filled with images such as Volkswagen mini-buses festooned with groovy graffiti, daisies and other flower power symbols, peace signs, psychedelic drawings in Day-Glo colors and "hair, long beautiful hair, shining, gleaming, streaming, flaxen, waxen" (to quote a lyric from the era). All that is missing are helicopters, tear gas canisters and riot police. The priceless folk-rock music legacy invokes the 1960s. Commercials on television, radio and on the internet play tunes by Dylan, Credence Clearwater Revival, Rolling Stones, Crosby, Stills, Nash & Young, Lesley Gore, the Lovin' Spoonful, the Spencer Davis Group, and Canned Heat.

The last thing in the world that Sixties Survivors want to hear are cutesy TV commercials with their music as background.

Many of the survivors found seclusion in their beach houses, mountain top hideouts, and isolated suburban McMansions. They retreated from inner cities as interstate super-highways and so-called California 'freeways' expanded, following the construction of energy-hungry new suburban homes with five-car garages and swimming pools on once verdant landscapes. These ozone-destroying energy-wasters constructed at a time when gasoline was 29 cents a gallon and ample tax money was available to build and staff high quality public schools in suburban neighborhoods. As children, many boomers biked or walked to neighborhood schools. Those days are over.

The American Dream has morphed into a separate but unequal urban ghetto or suburban enclave, replete with quickie drive-ins, meth labs, half-vacant retail shopping centers and smog. The tattered suburban exterior of abandoned buildings reeks with youthful repression which for some millennials quickly progresses from cruising aimlessly 'on the boulevard' to silent rebellion, theft, heroin and PCP use—all to escape the maddening boring manicured green lawns, golf courses, and the prospect of continued sub-minimum wage underemployment.

For many, the American Dream evaporated into a numbing white powder of boredom and underemployment. Can you blame anyone for being angry when the inflation-adjusted purchasing power of wages is virtually the same today as 50 years ago?[12] Selfish Republicans have repeatedly blocked increases in the minimum wage to serve their corporate masters. The federal minimum wage has remained $7.25 since 2009 and many states are even lower. Alabama, Louisiana, Mississippi, South Carolina and Tennessee have no set minimum wage. The Obama administration raised minimum wages for federal employees and contractors, and persuaded a few corporations (Target, McDonalds, and Walmart) to provide a starvation wage of $10 an hour for millions of retail workers. Why did it take so long? One of Trump's first actions will doubtless be to repeal those executive orders.

Boomers may be wealthier and more mobile than their parents or offspring, but they still had to make difficult personal choices: some accepted the draft, others joined voluntarily; some fled to Canada, others became protesters; a few dropped out to enjoy music and drugs. Activists pushed politicians hard enough to force passage of the 26th Amendment during the Vietnam War, providing the right to vote for individuals who were eighteen years of age. (Previously, the 14th Amendment had set the voting age at 21.) Congress and state legislatures finally listened to pleas from males who were old enough to serve and die for their country but unable to vote for those who were sending them to war. Such a simple addendum, but so costly to thousands of young lives.

****

Despite some progressive changes, citizens have less control now of their deep-pocket democracy than they did 50 years ago. According to a majority of members of the U.S. Supreme Court, money is equivalent to "free speech" and any type of campaign finance regulation, like machine-gun registration, would be anathema to basic Constitutional freedoms. Late Supreme Court Justice Antonin Scalia went even further in his derisive assessment, suggesting that certain protections granted under the 14th Amendment and the Voting Rights Acts were "racial entitlements" no longer necessary for the enforcement of federal laws in the states.

As a result, electoral processes have been turned upside down, with political parties now more dependent on candidates than the candidates need the major parties. Donald Trump is the Frankenstein created by our antiquated and vulnerable two-party winner-take-all electoral process. Family dynasties like the Bushes and Kennedys and now the Trumps—and soon possibly the Clintons and Obamas—dominate as much through access to economic power as partisan "dark money" political support.[13] Trump's campaign taught us that candidates must possess telegenic personalities transmitted via television and social media—but little else.

The 'reality show' charade of candidate debates and state primary electoral contests now revolve around contrived intra-party squabbles and 30-second TV sound bites sponsored by big money candidates and contributors who fund attack ads, attack ads, and more attack ads. Big money campaigns focus on early primaries with less than 2 percent of the nation's population: candidates have to pretend to care about these charades while seeking campaign funds from billionaires. Multi-billionaires are courted for their campaign 'donations' and candidates feed off interest groups and Super Pac money, laundered through thinly-veiled front organizations supposedly supporting the 'issues' rather than the candidates or parties. Money now screams louder than votes in politics. How loud?

The total amount spent on the entire presidential campaign by both parties in 1960 was barely $10 *million*. In stark contrast, the 2016 Presidential Election was the most expensive in history, likely to be the first $6 *billion* political campaign in American history (not including Russia's contribution). The vast sums raised and spent by the Democratic and Republican candidates undercut claims that the United States is a democracy in which the people rule. Big money rules, dominating the process of selecting the candidates and effectively determining the outcome of the vote on November 8, 2016.

The most significant statistic from 2016's election is the **massive drop in support** for both the Democratic and Republican candidates. Whether attributable to Russian Hackers, voter suppression, or just disgust about the campaign, Hillary Clinton received about ten million fewer votes than Barack Obama did eight years ago. Trump, who lost the popular vote but suspiciously won the electoral vote, received the least number of votes of any candidate from either party since 2000. These figures are even more striking because of an increase in eligible voters: 18 million more since 2008.

Far larger and more troubling, the **100 million eligible voters** who abstained from the 2016 election or voted for a third party. In Michigan, nearly 100,000 voted for candidates and ballot measures but failed to vote for either Clinton or Trump. In other words, while Clinton and Trump received the vote of 26.6 and 25.9 percent respectfully of eligible voters, 43.2 percent chose neither. Among those who voted, Trump received the votes of just over 27 million white men, less than the 27.2 million who voted for Romney in 2012. As for women, 35.5 million voted for Clinton, a significant drop from the 37.6 million who voted for Obama in 2012. Remarkably, just 30 percent of women eligible to vote cast ballots for Clinton in 2016, compared to 47 percent who did not vote. The Republican strategy of state-by-state voter suppression worked better than they imagined.

Clinton also suffered significant losses among African-American, Latinos and young voters. In 2012, Barack Obama won 16.9 million African-American votes, over 3 million more than Clinton's 13.7 million. Just over 9 million Latinos voted for both Obama and Clinton, despite a significant increase in the Latino voting population over the past four years. Among younger voters aged 18-29, Clinton's 13.6 million votes is roughly 8 percent less than Obama's 14.8 million figure from 2012, despite a similar growth in this age group.

As a percentage of votes cast, all racial groups swung toward Republican candidates in record numbers as compared to 2012. Asian-Americans showed the highest (11 percentage points), Latinos (8 percentage points), African-Americans (7 percentage points), with White voters having the lowest swing to Republicans (1 percentage point). Economic issues drove these shifts, which occurred amid the broader framework of massive abstention from political activity. Fifty-two percent of voters said the economy was the most important issue in the election, far above the second most important issue of honesty at 18 percent. Racial and gender issues failed to register, while 68% said their financial situation was the same or worse than it was four years ago. Thirty-nine percent said they were looking for a "change" candidate, and of these, 83% voted for Trump. This equals roughly 40 million votes, or two thirds of Trump's total.

Another indication that Trump was viewed as the anti-establishment candidate was the fact that, of the 18% of voters who said they disliked both candidates, Trump won 49% to Clinton's 29%. Fourteen percent said neither had the right temperament to be president, with Trump defeating Clinton 71% to 17% in this group. Remarkably, 57% of voters said they would be concerned or scared by a Trump presidency, but Trump still won 14% of these voters. These figures indicate the just how effective the big money and the media are in fomenting the hatred that exists for the political establishment.

The election saw a massive shift in party support among the poorest and wealthiest voters. Votes for the Republicans among the most impoverished section of workers, those with family incomes under $30,000, increased by 10 percentage points from 2012. In several key Midwestern states, the swing of the poorest voters toward Trump was even larger: Wisconsin (17-point swing), Iowa (20 points), Indiana (19 points) and Pennsylvania (18 points). The swing to Republicans among the $30,000 to $50,000 family income range was 6 percentage points. Those with incomes between $50,000 and $100,000 swung away from Republicans compared to 2012 by just two points.[14]

The affluent and educated voted for Clinton by a much broader margin than they had voted for Obama in 2012. Among those with incomes between $100,000 and $200,000, Clinton benefited from a 9-point Democratic swing. Voters with family incomes above $250,000 swung toward Clinton by 11 percentage points. Clinton was unable to make up for the voter decline among the former Obama Coalition: African Americans (-3.2 million), women (-2.1 million), and youth (-1.2 million). The 2016 Election was a populist revolt against the establishment, which decided beforehand that party nominees should be another Clinton or another Bush. Democrats sabotaged their populist candidate and lost. The Republicans failed to stop their populist candidate and won. The power of big money in the presidential campaigns has become so pervasive that even the corporate-controlled media cannot disguise it any longer. The *Washington Post*, for example, published a report July 16, 2016 whose headline left little to the imagination: "2016 fundraising shows power tilting to groups backed by wealthy elite." The article noted that "independent" expenditures by so-called super PACs—political action committees loosely linked to the candidates—would *exceed* the amount spent by the candidates and their official campaign committees. And the result?

Despite the massive influx of capital to influence the attitudes of voters and the outcome of elections, voter turnouts are far *lower* than they were in the 1960s. This paradox raises obvious and embarrassing questions: Where is all that money coming from, going to and for what purposes?

The answer is as simple as our campaign finance rules, television-advertising costs, and tax codes that have become so complex and obscure. Elections are playgrounds for billionaires running for office or seeking to promote candidates sympathetic to their narrow economic interests, while suppressing others from casting a vote. Plutocracy rules.

It has been real. Even though many of our futures were compromised by a succession of liberal and conservative presidents, we still had a bitchin' ride, while it lasted. We actually were 'out there havin' fun in that warm California sun,' as the *Riviera's* timeless lyrics express. Although aimless cruising, outdoor drive-in theaters, and gorgeous gas-guzzlers have all but disappeared, indelible memories remain. The muscle cars of the era, the ones that we so carelessly discarded, are now 'cherry' and have become collectors' prized objects of art; the lyrics of the priceless music collection of the era have now become elevator music. To the best of our recollection, our youth was 'otta sight' and the decade was 'far out.' No complaints. No excuses. No regrets. Our feeble attempts to undermine authority went down in flames as we passed age 30. God bless Castro, Cyclops, Daley, J. Edgar, Khrushchev, LAFCO, LBJ, Mao, Nixon, Reagan, the TF—and all the rest of those who tried to spoil the party.

Along the pathways to fulfilling personal goals, lofty civic aspirations, and patriotic obligations, the much-maligned boomers faced life-changing personal challenges. They were the first generation to witness horrific images broadcast nightly on the new mass medium of television; their minds were further corrupted by images of racism, repression and war. Hungry for mental escape, each one reacted differently to the external threats posed by political leaders—despite misgivings, most dutifully obliged and joined the establishment, some rebelled, and others dropped out. We were lucky enough to become part of a micro-group, a distinguished covey of individuals who, despite their flaws, formed lasting support networks.

Despite our various and nefarious pasts, thinking about the accomplishments of our absolute peer group makes us feel proud, honored, reconnected and reinforced by our affiliation with the Red House on Isla Vista. Despite a few standouts on both sides of the economic and social responsibility scale, most of the survivors simply lived ordinary middle-class lives—or at least tried to balance civic responsibilities with personal survival. In their dotage, they reflect among themselves and on experiences that formed lifelong friendships and relationships. Of course, we are not all equal in achievement, fame, income, procreation, health or personal stability. Even so, the bonds formed in the Red House a half a century ago supersede any feelings of isolation in our present world. Regardless of individual achievement, fame, fortune, or failure, we have a peer group, a baseline, a foundation upon which to judge our chosen career endeavors. We loved the challenge, and are proud to associate with others who practiced determined individuality, the Red House ethos that enriched our lives. What have we learned that might help our progeny survive?

Both Isla Vista and the United States are at an extreme crossroads stuck in political gridlock and suffering from decades of civic neglect. China will overtake us as the world's largest economy with little prospect for recovery. Unemployment rates for millennials have reached staggering rates of 16%--much higher for minorities and still rising. Colleges and universities will see rapid enrollment declines as students and parents question the costs and value of a traditional college degree. Employment data for graduates are not encouraging: 44% of college grads in their 20s are stuck in low-wage $10 per hour dead-end jobs, the highest rate in decades, and the number of young people making less than $25,000 has spiked to the highest level since the 1990s. Employers hesitate to hire new graduates because baby boomers are delaying retirement and holding jobs longer.

History teaches us nothing unless we change our collective spirit:

Schoolchildren practice "active shooter drills" and hide under their desks, cringing in fear of mass murderers with automatic weapons rather than nuclear holocaust.

High-tech drones are now used instead of conscripted combat soldiers to disguise the real purpose of global conflict.

In several states, gays, women and ethnic minorities are denied full rights of citizenship. Income inequality is greater now than at any time since 1929.

The United States still fights wars in far-off lands to protect the economic interests of multi-national corporations instead of ideological threats.

U.S. Special Forces conduct covert operations in 134 countries.

Bankers, billionaires and generals now dominate presidential cabinet positions.

There is a great deal more depth to those who grew up during the Sixties than the thin stereotypes of acid trips, drug dealers, hippies, free lovers, protesters, draft dodgers and war mongers. Although we left IV decades ago, IV never left us—we never forgot the lessons learned during those formative years. I hope that there is a vintage 'Isla Vista,' real or imaginary, in the minds of young hearts, whatever your age, ethnicity, gender, race, or religion.

APPENDIX

America by Alan Ginzberg (full version)

America I've given you all and now I'm nothing.
America two dollars and twenty-seven cents January 17, 1956.
I can't stand my own mind.
America when will we end the human
war? Go fuck yourself with your atom
bomb I don't feel good don't bother me.
I won't write my poem till I'm in my right mind.

America when will you be angelic?
When will you take off your clothes?
When will you look at yourself through the grave?
When will you be worthy of your million Trotskyites?
America why are your libraries full of tears?
America when will you send your eggs to India?
I'm sick of your insane demands.
When can I go into the supermarket and buy what I need with my good looks?

America after all it is you and I who are perfect not the next world.
Your machinery is too much for me.
You made me want to be a saint.
There must be some other way to settle this argument.
Burroughs is in Tangiers I don't think he'll come back it's sinister.
Are you being sinister or is this some form of practical joke?
I'm trying to come to the point.
I refuse to give up my obsession.

America stop pushing I know what I'm doing.
America the plum blossoms are falling.
I haven't read the newspapers for months, everyday somebody goes on trial for murder.

America I feel sentimental about the Wobblies.
America I used to be a communist when I was a kid and I'm not sorry.
I smoke marijuana every chance I get.
I sit in my house for days on end and stare at the roses in the closet.
When I go to Chinatown I get drunk and never get laid.
My mind is made up there's going to be trouble.
You should have seen me reading Marx.
My psychoanalyst thinks I'm perfectly right.
I won't say the Lord's Prayer.
I have mystical visions and cosmic vibrations.
America I still haven't told you what you did to Uncle Max after he came over from Russia.

I'm addressing you.
Are you going to let our emotional life be run by Time Magazine?
I'm obsessed by Time Magazine.
I read it every week.

Its cover stares at me every time I slink past the corner candystore.
I read it in the basement of the Berkeley Public Library.
It's always telling me about responsibility. Businessmen are serious. Movie
producers are serious. Everybody's serious but me.
It occurs to me that I am America.
I am talking to myself again.
Asia is rising against me.
I haven't got a chinaman's chance.
I'd better consider my national resources.
My national resources consist of two joints of marijuana millions of
genitals an unpublishable private literature that goes 1400 miles an hour
and twenty five thousand mental institutions.
I say nothing about my prisons nor the millions of underpriviliged who live in
my flowerpots under the light of five hundred suns.
I have abolished the whorehouses of France, Tangiers is the next to go.
My ambition is to be President despite the fact that I'm a Catholic.

America how can I write a holy litany in your silly mood? I will
continue like Henry Ford my strophes are as individual as his
automobiles more so they're all different sexes
America I will sell you strophes $2500 apiece $500 down on your old strophe
America free Tom Mooney
America save the Spanish Loyalists
America Sacco & Vanzetti must not die
America I am the Scottsboro boys.

America when I was seven momma took me to Communist Cell meetings
they sold us garbanzos a handful per ticket a ticket costs a nickel and the
speeches were free everybody was angelic and sentimental about the
workers it was all so sincere you have no idea what a good thing the party
was in 1835 Scott Nearing was a grand old man a real mensch
Mother Bloor made me cry I once saw Israel Amter plain. Everybody must
have been a spy.

America you don't really want to go to war.
America it's them bad Russians.
Them Russians them Russians and them Chinamen. And them Russians.
The Russia wants to eat us alive. The Russia's power mad. She wants to
take our cars from out our garages.
Her wants to grab Chicago. Her needs a Red Reader's Digest. Her wants our
auto plants in Siberia. Him big bureaucracy running our filling stations.
That no good. Ugh. Him makes Indians learn read. Him need big black
niggers.
Hah. Her make us all work sixteen hours a day. Help.
America this is quite serious.
America this is the impression I get from looking in the television set.
America is this correct?
I'd better get right down to the job.
It's true I don't want to join the Army or turn lathes in precision parts
factories, I'm nearsighted and psychopathic anyway.
America I'm putting my queer shoulder to the wheel.

Source: Online Poems by Allen Ginsberg
http://www.english.illinois.edu/maps/poets/g_l/ginsberg/onlinepoems.htm

Glossary armchair hactivists: younger tech-savvy millennials who possess the knowledge and moral consciousness to act, but fear the consequences or lack the motivation to engage in real civic participation, protests or political change.

Baby Boomers: the demoralized offspring of the "Greatest Generation" born between 1946 and 1964.

bitchin': superlative, as in "that's bitchin'" or good, great, superb.

beatniks: song writers, poets, and writers of the "beat" generation of the 1950s.

blacklisted: during the Red Scare of the 1950s, those who refused to take loyalty oaths, including artists, intellectuals, scientists, and writers suspected of having communist leanings.

BMOC: Big Man on Campus

bonged: double meaning, both loaded with marijuana and excluded from a fraternity.

Brew 102: popular beer of the day.

cannon fodder: ground troops ordered into battle and more likely to be killed or wounded.

carbon paper: before copy machines, a sticky paper with black or blue ink that is inserted between two sheets of white paper that would reproduce identical copy of document or letter.

caucus: meeting or gathering of the members of a legislative body who are members of a particular political party, to select candidates or decide policy or a group of people with shared concerns within a political party or larger organization.

chinks: derogatory description of Asians.

choom gang: youth drug gangs.

de facto refers to segregation by income, housing, neighborhood assumed to be beyond the scope of the judicial system to correct.

de jure means segregation by law or regulation such as so-called "separate but equal" facilities for blacks and whites.

Dixicrat: Southern Democrats who switched allegiance from Democratic to Republican Parties in the 1960s because of democratic politicians support of civil and voting rights.

Freedom Riders: Northern liberals who rode in busses during the 1960s to support Black civil rights causes and demonstrate against segregation and racism in the South. Many were injured and some killed by the Klu Klux Klan.

Generation X: includes anyone born between 1965 and 1982.

Generation Y: a term used to describe those who were "too cool" for generation X.

Gulf of Tonkin resolution: Congressional approval for LBJ to expand Vietnam War based on alleged attack on an American ship off the coast of North Vietnam.

Greatest Generation: a term used to describe those who endured the Great Depression and fought in World War Two.

gremmies: from the word gremlin, aka surfers.

grunts: enlisted men or women in the Armed services.

goat parties: chauvinistic contest between frat boys to see who could bring the ugliest girl to a party.

gotcha parties: parties based on game similar to monopoly and strip poker where players disrobe various items of clothes if their tokens land on certain squares.

iron triangle: represents the three powerful institutions in government: Congressional committees, interest groups, and the bureaucracy. Most decision-making takes place among those representing various entities in these three power sectors.

John Birch Society: conservative advocacy group and radical right-wing organization supporting anti-communism and limited government.

mimeograph: machines used to make copies using stincles (below)

My Lai hamlet in *Song My* village: locations of massacres by American troops of hundreds of innocent noncombatant civilians, women, and children during the Vietnam War.

Millennials: today's kids and young adults born between 1982 and 2000.

Obama Coalition: those who voted for Obama in 2012 and 2008, including African Americans, gays and lesbians, women and youth mainly from the poor and working classes.

peace nicks: those who opposed the Vietnam war.

plausible deniability: tactic used by presidential advisors to protect the presidency. See Ronald Reagan and the IranContra investigation.

plutocracy: rule by the rich. See, for example, Donald Trump.

rat fuck: World War II slang term for sabotage or dirty tricks.

ray box: before indoor tanning booths, large tables covered with tin foil used to reflect sun for faster tanning. Basically an outdoor frying pan; a bad idea then, worse now.

smudge pots: smelly oil burning devises used to keep fruit on citrus trees from freezing during cold weather. Banned in California and replaced by large wind turbines.

stincles: similar to carbon paper (above) only longer to fit in mimeograph machines. Sticky paper with green substance processed though a rotary drum to copy documents. Very messy.

stonewalling: delay tactic first used by Nixon and his henchmen to prevent further investigation of the Watergate break-in.

Symbionese Liberation Army (SLA): left-wing revolutionary organization active between 1973 and 1975 that committed bank robberies, murders, and other acts of violence.

techno-hippies: younger millennials infatuated with all types of Internet-related technology and generally unaware of its dangers.

Tet offensive: coordinated attacks by Viet Cong and North Vietnamese regulars on dozens of U.S. and South Vietnamese military bases in January 30, 1968.

turkies: reference to those who did not "fit" the house image. See also, bonged.

Yellow peril: refers to the Chinese Communists and, more generally and derogatorily, to persons of Chinese decent.

WASP: White Anglo-Saxon Protestant

ENDNOTES Chapter 1

1. p. 9 The transformation of political campaigns began in the first decade of the 21st Century when Democratic Governor and presidential candidate Howard Dean of Vermont used technology to reach out to ultra-wired Gen-Xers. Although Dean failed in his 2004 bid for the presidency, his campaign set the stage for smart Obama 'techno-wonks' to succeed by reaching a much larger audience of younger voters in 2008 and 2012.

2. p. 9 New Internet-driven civic organizations could be created to supplement hollow political parties and allow citizen voices to be heard between elections, if they only possessed the knowledge and power to influence Congress.

Chapter 3: Generations X-Y-Z

1. In June, 2014 a CNN/NORC poll found that only 34% of respondents believed that most children would grow up to be better off than their parents, while 63% expected their children to be worse off. The Heldrich Center at Rutgers' Bloustein School found that only 16% of Americans expect job, career, and employment opportunities to be better for the next generation than for the current generation, compared with 40% in November of 2009, just months after the official end of the Great Recession.

2. Declining confidence in the American Dream is concentrated among women (down 14 percentage points since 2012), young adults (down 16 points), Democrats (-17 points), and liberals (-16 points). Compare these numbers with the decline in voting among these groups on p. 189.

3. The detailed report can be found at: https://www.macfound.org/media/files/E11540_How_Housing_Matters_2015_FULL_REPORT.pdf

4. Boomer parent's heroic triumphs over the Japs and Nazis were and still are vividly documented and indelibly etched into war baby boomers' psyches, often in gruesome detail. (Recall the opening scenes of Steven Spielberg's epic WWII film *Saving Private Ryan.*)

Chapter 4

1. *The Catcher in the Rye* by J. D. Salinger is still required reading in many high school English courses today. The book is banned from many school libraries by conservative parent and teacher groups opposed to its use of profanity and perceived glorification of rebellion.

2. This resulted from a conspiracy between bureaucrats, cement contractors, car dealers, politicians, oil companies, and suburban real estate interests accurately depicted in the film *Who Killed Roger Rabbit?*

3. Quotation from "The New America" Foreign Service Journal, January, 1958.

4. Nixon's political career nearly ended when the press discovered an illegal "slush-fund" that he had used to solicit money from wealthy contributors. Rather than focus on the substance of the accusations, he diverted attention by delivering an emotional diatribe about gifts that he and his wife had received from local Republicans, one of which was a little dog named Checkers. His so-called "Checkers Speech" was vintage Nixon.

5. Everyone and everything in those 1940s films was so black and white, reflecting the hardships of the depression and war years, moral certainties and rigid behavioral codes evaporated as populations spread South and West. Certain social traditions were questioned by the best books and films of the decade exposing social problems such as alcoholism, single-parenting, wrongful convictions, post-traumatic stress disorder (PSTD), racism, and anti-Semitism.

Chapter 6

1. Described by Janis Carter, an actress who played John Wayne's wife in the 1951 film *Flying Leathernecks.*

2. Adrian Gronseth and Sean Nolan, "Isla Vista: Born from Fire," Opinion page of the *Daily Nexus* or UCSB. Opinions are submitted primarily by students. Daily Nexus, May 1, 2014.

3. In one of the rare acts of war on U.S. territory, a Japanese submarine shelled the Ellwood Oil Fields in Gaviota, just West of Isla Vista, in 1942. There was little damage, but local residents feared the worst.

4. Private correspondence, May, 2007.

Chapter 7

1. The Civil Right Project at UCLA found that segregation has been steadily increasing since 1990, and that black students nationally are substantially more segregated than they were in 1970. Nationwide, only 23 percent of black students attended white-majority schools in 2011. That's the lowest number since 1968 and far below the peak of 44 percent in 1988.

2. BYU Law School is being investigated for discrimination against gays and those who might have "lost their Mormon faith" before graduation. Source: Chronicle.com/blogs/ticker/bar-association-investigatingcomplaint-of-discrimination-at-byu law school.

3. Segregated dining routines varied with the cultures of different campuses. Thanks to the 2010 blockbuster film *The Social Network*, nearly everyone is now familiar with the exclusiveness of elite 'final clubs' at private institutions such as Harvard College. An earlier 2000 film called *The Skulls* dramatized the not-sosecret societies such as Skull and Bones at Yale.

4. The midterm Congressional elections in 2014 showed abysmal turnouts of less than 36% of all eligible voters—the lowest total voter turnout since 1942 when millions of eligible young males were overseas fighting in World War II. Not surprisingly, only 13% of those aged 18-29 bothered to vote.

5. The value of the maximum grant for tuition, fees, and room and board at the average four-year public university fell from nearly 80 percent in the 1970s to only 27 percent in 2012-13.

6. In 1977, state and local governments provided 57% of higher-education revenue; that share dropped to 39% by 2012 even as enrollments increased. Families and students saw their share increase from 33 to 49% during the same period.

Chapter 8

1. It doesn't take a PhD in sociology to recognize the trends clearly evident with the expansion of socially-conscious and female-oriented policies such as Social Security Disability Insurance, Medicare, and the Affordable Care Act—all passed or expanded under the Democratic administrations of Franklin D. Roosevelt, Lyndon B. Johnson, Bill Clinton, and Barack H. Obama.

Chapter 9

1. According to the Pew Research Center's Internet and American Life Project, over half of all adults in the United States used the Internet to ask questions and obtain information about candidates and issues during the 2008 presidential election. This trend continued in the 2012 election with about one-third of all voters saying that their vote was influenced by the opinion of friends on *Facebook* or other social media outlets.

2. Vaidhyanathan, Siva, *The Googlization of Everything (and why we should worry)*. (Berkeley and Los Angeles, CA: University of California Press, 2011).

Chapter 10

1. Once again, the all-seeing eye of the camera presented an entirely opposite picture to the viewing public. The film *Medium Cool* directed by Haskell Wexler in 1969 captures the street-level violence and tension through the eyes of a television cameraman. This was one of the first movies to employ documentary style film-making techniques showing how demonstrators were treated by police.

2. *First National Bank of Boston v. Bellotti,* (435 U.S. 765) defined the free speech right of corporations for the first time. The Supreme Court held that corporations have a First Amendment right to make contributions to ballot initiative campaigns. The ruling came in response to a Massachusetts law that prohibited corporate donations in ballot initiatives unless the corporation's interests were directly involved.

3. In his memoirs, Secretary of Defense Robert McNamara confessed that the entire "air mobile" strategy of moving troops rapidly by helicopters to engage the enemy was flawed. These giant 'grasshoppers,' as the Viet Cong referred to them, were loud and easily shot down with small arms.

Chapter 11

1. Portions of this section excepted from "Forty years ago, a mob of students stormed the Bank of America building," February 25, 2010 by Taylor Haggerty http://dailynexus.com/2010-02-25/fortyyears-ago-a-mob-of-students-stormed-the-bank-of-america-building/.

Chapter 12

1. Quote is from Peter Baker, *Days of Fire: Bush and Cheney in the White House.* Anchor: 2014.

2. When challenged by labor demands at home, owners of multi-national corporations simply follow cheaper global labor markets and move elsewhere, incentivized by U.S. tax laws which treat overseas income and investments more favorably than income generated by jobs created at home.

3. China is looking for productive investments to grow its record $54 *billion* monthly export trade *surplus* (as of January, 2016). Simply put, for every $1.00 in raw materials the U.S. exports *to* China, we import $4.00 worth of finished goods *from* China. It doesn't take a one-armed economist to figure which party is getting screwed. http://www.bloomberg.com/news/articles/2016-01-13/china-s-exports-unexpectedly-rebound-asyuan-weakness-kicks-in exports-unexpectedly-rebound-as-yuan-weakness-kicks-in.

4. Among the consequences, 80 global elite families now control half the world's wealth; 35 of those billionaires are Americans. Data from OXFAM, a confederation of 18 Non-Government Organizations committed to removing injustices the cause poverty.

5. Current unemployment numbers are more suspect today because of the growing *lumpen proletariat* of permanently unemployed who no longer even look for jobs.

6. Source:http://www.politifact.com/wisconsin/statements/2013/dec/08/one-wisconsin-now/just-how-wealthywal-mart-walton-family/

7. The income spread between the college-educated and those without degrees continues to expand. The Census Bureau reports that adults with bachelor's degree or more earned an average $81,761 in 2011. Those with high school degrees or GEDs earned an average $40,634; workers who did not finish ninth grade earned $26,545.

8. The January 2013 agreement to restore Clinton-level marginal income-tax rates for individuals making more than $400,000 (households making more than $450,000) did little to change this imbalance. Returns from Wall Street speculation by 1-percenters are taxed at a far lower rate than hourly or salaried income. This, in turn, results in lower tax receipts and prevents government from making necessary investments in infrastructure, education, and healthcare aimed at restoring economic strength and stability.

9. The International Monetary Fund (IMF) noted the systemic relationship between economic instability and income inequality, but few American leaders have absorbed that lesson. (https://financesonline.com/incomeinequality-views-solutions-from-experts/)

10. These and a number of other surveys corroborate the core finding of a dramatic decline in confidence about the future. For example, when the August 2014 NBC/WSJ poll asked *"Do you feel confident or not confident that life for our children's generation will be better than it has been for us?"* only 21 percent expressed confidence, down from 30% in 2012. During the same month, the CBS poll asked, *"Do you think the future of the next generation of your family will be better, worse, or about the same as your life today?"* only 23% responded "better" compared to fully 63% who said "worse."

11. The most recent solid data run through 2013. MONEY magazine recently reported the median wealth of a U.S. household, in inflation-adjusted dollars, dropped 36% from 2003 to 2013. During that same period, the richest 5% of household's median net worth increased by 12%.

Chapter 13

1. Social Security data confirm that over one-half the workers in the US earn less than $30,000 per year and 40% of those earn less than $20,000. The federal poverty line for a family of four is $24,250 and the line for a family of three is $20,090. The income gap is now twice as large as the black-white achievement gap. These types of statistics are rarely, if ever, found in the American mainstream media reports commenting on the crisis of schools. Just replace the incompetence teachers and privatize schools and, bingo, problem solved.

2. Today, it matters increasingly not just whether you go to college, but also what type of degree you seek. Prior to the steep drop in oil prices, starting salaries for petroleum engineers were $90-100K regardless of how much someone paid for college; psychologists are paid $30-40K whether they went to Harvard or Old State U. Many needy students are sequestered into separate and inferior institutions, including for-profits, from which they are likely to emerge without viable degrees and with crushing levels of debt.

3. The Center on Budget and Policy Priorities (CBPP) paints a devastating picture of a polarized society in which the prison and police-military-complexes continually expand while vital educational and healthcare programs are starved for funds. CBPP estimates that if state corrections spending had been held to mid1980s levels, adjusted for inflation today, the 50 U.S. states would have $28 billion more each year between them to allocate to non-prison related expenditures. Prison populations in most U.S. states are at historic highs and many states now spend more on prisons than on higher education. Plainly, state governments no longer treat public higher education as a high priority.

4. U.S. Department of Education data show that, from 1996 through 2012, public colleges and universities gave a declining portion of grants—as measured by both number and dollar amount—to students in the lowest quartile of family income.

5. According to Georgetown University's study "Separate and Unequal: How Higher Education Reinforces the Intergenerational Reproduction of White Racial Privilege," higher education has become a "passive agent" in perpetuating elite white privilege. (See, https://cew.georgetown.edu/wpcontent/uploads/2014/11/SeparateUnequal.FR_.pdf)

6. After counting the expected family contribution, grants, and loans, students in the lowest family-income quartile had $8,221 in unmet need in 2012—far more than students in any other quartile. That level of unmet need is twice as high as it was in 1990.

7. Stanford University studies confirm that the income achievement gap has been growing for at least 50 years, with the current gap 30-40 percent *larger* for children born after 2001 than for those born 25 years earlier.

8. Firearm homicides for those under age 50 is a stunning 20 times higher in the United States than in any other economically advanced country. For young Black males, the probability of being killed by police is 28 times higher than that of young white males.

9. Sanjay Gupta, CNN News *Weed.* Broadcast 8/13/2016.

10. Despite slight increases in recent years, to purchasing power of wages for a typical male worker, when adjusted for inflation, actually fell from $33,880 in 1968 to $32,986 in 2011.

11. One way to level the playing field is to prohibit lawmakers from accepting campaign contributions from lobbyists and their organizations. Another is to slow down the revolving door, introducing longer waiting periods and more-comprehensive limits on the extent to which individuals circulate back and forth among positions in Congress, industries subject to regulation, and executive agencies charged with regulating those industries. All are policies opposed by conservative Republicans.

12. Purchasing power for minimum wage workers is less now than in 1968! Pew Research Center. See chart below. Source: U.S. Census figures from 1940-2014.

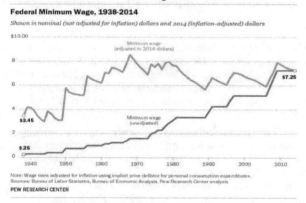

Federal Minimum Wage, 1938-2014

Shown in nominal (not adjusted for inflation) dollars and 2014 (inflation-adjusted) dollars

Note: Wage rates adjusted for inflation using implicit price deflator for personal consumption expenditures.
Sources: Bureau of Labor Statistics, Bureau of Economic Analysis, Pew Research Center analysis
PEW RESEARCH CENTER

13. Jane Mayer, *Dark Money: The Hidden History of the Billionaires Behind the Rise of the Radical Right.* Doubleday, 2016.

14. Statistics excepted from http://www.defenddemocracy.press/myth-reactionary-white-working-class/

BACK COVER: Stock photos of bank burning.

CPSIA information can be obtained
at www.ICGtesting.com
Printed in the USA
FSHW02n1311140618
49420FS